Spire Publishing

www.spirepublishing.com

Hearts and Diamonds

by

Patricia Robson

Patricia Robson

Spire Publishing

www.spirepublishing.com

Spire Publishing, September 2008

First published in Canada and the UK 2008 by Spire Publishing.
Spire Publishing is a trademark of Adlibbed Ltd.

A cataloguing record for this book is available from the Library and Archives Canada. Visit www.collectionscanada.ca/amicus/index-e.html

Set in Times and Times Italics.
Printed and bound in the USA or the UK
by Lightning Source Ltd.

ISBN: 1-897312-76-8

Cover Illustration by Caroline Robson

www.spirepublishing.com

For Sue

CHAPTER ONE

At the sound of the carriage wheels crunching across the gravel, Charlotte flinched. Then she steeled herself. She must not be afraid. She had acted for the best and nothing her stepmother could say would make her change her mind. Quietly she laid her book down on the library table and went out into the hall, ready to face Isabel in a fit of rage.

The maid, alerted by the sound of the carriage, opened the front door, only to find it pushed hard into her face. The girl fell back and with a terrified glance towards Charlotte, scurried back to the servants' quarters.

Isabel stood in the doorway, her eyes blazing, her face contorted with fury. As always, she was beautifully dressed, this time in a purple costume with matching hat. Charlotte's heart gave a lurch when she saw her stepmother wielding a riding whip which she tapped, restlessly, on her left palm. She had seen Isabel in this mood before. But she would stand her ground. Isabel's voice was thick with anger.

'How dare you? How dare you interfere like this?'

Charlotte took a deep breath and drew herself up.

'Daring does not come into it, Isabel. I did what needed to be done. I paid off your debts, all of them, and suggested that the tradespeople should give you nothing more on account.'

'Suggested! You have humiliated me in front of my friends! You had no right!' As she spoke, Isabel struck out with the whip, hitting the frame of a painting on the wall, sending it rocking crazily.

Charlotte's reply was cool and steady although her heart was thudding hard against her ribs.

'I had every right. You owed the jeweller and the dressmaker five hundred pounds between them, to say nothing of the smaller debts at various shops in Huddersfield for all the trinkets and finery you continue to buy.'

'And why should I not? It is what is due to me and my position! The position of the wife of George Blezard, mill-owner!'

A huge wave of sadness washed over Charlotte but she did not let it show. She kept her voice firm.

'You are not George Blezard's wife any longer, Isabel. You are his widow.'

Isabel glared at Charlotte and looked as if she would snarl back at her. But something in the younger woman's face seemed to stop her, at least for the moment. Charlotte continued.

'You should not need me to remind you of the state of Father's finances, which we discovered after his death. The cost of this house, and all you spent on it and on yourself, ran into thousands of pounds. Just at a time when the textile trade was facing its worst period for years.'

'Trade, trade! I forgot that was your favourite subject! The business expert – and still so young! Much good may it do you – when you're a lonely old maid, as no doubt you will be!'

This was one of Isabel's constant jibes. Charlotte ignored it, although it had the power to hurt her.

With a flounce of her skirt, Isabel swung round and began to mount the stairs. Having the last word was something she did well.

Charlotte stood at the bottom of the staircase, struggling with her feelings. If only her stepmother would go! She had parents still living in Scarborough. Perhaps she would go back there? Charlotte feared it was a vain hope. Being married to George Blezard for two years had given Isabel the taste of a life with money to spend, and spend it she did, until her husband's premature death in the mill.

At first, Isabel had enjoyed the attention paid her as the tragically young widow, elegant in her brand-new mourning clothes, touching in her pretence of grief. But she soon became bored with weeks without parties and months wearing black. She had recently moved into mourning purple, a colour more flattering to her brunette colouring.

Charlotte had borne it all as calmly as she could although the loss of her father had caused her much pain. Now she had taken a decisive step in the control of Isabel's spending, she felt a sense of relief, accompanied by a strong desire to get away from her, if only for a short while.

She summoned the maid.

'Bella. Please inform the mistress that I am visiting my friend Helen and will stay the night.'

The maid bobbed a curtsey and nodded. Charlotte packed a small bag and set off.

The walk to Honley would do her good.

As soon as Charlotte had gone, Isabel summoned the two maids upstairs and kept them busy for the next three hours. The coachman was sent on an urgent errand and told to wait for an answer before returning. In the kitchen, Mrs Burton prepared a light supper that could be sent up to Madam at a moment's notice. She had come to learn of her mistress's impulses, and her reaction if she was thwarted.

By midnight, the house was silent, the staff all asleep in the servants' quarters. Wearing slippers, Isabel stole downstairs, her crinoline swishing against the banister rails, her feet making almost no sound as they met carpet and then the hard smooth tiles of the hall floor. Moonlight filtered through the engraved glass panels of the front door, casting patterns on the dado, slantwise on the wall; it gleamed on the swinging brass pendulum of the clock, the tick tock loud in the emptiness.

Parlour, dining-room, library. She glided from one room to another, turning the brass doorknobs with both hands so as to make no noise. The business did not take long; she had already marked out the things she wanted. Gathering them up, she went back upstairs time and time again, her arms full, her hands grasping the cold metal and glass. Finally, the hall itself yielded up its only treasure.

She slept lightly and fitfully that night; she could not afford to do otherwise. As dawn was breaking, she went downstairs again, this time opening the door to the two poorly-dressed men who stood there, packers from Broomfield's factory. Without a word being exchanged, they followed her upstairs and immediately set to work packing the goods into the tea-chests they had brought with them. They worked fast, with the error-less speed of professionals, bending, wrapping, pushing the items into spaces which seemed made for them. With mounting excitement, heightened by the risk of discovery, Isabel stood watching them.

The task took them no more than twenty minutes. Soon they were carrying the goods downstairs, returning for the trunks and valises which the maids had filled with her clothes the day before. A few moments later, a sleepy coachman brought the carriage round to the side door. Again while she watched, the two workmen loaded up the carriage. They took the coins she proffered and left as silently as they had come.

There was no leave-taking. Wrapped in her warmest cloak and fur-trimmed hat, she clambered inside and sank down against the leather upholstery, luggage pressing against her on all sides. It was only just becoming light. With the sound of horses' hooves and heavy wheels on the gravel, the carriage moved slowly up the drive and out into the road. The four tea-chests were strapped and lashed outside. Each bore a label which read 'PROPERTY OF MRS ISABEL BLEZARD.'

It was late next morning when Charlotte set off for home, her heart heavy at the thought of facing Isabel again. She knew it would be up to her to create an atmosphere in which the two of them could live together. Isabel never apologised. And she could sulk for days, if she felt like it. Charlotte sighed at the thought of what lay ahead and kept on walking.

The lane skirted the lower slopes of Castle Hill, the great earth-work that towered above her. Down to her left, the land fell away steeply towards Huddersfield in the wide valley below. Smoke from the mill chimneys rose into the air, dispersing finally into the broad sky. A patchwork of fields, punctuated by stone cottages, encircled the town while away to the west, the dry-stone walls petered out and the moorland took over, rising to the sharp Pennine ridge in the distance.

Coming to a lane which spiralled downwards sharply to her left, Charlotte followed it towards the house her father had built for Isabel. Poor Father, his second marriage had brought him little but worry and debt. She was sure it had contributed to his early death. And now the new house would have to be sold in order to give Isabel the share of his estate that belonged to her.

The prospect of the sale did not distress Charlotte. It would not be like losing the old house in Lockwood where she had grown up and where Mother had died. Isabel had despised that house. 'Common' she had called it, in a 'common' area where 'common people' filled the streets on their way to work in the nearby mills and factories.

Charlotte had loved the house, thought it perfect. There she had a bedroom with a view of the distant moors. In the mornings, when Father had gone to work by walking the few yards to their mill, she would go into the room where Mother would be propped up on pillows and describe for her the scenes passing in the street below – the mill girls in their shawls and clogs, the men in their cloth caps and mufflers, and all manner of vehicles, from carts trundling past laden with bales of wool or hay, to smart carriages and gentlemen on horseback.

It had been a wrench when Father told her that Isabel, his new wife, refused to stay in the house where he had lived with Charlotte's mother. He had not expressed it in that way, of course, had made it sound like a good thing, praising the prospect of a brand-new house with a fine bedroom for Charlotte, higher up, further away from the mill dirt and closer to the surrounding countryside. But she had known what lay behind the decision without being told.

Looking at the move from a practical viewpoint, one that came readily to Charlotte, it had been sensible. The fine new house, built in the local stone, would fetch a good price, much more than the old one. Charlotte had already arranged to have it valued. It was not quite at its best now in autumn with the trees bare but was looking neat and well-kept, its gravel drive flanked by laurel bushes, their leaves glossy after a shower of rain.

Charlotte let herself in by the side door, startling Mrs Burton, who came out of the kitchen, wiping her hands on a tea towel.

'Miss Charlotte! We didn't know when to expect you!'

'That's all right, Mrs Burton. I wasn't sure myself. Is Mrs Blezard in?'

'No, Miss Charlotte. She's gone.'

'Gone? What? Gone completely?'

'Yes, Miss. She went early this morning.' Mrs Burton looked uneasy. 'Will you be wanting some lunch, Miss? I have some soup made.'

'Oh yes, thank you, Mrs Burton. That will do nicely.'

There was something odd about the hall but Charlotte could not, at the moment, see what it was. It was as handsome as ever, with its dark blue and ochre floor tiles, its walnut hat-stand, its rich mouldings. But something was different. She was sure of it.

Slowly, she put her hand on the newel-post at the foot of the banister and climbed the stairs to her bedroom where she removed her cloak and laid it in the chest. If the house was going to be sold very soon, there would be no point in moving into the largest bedroom where her father and Isabel had slept. Nevertheless, she crossed the corridor to see in what kind of state Isabel had left it.

It was exactly as she would have predicted. It looked not just empty but stripped. Every drawer was hanging out, every cupboard door open and chest-lid flung back. Charlotte allowed herself a wry smile as she wondered how long it had taken to pack everything. Isabel had possessed more clothes than Charlotte had ever seen together in one place at one time. There were day dresses and walking costumes for every season and time of day, blouses, skirts, cloaks, hats, gloves, boots, undergarments, nightgowns, evening gowns and even a ballgown, never worn.

Charlotte suddenly realised why the room looked so bare. The dressing mirror had gone, as had the silver candlesticks which had stood on the dressing table. Almost simultaneously she realised why the entrance hall had looked different. There had been a pretty oval mirror in a gilt frame at the end of the hall near the front door. Isabel had always used it to make a final check on her appearance just before leaving the house.

Her heart sinking, Charlotte ran downstairs, this time into the parlour. Sure enough, anything small and of value, was gone – the matching crystal lustres from the mantelpiece, several vases, an attractive French timepiece and most upsetting of all, a painting which Father had given to Mother in the early days of their marriage, rumoured to be not just beautiful but increasingly valuable.

Dismay turned to anger. How dare Isabel take things that did not belong to her? A swift glance round her father's library reassured her until she noticed that a silver and gold writing set had disappeared from the desk.

She felt a sickening sensation in the pit of her stomach. The silver! Pulling open the drawers of the mahogany side-board in the dining-room, she found her suspicions were correct. An entire silver cutlery service had been lifted.

There came a tap at the door. It was Mrs Burton with a tray of soup, bread, butter and cheese.

'I'm that sorry, Miss Charlotte,' she said, putting the tray down. 'I feared you'd be upset but there was nothing I could do. It was all done so quick. Very early. Like it was planned.'

'Don't blame yourself at all, Mrs Burton,' replied Charlotte. 'I can see that it was done with some forethought.' She bit her lip, feeling her anger, and her colour, rising. Thankfully, Mrs Burton was not looking at her. The woman kept her head down and left the room quickly.

Charlotte walked up and down, trying to compose herself. How often had she prayed for the day when her stepmother would disappear from her life! But not like this! Stealing precious things which Charlotte felt to be hers and hers alone – mementoes of her father, her mother, their marriage and her own happy childhood. Isabel had no right to lay her greedy hands on any of these.

Why should she be surprised? Isabel's actions were completely in character. The woman's exit was as heartless and selfish as her entrance. She had come into her father's life without loving him. She had fastened on to him like a leech, bleeding him and giving almost nothing in return.

Thank God she was rid of her – well, almost. There was still the settlement of her father's will. But the solicitor could see to that. She remembered the look of fury on Isabel's face, at the reading of the will, when she learnt that Blezard's Mill had been left to her step-daughter. Charlotte had been overjoyed at the news. It meant her father had trusted her to carry on the business. Not only that, it showed he had got the measure of his young second wife who had spent his money like water and refused to heed his pleas for restraint as the debts mounted.

Now Isabel was out of her life for good. She need never see that woman again. She had something much more important to concentrate on. She would run Blezard's Mill as her father had done. It was in her blood. She was sure of it.

'Station-master! Unlock this door at once! Do you expect us to stand here on the platform and freeze?'

The unfortunate station-master, portly in his smart uniform, bent to his task, unlocking and flinging open the door to the waiting-room at Wakefield station. Then he stood back politely to allow the well-dressed complainant, followed by her husband and Isabel, to enter.

Fortunately, the large cast-iron stove was well alight, the red-hot coals glowing through the grate. As if to offer some apology, the station-master prised up the cover on top of the stove and beckoned to a hovering porter who obliged by shovelling a fresh hod-ful of coals into it. Touching the brim of his peaked hat, the station-master withdrew.

Isabel and the couple stood as close to the stove as possible, the women stamping their feet to restore their circulation.

'Next time we have an invitation that means travelling this early on a cold morning, Hubert, remind me to refuse it,' said the woman, pulling her fur tippet tight about her shoulders. She seemed to find it hard to stay still; even when her body was quiet, her eyes darted back and forth. She could not fail to notice Isabel's great pile of luggage heaped on a station wagon, guarded by a porter who looked half asleep.

'Not just a social visit, yours?' she asked.

'No. No, indeed,' replied Isabel. She saw no reason to divulge her personal details to anyone, certainly not to this nosy woman.

As Isabel remained silent, the woman pursed her lips and began adjusting her hat, collar, gloves. But the impulse to chat soon overcame her. 'We travel this way to Leeds often,' she went on. 'Hubert more frequently, on business. I visit my dressmaker – and the shops, of course, which offer a superior range to that here in Wakefield.' She sniffed. 'In my opinion, anyway.' She looked Isabel in the eye. 'Are you going to Leeds as well?'

'No,' said Isabel, 'I'm travelling south. To London.'

'London is all very well, of course. One can't deny it. But it's too big, too scattered for me. So many unsavoury neighbourhoods! And the beggars and thieves in the streets! Hubert and I found Bath much more congenial. Have you ever been to Bath?' Her eyes glittered.

'Bath? No, no, I haven't.'

'Aah!' The woman smiled now, though it did not make her any more pleasant. 'Well, I do recommend it if you've never been there. It's very charming – fine houses, parks. And so compact. One can walk to all the places of entertainment. If one wishes to walk, of course.'

Isabel thought of something to say about Bath. 'I believe the Queen does not much favour the city.'

'Well no, but the poor lady favours very little. Apart from Scotland and the Isle of Wight. One wonders how long she will remain in this state of deepest mourning. One loses patience with her.'

Isabel made no comment. No doubt this inquisitive woman would leap upon the news of Isabel's own widowhood with renewed interest but she was not going to give her that satisfaction.

At that moment, the station-master re-appeared.

'The train for Leeds is approaching, Sir, Madam.'

The woman did not acknowledge him in any way.

'Come, Hubert,' she said to her husband who had passed the entire time in the waiting-room staring at the stove, both hands resting on his cane. 'The train is here.' Turning to Isabel, 'Goodbye. I wish you a pleasant journey.' She swept out, followed by the silent Hubert.

Isabel watched them go, admiring, in spite of herself, the fine quality of the couple's outer-wear. But then, if you could not find good cloth in the West Riding, where could you find it? Good Lord! It could be her late husband speaking. She had only begun to notice cloth since being married to George Blezard. How dull that made her!

About twenty minutes later, the link train that would take her to Doncaster arrived. Two porters lifted all her luggage into the guard's van and she settled herself, for the short journey, in a compartment close to it.

At Doncaster, there was about half an hour to wait before the arrival of the London train. A greater number of people were milling about on the platform than at Wakefield – business men, families, a miscellany of passengers with their own reasons for travelling south.

Isabel's belongings had been piled onto a station wagon but she had been unable to secure a porter to stand guard over them. One had taken her penny and then, annoyingly, gone off to carry someone else's portmanteaux. There was nothing for it but to stand close to them herself. Just before the train was due, she felt obliged to walk back and forth a little to keep her feet warm. It was while her back was turned that she heard a slight commotion behind her.

'Are these your belongings, Madam, if I may ask?'

The gentleman was well-dressed, in his late thirties perhaps, handsome, with shining blond hair. As he gestured towards the pile of luggage and tea-chests, Isabel saw that his other hand was holding an urchin by his ragged collar. The boy struggled and then, as the gentleman held on, kicked him sharply on the shin. With a grunt of pain, the gentleman released his grasp and the boy streaked off into the further reaches of Doncaster station.

'Oh dear! I'm so sorry!' exclaimed Isabel. 'Was he...?'

'Yes, I'm afraid he was. Or rather, was about to help himself to one of your valises.' The gentleman rubbed the front of his leg and smiled at her. He was certainly very attractive.

'I am much obliged to you, Sir. I'm afraid there is rather a lot.'

'May I suggest the assistance of a porter, if not two, is called for?' Without waiting for her reply, he threw up an authoritative arm and as if by magic, two porters scurried forward. 'I want these safely stowed in the luggage van,' he said. To Isabel, 'Do you wish to have some of the luggage with you, in the compartment?'

'Oh yes,' she replied, pulling two valises off the pile.

'May I lift these on for you?'

'Thank you, that is very kind.' Isabel rewarded him with her sweetest smile.

'You are travelling First Class, I presume, madam?'

'Of course.'

So it was that in a very short time, Isabel found herself safely and comfortably seated on the train, her personal belongings by her feet, opposite an obliging man who showed every sign of finding her a delightful travelling companion. After a few minutes in which they looked out of the window and commented on the weather, the gentleman leant towards her, legs astride, his hands resting on his thighs.

'Perhaps, Madam, as we are to spend a few hours in each other's company, I might be so bold as to introduce myself. Randolph Byrne.'

With a smile, he held out his right hand towards Isabel. She put her hand in his and was surprised at the effect. The feel of his warm, firm flesh, through her kid glove, sent a thrill of pleasure through her. She remembered that she had not lain with a man for many weeks. Byrne's touch and her own memory stirred her. She looked searchingly, meaningfully, into the eyes of the man not three feet away. But he did not respond as he might have done. His smile remained fixed and there was a sense of drawing back which Isabel recognised.

'Isabel Blezard,' she said, taking off her gloves. His gaze flickered towards her left hand. Of course! He would assume she was a married woman, would have seen 'Mrs Isabel Blezard' on her luggage labels. What was holding him back? Lack of interest in her person? Or morality? It would be interesting to find out. But not yet, not at the beginning of the journey. It would keep, at least until the final, tedious stages.

Byrne opened a carpet bag and took out a newspaper and several sheets of paper with columns of figures on them.

'You will excuse me if I...?' he asked.

'Of course,' Isabel purred, watching while he began reading. She had some magazines with her but lacked the will to get them out. Instead, she laid her head back and watched the landscape slip by. The rhythmic, repetitive noise of the train on the rails was strangely hypnotic but it would not do to fall asleep, even though her eyelids felt heavy. Her jaw might drop and make her look ridiculous. It was not surprising that she felt drowsy after the early start this morning. She would just rest her eyes for a while.

Suddenly the grinding shriek of brakes being applied woke her. She sat upright, aware that the left side of her face was hot and stiff. Despite her intentions, she had obviously fallen asleep. Discomfited, she looked across at Byrne and was relieved to see him smiling gently at her.

'We are just drawing in to Peterborough,' he said. 'I did not like to wake you. You looked so tranquil.'

Isabel was reassured. She had perhaps fallen asleep gracefully, charmingly even. Still, the sense of having been observed while she was not in control of herself was unsettling.

Any further conversation was halted by the opening of the compartment door by a young woman who, with the help of a porter, was assisting a white-haired old man up the steps. Holding him by the elbows, she turned him round gently so that he could sink down onto the seat with a minimum of effort. She gave him a quick kiss, patted his hand and gingerly descended. The porter closed the door and very soon the train was on its way again.

Isabel fidgeted with annoyance, un-doing the velvet ties of her cape at the neck and pushing it back over her shoulders. Another passenger was not welcome, disturbing the intimacy she was enjoying with Randolph Byrne. But she need not have worried. Within minutes, the old man, having consulted a gold watch that he took from a waistcoat pocket, leant back and was soon asleep, puffing slightly between thin lips.

Isabel and Byrne exchanged a conspiratorial look. Noticing that he had put his reading matter down, she nodded towards it.

'You have been busy with your reading. Business rather than pleasure, perhaps?'

'Yes, I'm afraid so.'

'May I ask in what line...?'

'Business in general. Hotels, entertainments and the like.'

Isabel sensed a trace of evasiveness in his reply.

'Indeed?' she said. 'My parents own a hotel on the Yorkshire coast.'

'Ah,' he said. 'Then you will understand something of the vagaries of pleasing the public.'

'Yes, indeed.' As she spoke, she stroked her jewelled rings, the expensive ones which overshadowed the plain gold wedding band. 'Well, I can't say that I have any great understanding of the subject but I remember it was something my late husband complained of.' Her pulse quickened. The fact of her widowhood had registered with her companion. His interest, she could see, rose by a notch. She could not resist the urge to raise it still further. 'He was a mill-owner in Huddersfield and used to say you could never be sure you'd be able to sell your cloth after all the trouble you had gone to in making it.'

'Exactly,' he murmured.

Rain was now beating against the windows, sending rivulets quivering down the panes. The sky was an ominous dark grey and soon the rumble of thunder could be heard over the noise of the train. Minutes later, a flash of lightning streaked across the sky. Byrne glanced at Isabel.

'You are not nervous, Mrs Blezard?'

'No, not at all. Thank you.' Isabel knew of fears amongst railway travellers of being struck by lightning but it did not worry her.

By now, as the train began to approach the outskirts of London, the rain was coming down in sheets. All three passengers watched it, the old man now awake and plucking at his clothing.

'This weather will be good for the cab-drivers,' said Byrne. 'But I think we shall have little difficulty at King's Cross. There are always several cabs meeting this train.'

'I see,' said Isabel. In her bag she had the name and address of a small hotel near King's Cross where she had planned to stay until she could find an apartment to rent in a suitable district. Suddenly, the idea of being alone in a strange city seemed unappealing on this gloomy, rain-sodden afternoon.

'You will be hiring a cab?' she asked.

'Yes,' he replied, 'to take me across the city to Paddington. I am travelling on to Bath.'

It took no more than a second for Isabel to make her decision.

'How interesting!' she exclaimed. 'That is my destination too.'

'Then we will share a cab? If that is agreeable.'

'By all means! I should be most grateful to do so.'

'As soon as we stop, I will go out and secure one. And find porters to carry your luggage.'

Isabel rewarded him with her fullest, most alluring smile. Her cape was completely off her shoulders now and the top buttons of her blouse undone. She shook her head slightly, just enough to stir the shiny ringlets about her throat. It was all falling into place, quite wonderfully. Sure enough, as the train came to a halt, Byrne was out on the platform and immediately disappeared from view.

The old man was peering at his watch and tapping its face. Grunting, he fumbled as he sought to return it to his pocket. At that moment, a young man appeared at the doorway, a look of recognition on his face, and clambered in.

'Good day, Father! I'm glad to see you.'

The old man mumbled and allowed himself to be helped to his feet by his son. Isabel watched without interest while the old man turned and grasped the sides of the door with trembling hands. As he began to descend the steps, she saw his gold watch lying on the cushions where he had been sitting. Her right hand slid towards it. A moment later, it was in the side pocket of her skirt.

CHAPTER TWO

Charlotte took a deep breath before she opened the huge wooden door of the mill, preparing herself for the onslaught of sound she knew awaited her. Even so, the noise was deafening as she pulled the heavy door back and slipped inside – the incessant clacking of the looms as the shuttles rattled back and forth, the slapping of belts and pulleys overhead and the undertow of the engine powering them all.

Against the continuous movement of the machinery, the women tending the looms were strangely still, as if posed for a photograph, until one of them destroyed the illusion by bending forward to perform some necessary action. Speech was impossible above the din but this was no handicap. As Charlotte stood in the doorway, collecting her wits, she saw several of the women speaking soundlessly, their lips sending the message 'Miss Blezard is here' along the length of the mill floor.

By now, the smell of the mill had reached Charlotte – a strange oily smell, made up of the lingering animal scent of the wool and the hot engine oil that licked the machines into efficiency. She did not find it unpleasant; she associated it with her father who would carry her proudly into the weaving shed as a child for a brief glimpse of 'Father's work.'

The women nearest to her nodded, their hands and faces grimy above the long drab overalls. Sam Armitage, now not only Chief Engineer but Mill Manager, was at her side immediately, miming over the noise and gesturing that they should go upstairs to the office in the gallery. After he did so, she saw his face flush with embarrassment. She thought she could guess why. The steps to the office were new, glaringly new, pink-ish pine, installed after the fire which had swept through that corner of the mill, the fire in which Charlotte's father had died. The over-turned oil lamp on the ground had told its own story. It did not take much imagination to picture the mill-owner crashing down the stairs in the dark, the oil lamp flying from his grasp.

Charlotte swallowed the lump in her throat.

'Yes, of course,' she replied.

The office was a good deal tidier than it had been in her father's day. His old leather-topped desk was still there but Sam had bought new chairs, cupboards and trays to hold orders and invoices. The view downstairs over the mill floor was clearer now that the windows had been cleaned on both sides. Sam spoke hesitantly. 'I've made a few changes. I hope that's all right?'

'Of course, Sam. Whatever you think fit. It's your office now.'

The young man relaxed and invited her to sit down on a new chair meant for visiting clients. Charlotte thought it best to begin by dealing with gossip.

'I don't know if you have heard but Mrs Blezard has left.'

Sam raised his eyebrows.

'No, I hadn't heard. Where's she gone?'

'I'm afraid I don't know yet. No doubt she'll write and tell me. There's money owing to her.'

They exchanged a grim smile.

'Well, I should say you're well shot of her.'

It was a slightly impertinent thing to say but Charlotte did not mind, in fact, did not mind anything Sam might say. He was looking at her now without shyness. She noticed how attractive his eyes were, green, with hazel flecks in the iris. His short top lip curved upwards at the centre of his mouth. It was a nice mouth. He went on, seemingly unaware of her admiration.

'I've got all the accounts here ready, as you asked.'

'Thank you. And Sam –'

'Yes?'

'I'm thinking of investing some money, when the house is sold, in business. What do you think about another mill?'

Sam frowned.' I'm not sure. It's not a right good time. Competition, specially from abroad, is pretty tough. We know we've a good market for our worsted coatings but even there... Why don't you ask some of your father's friends? Other mill-owners, business men and such-like? They're better placed than I am, I would say, to give you advice.'

'Thank you, Sam, I will. And thank you for your help. All of it.'

He looked embarrassed again, easy to discern in someone of his fair, sandy colouring.

'Not at all, Miss Blezard. It's a pleasure.'

'Charlotte, not Miss Blezard, please,' said Charlotte daringly.

His blush deepened. Charlotte found herself liking the situation. But she would not prolong it, for his sake. She stood up.

'Good day, Sam.'

'Good day, Charlotte.'

He led the way down the stairs, putting out his hand to help her down the last few. As he went forward to pull open the mill door, she saw the women glancing at each other. Lip-readers or mind-readers? One did not need to be very clever to know what they were thinking.

Later, as Charlotte approached the impressive home of Seth and Jemima Broomfield, her apprehension was as great as it had been outside the mill. There, she had been shrinking from the noise and, if she was honest, from the stares of the mill-workers. Now she was about to enter the social world of local mill-owners and business men and their no less formidable wives, the world in which her father had lived.

For the first time in her life, Charlotte thought how much easier it would have been if her step-mother had been with her, Isabel, resplendent in some new and fashionable dress, confident of her own charms and her ability to dominate or join the conversation at will. These dinner parties had been her favourite form of outing, less frequent than the tea-parties and immeasurably superior because of the presence of men. Charlotte knew how much Isabel liked men and how, in the main, they liked her. With her big dark eyes and lustrous brown hair, she had dressed in such a way as to draw attention to her colouring and her voluptuous figure. She always looked right and was able, if she wanted, to make other women look wrong or at the very least, dowdy and colourless.

Charlotte shifted uneasily in the carriage and re-arranged the folds of her cloak. She was still in her mourning black after the death of her father and this evening was neatly dressed in a bombazine dress with matching cape, her only ornament a jet brooch her parents had brought her after a trip to Whitby. She had thought, as she looked at herself in her wardrobe mirror, that she did not look so very different from the queen who was still in deep mourning six years after the death of Prince Albert. She was taller, of course, than Her Majesty and very much younger but she was rounded in figure and not a woman who could be called pretty. She had been told once that she had a lovely smile but had never managed to catch herself in a mirror in the act of smiling spontaneously. Perhaps it was true. It was nice to think it might be true.

The carriage turned into the long curving drive that led up to the Broomfield house. One could almost call it a mansion although that was not a word used much in this Yorkshire town. Lamps illuminated the long row of windows on the ground floor; maids were just starting to draw heavy curtains across them.

The Blezard carriage was the first to arrive. Charlotte had arranged it this way. She was laying her cloak in the arms of the waiting maid when Seth Broomfield, a heavily-built man in his forties, came down the richly-carpeted staircase to meet her. He had never been a man she much liked, had always thought him somewhat coarse and ungentlemanly but he had been a friend of her father's and she was grateful for any help he might give her.

'Eeh, Charlotte, lass! It's grand to see thee.' He took both her hands in his, eclipsing them with his own, hairy-backed ones. 'And how are ye getting on?' Without waiting for an answer, he continued. 'Good! Good!'

'I'm very grateful to you, Mr Broomfield, for seeing me like this, before the others arrive.'

'Not at all, not at all, lass,' he boomed, ushering her into a small parlour. 'Sit thee down. Now what's to do?'

He twinkled at her under his bushy eyebrows but failed to put Charlotte at her ease.

'You know that my father left the mill to me.'

He nodded.

'I have made Sam Armitage Mill Manager – '

Broomfield threw back his head.

'Well done, lass! That's a right good move, that is. He knows what he's doing, that lad. A wise head on young shoulders. I thought so when your father took him on.'

Charlotte was cheered. This was exactly her opinion of Sam. She carried on, her confidence rising. 'But I shall be in overall charge. Since my father died, I have read all the relevant trade journals, the reports of recent exhibitions and am trying to keep up with trends in the cloth trade.'

'Well done, lass,' said Broomfield although Charlotte had a sinking feeling that he wasn't really listening. But she had to finish.

'I wanted to ask you, first of all, whether you think it a good time to buy another mill, as I shall have some money to invest, or whether it would be better to look elsewhere, to go into other ventures.'

'By!' Broomfield sounded impressed. 'I don't think I've ever heard – How old are you, lass?'

'Nineteen,' Charlotte replied, flushing. This was not the response she wanted.

'My advice is – ' He leant forward and again, with both hands, took hold of hers. 'Look, lass. You've a good man in Sam Armitage and as for the brass, well, go to t' bank manager and let 'im invest it for you. Best way.'

Charlotte pulled herself free.

'Thank you, but I do really want to be involved in business in the town. I hoped that if you or your friends were thinking of some new project, whether in cloth or something else, you would let me come in with you.'

Broomfield looked for a moment as if he was going to laugh but thought better of it. 'Charlotte. Your father would be that proud!'

She ignored the remark.

'I wondered, for example, if you thought of putting in a bid for Schofield's mill. Now that Mr Schofield's gone, I've heard Mrs Schofield is thinking of giving up.'

Broomfield's eyes widened.

'Have you now?'

'Yes. And I think we should move quickly if we think of making an offer. It's a good site, right on the canal. So I would be interested in coming in on such a venture, Mr Broomfield, should you think of proceeding.'

'I'll think on,' he said, lowering his eyes.

To Charlotte's annoyance, the door bell rang. The other guests were arriving. She saw Broomfield's eyes slide towards the door.

'Thank you very much, Mr Broomfield. I hope you will keep me in mind if something comes up.'

'Right, right, lass. It's been grand talking to you. Now come and enjoy a good dinner.'

He put his arm round Charlotte's shoulders as she stood up and guided her towards the doorway. She let herself be shepherded, confident that she had said all she meant to say, even in such a short interview.

As they returned to the entrance hall, his wife, Jemima, was coming along the corridor, a very pretty young woman, becomingly dressed in a ruby-red silk gown. Charlotte happened to look at Broomfield's face at that moment and was struck by its vulnerability. 'The face of a man desperately in love' was the thought that came into her mind.

Broomfield strode forward and clasped his wife round her slim waist.

'Thou'rt looking lovely tonight, lass,' he murmured and bent to kiss her neck.

She submitted for a moment and then twisted away.

'Seth! Seth! The visitors are here!'

Charlotte felt sorry for the man who looked hurt. He seemed reluctant to tear his eyes away from his wife and towards the guests who were now thronging the hall. Most of them were known to Charlotte. Frederick Thorpe greeted her charmingly.

'My dear Charlotte! How good to see you! You must come and visit us in Edgerton before very long.'

'Yes indeed,' echoed his wife Ellen, a Londoner always dressed in the latest fashion.

'Thank you, Mr Thorpe, Mrs Thorpe. And are you enjoying living in your new house?'

'Oh yes,' said Ellen Thorpe. 'It is very fine. Such pleasant, wide roads and some elegant neighbours.'

'And still more houses being built, I believe,' said Charlotte. Ellen Thorpe looked less pleased but her husband responded with a brisk 'Yes, yes. Many more planned.'

Charlotte wondered whether to ask about building contracts but decided it wasn't the right moment. Perhaps later. Thorpe had already turned away to speak to his hostess who was dimpling prettily in response. Behind her stood her husband, the welcoming smile fading from his face.

'How are you managing, my dear, by yourself?'

It was Mrs Littlewood, wife of Dr Littlewood who had just arrived, along with their unmarried daughter Grace.

'Quite well, thank you, Mrs Littlewood,' replied Charlotte, sensing the older woman's genuine concern and grateful for it.

'I hear Mrs Blezard has vanished,' said Grace.

'She has left, it is true,' said Charlotte, hoping her tone suggested the matter was closed. Grace Littlewood, eyes sharp as needles, opened her mouth and then shut it again. Her mother took hold of her sleeve and pulled her gently away, Dr Littlewood contenting himself with a grunt and a nod in Charlotte's direction.

Soon the guests were seated in the large dining-room, several of them exclaiming at the beauty of the gleaming crystal and silverware reflected in the surface of the mahogany table. Gas lamps were turned low and many candles softly lit the faces of the dinner guests, the dense black of the men's suits acting as a foil for the jewel colours of the women's glistening evening gowns.

Charlotte felt her spirits lift. These were good people, for the most part, and she was very lucky to have an established place in their company. Plate after plate of delicious food came and went, glasses were constantly filled and refilled. Chatter rose and fell in waves.

To her left was a man she did not know – James Hallas, a young widower new to the area and owner of an engineering firm in the town. She was just beginning to learn something of his business from him when plates were cleared and the signal given for the ladies to retire while the men remained. This social custom had irritated Charlotte ever since she had learnt of its existence; she much preferred to listen to what the men were talking about rather than be banished to another room where the conversation centred on gossip, fashion and children.

So it was this evening when she found herself shown into another room, as beautiful as the last, where tea, coffee and sweetmeats were being handed round by obliging maidservants. The woman she most liked and respected, Mrs Littlewood, was unfortunately on the other side of the room, deep in sympathetic conversation with a woman whose children were just recovering from a serious illness. On Charlotte's left, Ellen Thorpe and Jemima Broomfield were exchanging news of recent fashions in hats so she was forced to turn to Grace Littlewood on her other side.

'So where has Mrs Blezard gone?' asked the woman.

Charlotte stifled her irritation and strove to answer calmly.

'To London, I believe. I shall know more precisely when she writes to me.'

'Oh, so she'll be writing, will she? No doubt asking for money.'

Charlotte said nothing, hoping Grace would realise that questions were not welcome. After a few moments glancing round the room, the woman tried another tack.

'I see you were getting on well with James Hallas at dinner.'

Charlotte's interest quickened although she felt slightly ashamed that she was now happy to draw on Grace's fund of gossip.

'Yes. He seems an interesting man.'

'He's about thirty-five, from somewhere near Oldham, wife and child died o' typhoid last year. Plenty o' brass. Taken over his uncle's business on Leeds Road. Doing right well, I hear.'

The young woman paused, fixed her eye on Charlotte and said with a slight sneer, 'Should be a pretty good catch, I'd say.'

Charlotte drew back. This was not what she wanted to hear. With a coolness she hoped Grace would notice, she said 'Indeed? I should be interested to know more about his engineering firm.'

Grace grimaced and called out.

'Jemima! Here's Charlotte wanting to know about James Hallas's business!'

Charlotte flinched but Jemima smiled pleasantly.

'I'm afraid I can't tell you much about that. Although I know he and Seth were talking about Schofield's mill last night. I think they're going to approach Mrs Schofield before she puts it on the market. It's going downhill, apparently.'

Charlotte stared at her, conscious that her heart had begun to beat faster. As she sat there, surrounded by conversation about hats, children and sickness, she felt her cheeks beginning to burn. She lowered her head and gazed fixedly at her skirt, pleating and smoothing the corded silk fabric with trembling fingers. What a fool Broomfield must have thought her! He had treated her like a stupid girl. But she was not, she was not! She felt mortified but there was nothing she could say or do at the moment.

Later, when the party re-assembled, she was glad to find she was nowhere near her host or James Hallas. She managed to spend the rest of the evening talking to Mrs Littlewood about greater provision for patients at the Infirmary, a subject of apparently little interest to her husband who retired to a corner where he helped himself liberally to the Broomfields' Scotch whisky.

Charlotte was relieved when, at last, there was a general movement to call for carriages. Hats and cloaks appeared and the process of lengthy farewells began. Charlotte thought she detected a hint of special interest in the way James Hallas shook her hand, holding on to it just a moment longer than necessary. But she held her face firm and was glad to make her escape into the familiar interior of the Blezard carriage.

She sat tensely on her seat, as the carriage rolled along Wakefield Road, recalling the conversations of the evening. It was clear that if she was to succeed in local business, it was up to her and her alone.

For a moment Isabel did not know where she was. The light between the curtains revealed a high ceiling, a chair and a pile of luggage. A hotel room!

She stretched her limbs with pleasure. Yesterday was full of memorable moments – the handsome escort shepherding her through the crowds at Kings Cross with its noisy throng, the cab-horses stamping and snorting; the speed and comfort of the Great Western train to Bath, roaring through the countryside, disappearing into tunnels and then screeching out into the light; the arrival in the city, its station aglow with light in the darkness of an autumn evening.

Whenever she could, she had rested her gaze on the man sitting opposite, his thick fair hair falling forward as he read, or leaning back with his eyes closed. Whenever they had the compartment to themselves, she imagined what it would be like making love to him. How exciting to do it on a speeding train!

When they reached their destination, she had asked him to recommend a hotel nearby. He had brought her to the Royal facing the station and left her, with a pleasant smile. Would she be seeing him again? She hoped so.

An hour later she was out on the pavement, ready to view her surroundings. As she walked from her hotel towards Pierrepont Street, flanked by terraces of Georgian houses, she gave way to a feeling of pleasurable amazement. She had entered the city, one she knew nothing of, by night; now, in the light of day, both the buildings and the passers-by possessed the two qualities she had always valued – elegance and style.

This first exploratory excursion was lifting her spirits. She paused as she drew abreast of South Parade, with its fine wide pavements and carriages drawn up alongside. And there was a river! Summer days and reclining in a boat under a parasol! It grew better and better.

When she came to North Parade, she crossed the road, avoiding a smart gig and a high-stepping horse, and stopped by a stone balustrade set high above gardens. On the far side of the open space stood the great shape of an abbey and behind it, more and still more imposing buildings.

This seemed a very different place from Huddersfield, with its working people filling the streets as they walked to and from the mills and factories and with the rumble of carts laden with bales of wool, machinery and goods of all kinds. She could remember George, who admired the town's industrial energy, saying 'You can almost hear it earning its living.' The comment touched no chord with her; she was just glad to find herself out of such surroundings. Bath seemed to her, even on such short acquaintance, to be designed for leisure and pleasure. It was a place where she felt at home.

It reminded her of the town where she had grown up, Scarborough, on the Yorkshire coast. However, the memories were not pleasant. To her, Scarborough meant the small hotel in the back streets of the South Cliff where her mother had worked from morning till night, cleaning and cooking, unable to afford staff to help her. Isabel, as receptionist, tried to give an impression of elegance, despite owning just one best black gown and eating, more often than not, the leftovers from visitors' plates. Her father's handsome face flashed into her mind but she dismissed it immediately.

Her hotel experience told her that the passers-by were the kind of people she had always welcomed as guests. The men and women seemed well fed and looked as if they had money to spend. A pale sun gleamed in the wintry sky and down below her, people strolled in the gardens, warmly wrapped in fur hats and woollen cloaks, seeming in no hurry to go anywhere. True, people of a poorer class could be seen on the streets but one found them everywhere.

As she leant against the balustrade, taking in the scene, Isabel became aware of a young couple standing not far away, deep in conversation. At first she thought they were man and wife but as she looked more closely, it seemed more likely that they were brother and sister. Both had light ginger hair showing beneath their hats, in the woman's case, a fashionable one tilted at a rakish angle. They were an attractive pair, both very slim with large eyes and mobile, expressive faces. Although they looked smart, Isabel's residence in one of the textile capitals of the world enabled her to see that their garments were in fact made of cheap cloth, of little wool content. Their conversation at an end, the couple began walking slowly towards the centre of the city. Isabel followed them, mainly to get away from a gaunt-faced woman selling flowers who was bearing down on her with a determined air. Before long she found herself in Milsom Street which to Isabel's delight was obviously Bath's best shopping area. Her spirits rose and she strolled along, noting tailors, goldsmiths, photographers, banks, haberdashers, glovers, jewellers, haircutters and perfumiers, linen drapers, milliners, outfitters – in fact, providers of goods and services which, to Isabel, were not just desirable but necessary. This was a place in which she could enjoy herself, always supposing she had enough money to do so. She was fully confident this could be achieved, by some means or other.

At the top of Milsom Street, the ground began to rise steeply. Here, on these slopes, Isabel thought, would be the houses where the quality lived. She was right. As she strolled round an almost complete circle of splendid terraced Georgian houses, she saw lamps and chandeliers being lit, illuminating magnificent drawing rooms at first floor level, strains of music and laughter reaching her as front doors were opened and shut. This was the life Isabel wanted; she had known it, deep down, all along and now here it was before her, in real life. Carriages drew up at the kerb-side, sometimes setting down guests or carrying passengers away to no doubt delightful places of entertainment. Behind the iron railings, she could see into basements where servants were cooking, cleaning, scrubbing, arriving with trays of dirty dishes and leaving with fresh ones. One glance down there was enough.

Isabel walked back slowly to the Royal Hotel. She felt that Bath would suit her very well, once she had established what her income would be. She had goods to sell and then there would be her share in the proceeds of the sale of the house in Huddersfield which Charlotte would be sending her. She had no worries that her step-daughter would cheat her; the girl was ridiculously honest. Still, she must make sure the sum was more than adequate; she could see that life in Bath would not be cheap – not unless she could find another man to support her.

The Royal did not appear very favourable on that score. The guests sitting in the drawing-room waiting for dinner to be served seemed universally undistinguished. True, there were a couple of good-looking men but they were firmly attached to wives. Isabel arranged herself becomingly in a comfortable chair and kept her eye on the door.

Almost immediately, a faded-looking woman on her left began to speak to her.

'May I introduce myself? Ada Cleaver.' She proffered a blue-veined hand and smiled, revealing discoloured teeth.

Isabel responded. 'Isabel Blezard. I'm very pleased to make your acquaintance.' How easily we lie, she thought. Still, the woman might be useful.

'Is this your first visit to Bath, my dear?'

Isabel saw no reason to dissemble. 'Yes, it is. But not yours, I presume?'

'Oh dear me no! I have been coming here for many years. My husband and I always paid a visit in the autumn and although he died a few years ago, I like to keep up the tradition. So much to see and do! And the shops! We have nothing like them in the countryside where I live. You are very fortunate, my dear. A first visit to Bath – the Pump Room, the Assembly Rooms, the Guildhall! Have you come from afar?'

'From the north.' There was no need to be specific. 'My late husband was a mill-owner.'

The effect on Mrs Cleaver was gratifying. Her lined face wrinkled further. 'Really, my dear? Well, I hope for your sake that the pleasantry I saw in *Punch* the other day had some truth in it. That it's easy to confuse 'mill-owner' with 'millionaire' because there isn't much difference between them!'

The woman gave way to a sniggering laugh which Isabel did not feel disposed to echo. Still, let Mrs Cleaver think that if she wished. That kind of reputation did one no harm; people were more keen to make your acquaintance if they thought you were wealthy.

At that moment, an elderly, well-dressed man entered, glanced round the room and recognising Mrs Cleaver, made his way towards her and

Isabel. A nod, a smile and 'If I may be so bold?' and he sat down beside the women, nipping up his natty trousers at the knee as he did so, his single eye-glass twinkling in the light.

Introductions were made. Isabel noted the man's look of delighted interest as he feasted his eyes on her. She was glad she had put on one of her better gowns that evening, a soft purple silk with a grape-like sheen which fitted snugly across the bosom revealing the swell of her breasts.

Charles Lester said he was a regular visitor to the Royal.

'It suits me very well, Mrs Blezard. I have a son in London and while I am here in Bath, he comes to visit me or I travel up to see him so a hotel close to the railway station is very convenient. You perhaps arrived that way yourself?'

Isabel agreed that she did. The dinner gong sounding at that moment brought them to their feet. Lester was swift to offer an arm to both ladies.

'May I have the pleasure of your company at dinner?'

Both ladies proving agreeable, the trio made their way to the dining-room where they secured seats at a table for four and successfully deterred anyone else from joining them. Isabel was pleased by the conduct of her new male acquaintance. He saw that every comfort the two ladies might desire was provided, had a serving-man move an ornamental palm that was brushing Isabel's shoulder and ordered a bottle of excellent wine, charging it to his room number. He displayed a polite curiosity about Isabel which she was happy to satisfy.

'I understand this is your first visit to Bath, Mrs Blezard. May I ask what has brought you –?' He hesitated as if he was suddenly aware that this might be too intrusive.

'Yes, it is. I wished for a change of scene after my husband died earlier this year. My doctor...'

Isabel wasn't quite sure why the final two words came out. They weren't true but they seemed to fit the situation in which she found herself. Her listeners seemed to crave a degree of pathos; it felt natural to supply it. She added a gesture to lend credence to the drama by taking a wisp of lace-trimmed lawn from her sleeve and pressing it to her eyes.

'Oh my dear!' Mrs Cleaver was moved. So, apparently, was Charles Lester who looked at Isabel now with an expression of lascivious tenderness. Mrs Cleaver patted Isabel's hand, the hand adorned with beautiful rings as it rested on the white tablecloth.

'Be of good cheer, my dear. You have come to exactly the right place to have your spirits lifted. Hasn't she, Charles?'

'Yes, indeed. And I hope Mrs Blezard will allow me to show her some of the sights of this delightful city.'

'How kind of you, Mr Lester! I shall be most grateful. And please, I hope you will call me Isabel – Charles.'

Charles Lester was as good as his word. A maid delivered a note to Isabel's room next morning. Did she feel ready to take a stroll around Bath later that morning and take the water and coffee in the Pump Room?

Isabel was decidedly ready. The only thing that delayed her was choosing which walking dress to wear from the considerable stock she had brought with her. She had unpacked only a few of her portmanteaux; the rest were stacked up beside the wardrobe. Her hair brushes and combs, face creams and perfumes filled the top of the dressing-table; her jewellery was in a small, locked, walnut chest that she had locked in a drawer. She kept both keys on a ribbon which she wore round her waist over her stays.

The weather had improved since the day before, the sun stronger, the temperature milder. Isabel and Lester walked slowly along the wide pavements, Isabel appraising every person and carriage that passed by. They had not gone very far before Lester stopped and turned to her, raising a bent arm and smiling.

'Would you do me the honour…?'

Isabel acquiesced charmingly, slipping her arm through his and resting it lightly on his jacket sleeve. She thought they probably looked like a handsome married couple; it was certainly much more comfortable than walking unsupported. She could feel that he was a leaner man than her ex-husband, healthier probably too; he certainly did not drink as much as George had done. He also gave an impression of cleanliness. His clothes were immaculate, clean and well-pressed as if they had come fresh from the laundress, which was a relief in an older man. Later, when they were standing in the Pump Room, she wondered how old he was. Late fifties? Well-preserved sixties? It was difficult to tell. No doubt there would be clues to come.

'Are you going to try a cup, my dear?'

Lester gestured towards a table where a smartly-dressed serving-man was dispensing small cups of Bath spa water. Several people behind her were jostling Isabel to reach the table. The competition sharpened her response.

'Of course, Charles! One must partake if one is in Bath!'

The spa water was not pleasant and tasted of metal and sulphur but she swallowed it quickly with a grimace, much to Lester's amusement. He gave a laugh which was more of a giggle and which Isabel was beginning to find irritating. She laughed herself to drown it out.

'Now that I have taken my medicine…?'

He giggled again. 'Oh yes, I think coffee and cake are now called for.'

Lester found a table in a corner of the Pump Room and summoned a waiter to take their order. The large, lofty room with its elegant windows was thronged with people, some in invalid chairs but the majority not so and in apparent holiday mood. Isabel's eyes darted from woman to woman, noting fashionable dress here, a new hairstyle there. She was happily occupied for some time, drinking in the scene along with the small cup of sweet coffee. Lester was speaking, saying something about Christmas.

'I had intended to spend it with my son but his wife's family have insisted they spend it with them in Norfolk. I am invited too but I fear the inducement is simply not enough to tempt me into making what is always a lengthy and awkward journey, travelling up to London from Weymouth and then out again, to say nothing of the final coach journey into the depths of the Norfolk countryside. And at that time of year when the weather can be treacherous. No indeed, no Norfolk Christmas for me.'

Isabel's attention was held; she was now fully alert.

'So will you be returning to Weymouth?'

As conversation buzzed around them, Charles Lester fixed his hooded grey eyes upon her. His lips were moist between the grey moustache and beard.

'Is it of any consequence to you – if I go or if I stay?'

Isabel felt his words to be slightly ridiculous; they were more suited to a lover half his age. But she showed no sign of this reaction.

'Of course it is – Charles.' She smiled and placed her warm hand over his. It felt dry and scaly but she left her hand where it was.

'So shall we both be staying on at the Royal?' There was a pleading note in his voice that was almost touching.

'Yes, of course, Charles. If that is what you wish. I have no other place to go – as yet.' Isabel squeezed his hand and took her own away. As the waiter removed their empty cups and plates, she dabbed her lips with her napkin. She could feel Lester's eyes boring into her.

'Tell me about your home in Weymouth.'

Lester looked extremely pleased to be asked.

'Well actually, I have two. One is a small country estate a few miles inland but I spend most of my time at Melcombe Regis where I have a house on the harbourside. A handsome terrace. In Ralph Allen's day, he owned the house next door so that he and his family could spend time beside the sea.'

Isabel had never heard of Ralph Allen but the air with which Lester delivered the information suggested he was a person of some note.

'It sounds delightful. I should like to see it – perhaps one day.'

'Perhaps indeed,' he replied, giving Isabel what could only be described as a meaningful look.

That evening they attended a concert together. Isabel had not the slightest interest in music and was preparing to be thoroughly bored but the setting in the Assembly Rooms was splendid and she was content to derive pleasure through her eyes and ignore the assault on her ears. Lester seemed to enjoy the music nearly as much as he enjoyed pressing his thigh against hers as they sat close together on the upright gilt chairs.

When they returned to their hotel later that evening, he accompanied her along the dim, gas-lit corridor to her room. At the door, he took her hand in his, kissed it and shot her a burning look. Isabel knew what he was hoping for but disengaged herself from him gently, said goodnight and backed into her room as smoothly and swiftly as she could. She was not going to grant any favours freely which she might wish to use for profit in the future.

The next evening he was absent at dinner. Isabel dined with Ada Cleaver who was leaving a few days later.

'Charles not here this evening? Has he left Bath?' the old woman enquired, her pale face alight with interest.

'No, no. Oh, I don't think so. He speaks of spending Christmas here. At the Royal.'

'Oh, does he?' said Ada Cleaver archly. 'Well, we know whom we have to thank for that, don't we?' Seeing that Isabel did not answer, she went on. 'Seriously my dear, I am very pleased to see how well you have been getting on together. You both look better than you did when you first arrived.'

'Thank you, Mrs Cleaver. I am very grateful you were able to introduce us. I have had a most pleasant time.'

'And I know that Charles Lester has had a most pleasant time also. He told me so himself. Oh, don't worry, my dear. I have been most discreet in answering his questions.'

Isabel was momentarily thrown off balance. She did not like the idea that she had been discussed behind her back.

'May I ask what you have told him?' She could hear her voice hardening.

Ada Cleaver's face flushed. 'Oh, only what you told me, my dear. About your being a widow. Of a Yorkshire mill-owner.'

When dinner was over, which had been continued in silence on Isabel's part, the two women separated. Isabel went straight to her room where she sat down and picked up a fashion magazine. But its usual allure had evaporated. She paced up and down the floor. What was that stupid joke Ada Cleaver had made when they first met? Something about a mill-owner being very like a millionaire? If only that were true! Did Charles Lester really think she had a large fortune? Was that the reason for his warm attention? Pausing in front of the fireplace, she leant her arms on the mantelpiece and studied her face in the mirror, as if it would somehow provide the answer to her questions. It was, she knew, a face that men found attractive, with its large dark eyes and the red, full-lipped mouth.

How much should she trust Charles Lester? He appeared to be comfortably off, spoke of not one but two properties in Dorset, stayed regularly at the Royal according to Mrs Cleaver. Mrs Cleaver? How much did she know of her? Only what the woman had told her.

An ugly thought struck her. Could these two people be in league together to entrap her, the woman's task to pick out a likely victim, the man to close in and play the part of an interested suitor? Their joint prize – a very rich widow? Except that she wasn't.

For a few moments she struggled with her doubts. Could she have been taken in by a pair of rogues? Or were they what they appeared to be – innocent, regular visitors to Bath, one an ageing widow looking for diversion, the other an ageing widower hoping to marry again before too long? Whatever they were, they had not penetrated her defences. She could at least be sure of that.

Unable to sit still, she went over to the window and pulled back the thick, lined curtains. Gas lamps cast a yellowish glow on the wet paving stones and pools of rainwater outside the hotel. Across the road, the station entrance was clogged by cabs drawn up in front of it, the horses fidgeting as other conveyances came too close. A train had obviously just arrived; passengers came streaming out of the station doorways, accompanied by servants and porters carrying luggage. Cabs were hailed, loaded and began to move slowly out of the station approach. Crowds clustered outside the Royal and other nearby hotels.

The message became clear to Isabel. Bath was full of people among whom there would be men worth cultivating, possibly younger, richer and more handsome than Charles Lester. Still, the man had been useful and could be again. She would let him know her financial situation. If it did not deter him, then all well and good. If it did, she would lose nothing but a false admirer.

CHAPTER THREE

It was a raw wintry afternoon when Charlotte set out for Schofield's Mill the day after the Broomfields' dinner party. She kept her head down against the keen wind and pulled her cloak more tightly about her. There were few people about as she walked down from Newsome, mostly carters, closed against the cold, hats pulled low, hunched down into mufflers and turned-up collars behind heavy, slow-moving horses.

She passed terraces of poor-looking houses, cheek-by-jowl with warehouses and workshops. Behind her the green mound of Castle Hill loomed on the horizon but she hardly noticed her surroundings, partly because they were familiar and partly because her mind was full of what she was about to attempt. Her venture might fail but she could not rest until she had tried to achieve it.

Her mind kept returning to the scenes of the night before – Seth Broomfield, with his thick dark whiskers which grew low on his swarthy cheeks; his apparent bonhomie towards her; the news that he and James Hallas were already planning to approach Mrs Schofield about the mill. She hated the feeling of helplessness which swept over her when she realised how he must regard her – as a stupid young girl who was trying to enter the world of business men.

Fortunately she was also driven by the fury which accompanied that emotion. She had as much right as he had to make an offer on the mill and make it she would. There was enough money in her own mill account for part payment and she would find the rest when she had sold the house in Wood Lane.

She already had a good idea what use to make of the Schofield mill building. She passed it now and gave it a searching glance. The stone building, with its rows of large windows, looked as strong and sturdy as the day it had been built. Its position by the side of the canal was a definite advantage.

The mill-owner's house was only a short distance from the mill yard. Its front steps were swept and clean, neat curtains framed the windows and yet it had a desolate air as the life had gone out of it. An elderly servant, more like a cook-housekeeper than a maid, opened the door and ushered Charlotte into a parlour where a good coal fire roared in the ebony grate.

Mrs Schofield, dressed entirely in black, sat motionless beside it. When she turned her head, Charlotte gave a slight start, as if a statue had suddenly moved. The old woman's face was pale, the hand she placed in Charlotte's dry, limp and cool. The smile seemed an effort.

'Good day, my dear. What can I do for you? Will you take some tea?'

'Good day, Mrs Schofield. No, thank you.' Drinking tea was too social and too distracting. 'I hope you are well?'

The old woman grimaced.

'As well as can be expected at my age. And yourself?'

'Oh yes, I am very well, thank you. It is good of you to see me.'

Mrs Schofield seemed to relax a little. This time the smile reached her eyes.

'I get little enough company these days. It's good to see someone young now and again.'

Charlotte smiled gently.

'I was very sorry to hear of the death of Mr Schofield.'

The words had to be said although they brought a veil of sadness to the old woman's face. She simply nodded, as if further speech would be too painful.

Charlotte spoke again.

'I lost my father, George Blezard, earlier this year.'

At this, Mrs Schofield's face flushed and she suddenly became agitated, leaning forward, twisting her hands in her lap.

'Of course, my dear. Miss Blezard. Charlotte. I should have realised as soon as Mary said your name. You will think me a cold, selfish woman.'

'No, no, Mrs Schofield. Not at all.'

'And how are you managing, my dear, without him?'

The question was kindly meant but Charlotte felt her throat contract with suppressed tears.

'I miss him very much. He was very dear to me.'

Now the older woman seemed the stronger of the two.

'Of course he was, Charlotte. He was fair grand. As was your mother, Betty Gledhill. I knew them both when we were young.'

'Did you?'

'Yes indeed. I remember Betty very well.' Her face glowed with recollection. 'When we were girls. We sang in the same choir for a few years. I remember your mother and father courting.'

'There was a bit of trouble, I believe. With him being one of her father's workmen.'

Mrs Schofield gave a slight snort. 'There always is when that happens. But anyone who knew him would have known his motives were what they should be.'

'I think my mother had a job persuading him to propose. With her father owning the mill.'

'Yes, she did that. But your mother had a will of her own. And her father couldn't deny her anything. He fair doted on her.'

Charlotte was torn by conflicting emotions. She had a clear-eyed sense that this meeting was going just as she wanted but kept finding herself disturbed by a rush of painful feeling.

Mrs Schofield's next remark restored her equilibrium.

'After Betty, your mother died – well, we were all a bit surprised when your father married again. So soon after. Not that I'm criticising, you understand. A youngish woman from Scarborough, I heard.'

'Yes.' How much should she say? That she had felt exactly the same, that she had resented the idea of a stepmother but had wrestled with herself to see the situation from her father's point of view – a lonely and loving man who had enjoyed being a husband and was, as a widower, adrift in every sense. And that the reality of Isabel, the second Mrs Blezard, had been the hardest thing of all to bear.

'Are you living together now, you and your stepmother?'

'No, no, she's gone. Possibly to London. Or perhaps back to Scarborough.'

The old woman raised an eyebrow but said nothing.

'Do you think I might change my mind, Mrs Schofield, and have a drink of tea with you?'

It was the right thing to say, at the right moment. With Mary busy in the kitchen, Mrs Schofield got to her feet and took Charlotte to the windows, pointing out the marshalling yard, the storage premises backing on to the canal bank and the weaving-sheds, all now empty and still.

Charlotte could imagine the scene.

'It must have been a rare sight, and a noisy one, when the business was thriving.'

'It was, lass, it was.' Mrs Schofield became quite animated, leaning heavily on Charlotte's arm and using her stick to point out areas of interest. 'You'd see them unloading the bales of wool, great fat bales, right there and carrying them inside. I used to like watching the mill girls, on a fine day, coming outside and going down to the canal bank to eat their dinners. And I always liked the fact that we were making something – something good. Which made us some brass, of course.' Mrs Schofield laughed but sobered almost at once. 'But them days are long gone. We'd not been making much profit when Edgar died.'

'I know. Times are hard in wool just now. I'm keeping Father's mill going, but not extending it.'

Mrs Schofield's eyes grew dark with sorrow as she turned her gaze outside again.

'I don't know what's to become of all this. The agent says the market's very low at the moment.'

Charlotte took a deep breath.

'May I suggest something, Mrs Schofield?' She took the woman's silence as agreement. 'It's true that weaving's not doing right well but I've heard that other mills have got rid of most of their looms and are renting the premises out to other trades – several under one roof – and that's keeping business going.'

Mrs Schofield looked at her in surprise.

'You've heard that, have you? Are you getting help from your father's business friends? Is that what they say?'

'No,' Charlotte said. 'I've found it out myself. I should like to get into this, Mrs Schofield. And I think your premises would be just right. If I could buy them off you, I would go ahead on those lines.'

The old woman seemed unsure.

'If Edgar was still living – but that's foolish talk. I've to decide this myself.' She looked at Charlotte with something like respect. 'Do you think you can do this, all on your own?'

'I do,' declared Charlotte. 'I'll take advice if I need to. But I don't see why we women can't do as well as any man. We understand money as well as they do and I think we're better at keeping our feet on the ground. Not just trying to look important.'

Mrs Schofield's face shone with agreement. The conversation appeared to be bringing her back to life. She chuckled.

'You seem to have learnt a lot for so young a woman! So you're going to carry on the name of Blezard in Huddersfield business, are you?'

'I am that,' replied Charlotte. 'But, I thought, if you wished it, we'd still call your building 'Schofield's Mill' – like it's always been.'

Mrs Schofield leaned forward and patted Charlotte's knee.

'You call it what you like, my dear. I shan't mind either way. It sounds a grand idea to me, what you've suggested. I'll take advice on it, of course, and then we'll talk terms. I've been thinking I ought to sell up and go and live with my sister in Holmfirth. She's asked me often enough. Now before you go, come into the bedroom and look at this view.'

Charlotte was buoyed up with the feeling of success for the best part of a week. Just when it was beginning to fade, it received a welcome fillip. Tonight she would tell the one person who would respond to the news as she wished – Sam Armitage.

She had invited him to take supper with her on Friday evening. Although he always seemed hesitant when he arrived, the combination of hot food and a glass of wine soon had him relaxed and talking to her as the good friend he was. She didn't know why it cheered her so much to sit opposite him and watch him enjoying his dinner.

She had decided not to call and speak to him at the mill, remembering all the interested onlookers last time she went there. So she had arranged with Sam that he would come and bring her news of mill business regularly, at her invitation.

Preparing for his visit was pleasantly stressful.

'I think we'll have lamb chops again, Mrs Burton. Mr Armitage is very fond of them. With a bottle of Father's red wine from the cellar. And apple pie – will you make one of your apple pies please?'

Charlotte fidgeted with the place settings as the maid laid the table, moving the cruet nearer, the cutlery further apart, until it satisfied her. She watched as the servant put coal on the fire.

'A small fire here while we're eating, please, but keep the parlour fire well built-up for when we have our coffee in there.'

She caught sight of herself in the mirror over the mantelpiece and was startled to see how well she looked. Her skin glowed with rosy warmth, her eyes sparkled. Even her light brown hair seemed shinier than usual.

In her black dress, she could see that the slight loss of weight she had experienced after her father's death had improved her figure. She stepped back and turned sideways to see more of herself in the glass. Goodness! How vain she was becoming!

A knock at the door caused her to flutter even more. She went out to greet Sam in the hall instead of waiting for him to be announced and brought to her. He stepped inside, bringing a rush of cold air with him.

'Come inside, Sam, and get warm! Bella, will you bring us some sherry? Here, Sam, let me take your overcoat.'

Soon, even before they had reached the soup stage, she had told him of her visit to Mrs Schofield, the pleasing outcome and the progress she had already made in finding tenants for the mill. Sam was amazed and delighted, as she knew he would be.

'And you did it all by yourself? Not with any help from your Father's friends?'

'No indeed. In fact,' Charlotte smiled impishly, 'I think I rather stole a march on them.' She chose not to recount her experience at the Broomfield dinner party. 'And I'm seeing the bank manager next week about investments.'

Discussion of mill business accompanied the main course and after Sam had had a second helping of apple pie, Charlotte drew him on to more personal territory.

'Have you been anywhere interesting this week, Sam?'

'Yes, on Monday night,' he said, dabbing his mouth with his napkin, 'I went to a meeting of the Literary and Scientific Society. George Jarmain was giving a paper about how we local manufacturers depend on chemistry. It was right good. A lot there.'

'Oh, I wish I could have come with you, Sam! Do any women go?'

'Yes, there were quite a few there. Here –.' Sam pulled a folded copy of *The Huddersfield Weekly Examiner* from an inside pocket. 'There's a report of the meeting here.'

Charlotte scanned the article and read the final words aloud.

'*"the room was fully occupied by a highly attentive and appreciative audience, which included an interesting sprinkling of the fair sex."* Oh, then I will go next time. You must tell me when.'

'Well,' said Sam slowly, as if unsure of broaching the matter, 'they're having their annual conversazione soon in the Assembly Rooms in Queen Street.' He pronounced the foreign word slowly.

'What's –?'

'It's a meeting, with discussion. There'll likely be displays as well.'

'Then we'll go,' said Charlotte decidedly. 'Together.'

Sam looked up at her and blushed.

'That'll be grand,' he said quietly, his colour deepening.

Charlotte looked into his eyes and held her gaze steady. The room suddenly felt very warm. How long they looked at one another was impossible to say but for Charlotte, it was as if they had moved to a different level of intimacy. She felt confused, stirred and foolishly happy all at the same time.

What might have been said next would not be known because at that moment, the maid tapped on the door to tell them that coffee was ready in the parlour.

The business of pouring coffee and offering cream and sugar broke the mood. Charlotte could not tell if she was relieved or disappointed. She sought a new subject.

'Did I tell you that I've received a very good offer for the house? Very much more than Father paid for it, even with adding on the extra he paid for the special woodwork and fireplaces.'

'Good! I'm glad to hear it. I thought you had a mind for somewhere fresh.'

'If I could go back to our old house in Lockwood, I would do. But it's been sold. This one is very fine but it's too big and – .' She refrained from giving the main reason for moving, that it was Isabel's choice of house and still largely filled with her presence.

'Where do you fancy going? There's a lot of fine new houses being built up Edgerton way.'

'I know but I like old houses better than new ones. I thought I'd have a good look round Almondbury. My friends, the Brooks, live there and the Haighs at the farm at the top of Kaye Lane. And Castle Hill and the Woodsome valley take some beating. Where exactly do you live, Sam?'

'On Town End. With my parents. Not one of the loveliest spots in the area but it's gain for walking into town. And there'll be fewer carts and carriages down Old Bank once the new road down to Aspley is finished.'

'You must help me choose,' said Charlotte, re-filling his coffee cup. When he smiled back, she felt a surge of something like joy.

Charlotte's opinion of Edgerton was confirmed a week later when she arrived at the new house where Frederick and Ellen Thorpe now lived. It was true that the road was commendably wide, edged by young trees, and the handsome houses spacious and set on good-sized plots. But it was not her Huddersfield. She would look hard for just the right house in Almondbury.

However, she could not but admire Ellen Thorpe's taste as she entered the hall and was shown into the drawing-room. Used to Isabel's preference for ruby red and purple, it was refreshing to move into lighter surroundings of delicate green and shades of lilac and pale blue. Ellen was dressed in a pale lavender day gown which suited her colouring, and her décor, perfectly.

'My dear Charlotte ! So good to see you! Do come and sit down and have some tea and cake. I think you know most people here.'

Charlotte nodded and smiled at the nine or ten women seated on the new upholstered chairs, their full skirts overflowing on both sides. Most of them had been at the Broomfields' dinner party and were either married to, or the daughters of, business men in the town. They all had an air of prosperity about them and were well-dressed in clothes of more or less recent fashion. Charlotte was the only one wearing black.

She took a chair near to Jemima Broomfield, Mrs Littlewood and Grace. For the next half an hour, drinking tea out of expensive china cups, they chatted companionably enough. The Littlewoods had been away visiting relatives, Jemima and Ellen had been to London on a shopping trip so that Charlotte felt compelled to add her own recent experience.

'On Thursday night I went to the annual conversazione of the Literary and Scientific Society. It was most interesting. There were some beautiful exhibits on display – some very tiny curios, paintings and Venetian glass.'

Her words evoked some polite response. Thinking to find something relevant to the listener, she turned to Grace Littlewood. 'Your father, Doctor Littlewood, might have been interested in the collection of stethoscopes on show.'

There was no response from Grace Littlewood who was busy stirring her tea and apparently trying to listen to another conversation on her left. Her mother made an effort.

'Possibly so, my dear. And are you interested in science – medical and other kinds perhaps?'

'Oh yes, very much!' said Charlotte. 'When we look around the world today, we cannot fail to be interested. So much being discovered. And invented. And being put to the service of mankind.'

Mrs Littlewood smiled encouragingly. Grace suddenly jerked to attention.

'How long have you belonged to this society? I didn't know you went to such things.'

'I'm not a member. I went with Sam Armitage who is. I met several other members there. It was most interesting.'

'Sam Armitage! Your mill manager!' retorted Grace, so loudly that the other women stopped talking and turned their heads.

'Yes,' said Charlotte, sensing unpleasantness.

'Well, I must say I'm surprised at you, Charlotte. Going about with one of your workmen. I should have thought you could do better than that.'

'I don't know what you mean,' said Charlotte quietly but very clearly. 'Sam Armitage is a fine man in every respect and I'm proud to be his friend.'

The room had fallen silent. Everyone was listening.

'You know best, of course,' sneered Grace. 'But don't expect me to mix with such company.'

Charlotte bit her tongue. She wanted to say that Sam was worth ten of Grace Littlewood who was not only idle and stupid but showed no concern for anyone whether they were people she knew or not, such as the poor children you saw in the streets. But this kind of rejoinder had no place in a tea party.

Raging inside at Grace's words, she stood up slowly, as if she had just remembered another engagement. Grace, lip curled, was still glaring at her; her mother, with raised colour, was looking away, avoiding Charlotte's eyes.

Ellen Thorpe, an assiduous hostess, was at her side, visibly nervous.

'My dear Charlotte. Must you go?'

'Yes, Ellen. Thank you very much for the tea.'

As Charlotte reached the entrance hall, she heard voices raised in the drawing-room behind her. 'Who?' 'What did she say?' 'I couldn't hear.'

A maid appeared and began helping Charlotte to find her cloak among those hanging on the hat-stand. As Charlotte reached up to lift hers off the hook, she was jostled, much to her surprise, by Jemima Broomfield, who was tugging her cloak off its hook with near-feverish haste.

'He's come to collect me,' she said, throwing her cloak round her shoulders and trying to fasten it at the neck with trembling fingers. Who she was referring to became clear. A dark shape suddenly blotted out the light coming through the glass panels in the front door. Standing on the doorstep was Seth Broomfield, clothed in black from head to foot, eyes staring in his saturnine face.

As the maid opened the door, he strode forward and threw searching glances at all the doors and up the staircase, as if looking for someone.

'Jemima! Are ye ready?' he barked, the scowl on his face deepening.

Charlotte's heart gave a lurch. Had he heard yet about her agreement with Mrs Schofield? She steeled herself for some hostile remark. But she need not have worried. Whether he knew of the deal or not, at that moment Seth Broomfield was in the grip of something that blotted everything else out of his mind. He looked at Charlotte without recognition and grabbed hold of his wife.

Then the sound of a door shutting. It was Ellen Thorpe, her hand firmly on the handle of the drawing-room door.

'Goodbye, Charlotte. Jemima. I'm sorry you both have to leave so soon.' A slightly glazed look in her eyes betrayed her effort to give the impression that everything at her tea party was entirely normal. Broomfield gave a grunt and swung away towards the front door, pulling Jemima behind him, her face registering both alarm and defiance.

Charlotte held out her hand to Ellen.

'Good-bye, Ellen. And thank you. I hope to see you again before too long.'

The feeling of relief was overwhelming as she climbed into the Blezard carriage which was soon rolling down New North Road into town. She wondered whether she needed to keep attending these foolish tea-parties where little of any interest was ever voiced. But as soon as this thought had crossed her mind, she dismissed it. It smacked of pride. Who was she to judge people? This was not how she had been brought up. She remembered that her father had valued this group of people and would have wanted her to remain on good terms with them.

As the carriage slowed to let some heavily-laden carts cross its path, she thought about Seth and Jemima Broomfield. What had been the reason for his unexpected arrival at the ladies' tea-party? Unusual, surely, to be collected at such an hour by one's husband? She knew Jemima had her own carriage. Perhaps they had another appointment somewhere else. That could be it. But the uneasiness the episode had created in her did not dissipate as easily as she hoped.

On arriving home, she found two letters awaiting her. She opened the one from Sam first. He could obtain tickets for a concert in town next week. Perhaps she would let him know if she would care to accompany him. He would quite understand if it were not possible. Charlotte replied straightaway. She would be delighted to attend the concert and looked forward to hearing more details.

The other was more expensive-looking, the handwriting all too familiar. She sat down and drank some more tea before she read what Isabel had to say.

The Royal Hotel
Bath
30th November 1867
Dear Charlotte

You may perhaps be surprised to see my address. But having made an acquaintance on the journey south, I was persuaded to travel on to Bath where I was assured of finding congenial surroundings. I am at present staying in a hotel as you see but hope soon to move into an apartment of my own. To this end, it has become pressing for me to receive some money from my late husband's estate. If the house is not already sold, perhaps you would be so good as to send me an advance, which I know you are well able to do.

Yours truly,
Isabel Blezard

The restaurant had been a good one and well patronised by diners of importance. Isabel was sure she had heard French being spoken at a nearby table. Lester had apparently enjoyed himself, discussing and ordering the wine with great relish. Isabel watched how carefully he chewed his beef steak with his pointed yellow teeth. She approved of the care with which he wiped his moustache and beard clean after eating.

He had been willing to hail a cab to take them back to the hotel but it was a fine, dry night and Isabel chose to walk. The stroll back, with the gas lights creating shimmering pools along the darkened streets of Bath, was pleasant, with her arm tucked comfortably into his. Yet she occasionally sensed some impatience on his part, a slight tension in his demeanour, as if he was only just managing to bide his time before seeking some other, more exciting destination. It did not bother Isabel. Her experience was that men were usually restless and desirous of moving on to something, or someone, else.

It was one of the things she had found so tedious about life with George Blezard. His main aim seemed to have been a quiet domestic existence, with his wife and his daughter near him, along with a ready supply of food and drink, especially the latter. Not for the first time, she wondered how long she would have been able to endure being married to him, if an unexpected heart attack had not conveniently carried him off. True, she had enjoyed the courtship and the wedding, and most of all, the excitement of the new house which had given her the opportunity of furnishing and decorating it exactly as she wished.

She recalled the time she had commissioned the handsome John Brook, the skilled cabinet-maker from Almondbury, to carve some walnut and mahogany over-mantels for the fireplaces and a fine, curving banister that swept down from the top of the house to the bottom. *He* was a man who could have made her life interesting. Indeed, she had succeeded, just once, where he was concerned but she had been thwarted by a rival in love. Isabel instantly dismissed those memories from her mind; one did not acknowledge failure, much less revisit it.

But other, more recent thoughts were not so easily swept away. She remembered the handsome man she had met on the train – Randolph Byrne. Where was he now? Would she meet him again? She admitted to herself that she wanted to, very much. She had found him attractive in every way – his appearance, his poise, his apparent success in his business and even his conduct when he left her without disclosing his address. She found a certain amount of mystery fascinating; it whetted her appetite to know, and possess, more of the man.

At the moment, however, the man on whose arm she was leaning was opening the door of the Royal Hotel and guiding her gently through it. The contrast with the cold, dark street was startling. The foyer was warm and bright and from the dining-room came the sound of voices and the smell of cooked food and tobacco smoke.

Lester nodded in the direction of a small parlour.

'Perhaps a nightcap, Isabel? A little port? Cognac?'

'A cognac would be very nice. Thank you.' Isabel favoured him with a smile and sank down into a chair while he placed the order. Soon the spirits were having their effect, Isabel warmed by the brandy while Lester, no doubt, enjoying a similar experience from his whisky. The moment was right.

'Charles. I wonder if I might ask your advice.'

Lester's eyes brightened.

'Of course, my dear. Anything at all.'

'The fact is, Charles, that I am experiencing a little financial difficulty. Only a little, you understand, no problem with settling my hotel bill or anything like that – but I need to raise a little cash for current expenses. I may have told you that I am awaiting the settlement of my late husband's estate, in particular, the sale of the house we occupied. In fact, Charles, that is *all* I am expecting. The mill business has been left to my step-daughter. I shall not inherit a penny from that enterprise.'

There! It was said. She watched Lester's response beneath lowered eyelids. He appeared shocked.

'Indeed! Is not that somewhat unusual? Would not the widow normally be the one to inherit everything, there being no son in the case? With a bequest to a daughter of the first marriage?'

Isabel shook her head sadly.

'Normal. Usual. As you say. But you, with only a son, are perhaps not aware of how a daughter might manipulate a doting father – not just the heart-strings but the purse-strings as well.' It was diverting to see how offended Lester appeared to be on Isabel's behalf.

'Well, I'm sorry to say it, Isabel, and I hope you will forgive me using these words but I think the arrangement not the act of a gentleman.'

Isabel shook her head.

'You would think that, Charles, because you are a gentleman yourself. Perhaps, to be fair, Mr Blezard expected me to remain living in the family home with my step-daughter and consequently sharing the living costs with her. But I needed to get away – the memories…'

'Of course, of course, my dear,' said Lester, edging his chair nearer to Isabel's so that their arms were almost touching. 'And if you had not come to Bath, then I should not have met you.'

Isabel opened her eyes to their widest extent and bestowed the full beam of her long-lashed smile on him. The man looked as though he had gone weak at the knees. For a moment he was speechless, then asked in a croaking voice, 'What can I do for you?'

'Well,' said Isabel, glad to have returned to the main point of the conversation, 'I have a few items with me, of sentimental value but needs must. Could you advise me how to sell them to get the best price? At auction perhaps? Or at an antique shop? I really have no experience of this kind of thing.'

With pawn-shops, with pulling their jangling bells just before closing time, her arms full of hotel silverware, Isabel was well acquainted.

'Oh, I think an auction much the best way. There should be a few going on in the city. You can always place a reserve on the goods so that they are returned to you if the bids do not come high enough. Perhaps I could take a look at the items in question?'

Isabel downed her brandy in one gulp and stood up, leaving Lester to do the same. Upstairs, allowing him into her room was done with all speed and without any of the allurement such an act might previously have suggested. She had already sorted through the tea-chests she had brought with her and taken out the things she felt she could do without, at least for the time being. The remainder, along with the painting, still secured in its hessian wrapper, were locked up again in the small box-room she was renting from the hotel for a trifling sum.

Lester inspected the silver candle-sticks, the pair of crystal lustres, the assortment of vases.

'These should sell well, all good quality. And this is beautiful,' he said, picking up the gold and silver writing set on its silver tray and looking for hallmarks. 'I'll call in to some auction-houses tomorrow. Leave it to me.'

Sure enough, Shepherd's, the auctioneers, were holding a pre-Christmas auction sale in a few days' time.

'A pre-Christmas sale! Could not be better!' declared Lester. 'People will be ready to spend more than usual and will buy goods as gifts for others, not just for themselves.' Turning to Isabel, he leant towards her and said in a hoarse whisper, 'I feel this is going to be a happy Christmas. For both of us, I am sure of it.'

Isabel smiled. Perhaps it would.

The doors were open early the day before the sale to allow the public to view the lots on display. The smaller goods were set out on trestle tables, numbered by lot. Around the edges of the huge room stood wardrobes and tall-boys, whatnots and wash stands. Rugs were half-rolled, half-displayed, many looking as if they held the dust of decades. Miscellanies of small objects were grouped together; Isabel saw her vases forming one lot, the lustres and candle-sticks another.

'Where is the gold and silver writing-set, Charles? I don't see it.'

'It's over there. In a display case. They lock up the more valuable stuff. There are always a few of our light-fingered brethren about, looking to slip a tasty object into an inside pocket.'

Isabel looked more intently at the people strolling past. Two elderly women, down-at-heel and wearing coats greasy with wear, were bent over, prodding the seats of chairs and a matching sofa. Next to them, a young man and woman in good winter coats and hats cast appraising glances at the jewellery in the glass cases. The young woman pointed to something she obviously liked and drew her companion's attention to it. He smiled down at her, murmured something and lifting her hand to his lips, kissed it. They continued to hold each other's gaze, faces close together, oblivious of everyone else. Isabel looked away. It made her feel uncomfortable.

Lester returned to her side.

'Nothing very special, in my opinion. But that may not be a bad thing. All your stuff is very fine.'

'Yes,' said Isabel, heaving a sigh. 'I expect they are. Wedding presents, you know.' They weren't but her ready lie prompted extra attention from Lester who laid a protective arm across her shoulders as he drew her towards the exit.

When they arrived for the auction sale the next day, the room was already agreeably full. Conversation buzzed. Groups of dealers huddled together, friends chatted and a few determined-looking women in old-fashioned hats settled themselves in the front row.

Isabel was relieved that all her lots came up for auction early on. She hated sitting still for long, especially on a small uncomfortable chair. Lester said they would not reach the final lots, usually the carpets, until the evening.

The candle-sticks, the lustres and the vases attracted reasonable bids. When, however, the porter lifted the gold and silver writing set out of the glass case and held it aloft, rotating it slowly so that it caught the light, there was an audible ripple of interest.

'Now, ladies and gentlemen, a very fine object indeed. Lot 37. Gold and silver writing set, hall-marked, with inlaid inkwell, matching letter-opener and pens. Albert, let the ladies in the front row take a closer look.'

The auctioneer paused while the porter dipped and twirled the object to maximum effect. The artificial bird on one woman's hat fluttered on the front row.

'A quality object indeed. Would add distinction to any desk or writing table. What am I bid? Shall we start the bidding at £20?'

The bidding began, slowly at first then picking up speed as the auctioneer sensed the interest in the crowd. The main bidders were three elderly women in the front row and the young man. The bids rose higher. Isabel felt her heart beating faster, her face flushing. Two of the women dropped out as the bids increased. Now it was just the young man and the bird-hatted old woman in the front row.

'£50. Any advance on £50?'

The bid was with the old woman. The young man turned to his companion for assent but she shook her head. It was too much.

'£50 then. £50 for the writing-set.' He paused but the room was silent and motionless. There was a throbbing sensation at the pit of Isabel's stomach.

'Sold then for £50 to the lady in the front row.'

Lester clutched Isabel's arm.

'There, what did I say? A very good price indeed. Shall we go now?'

Isabel was glad to stand up and move away. Her under-garments were sticking to her body with sweat. The cold air hit her as they gained the pavement, chilling her perspiring face and neck.

'Come! We must get you home,' said Lester. Hurrying along, Isabel found herself shivering. Once inside the hotel foyer, Lester ordered drinks without delay and ushered her into a parlour which they had to themselves.

'Well, are you pleased, my dear?' Lester looked as if he was, without question.

'Oh yes! Definitely. Good prices. All of them. And it was all very – .' Why shouldn't she say it? 'Exciting. It was very exciting.'

Lester's face was aflame. 'Yes. I thought so too.' He moved closer and placed a hot hand on her knee. 'You like excitement?'

Isabel did not need to consider.

'Yes, I do. Very much.'

Lester's face broke into a wide, satisfied smile.

'Good. That's what I like to hear. A woman after my own heart.' He leant forward again, so close that she could smell the whisky on his breath. 'It's the uncertainty, isn't it? The sense that you might just be on the verge of winning everything!' His eyes glittered. Slowly he opened his mouth and bit his knuckle. 'Tell me, have you ever visited a gaming club?'

It was the same evening. Isabel came downstairs slowly in her black evening gown with its deep, scooped neckline, diamonds gleaming at her throat, her velvet cloak draped around her shoulders. Lester stood at the bottom of the stairs waiting for her. He looked stunned, as Isabel intended him to be. He lifted his arm, taking her hand as if for some old-fashioned minuet. He too was in evening dress, with cloak and top hat. In the darkness outside, he could have passed for a younger man.

As they turned the corner, a cab-horse came frighteningly close to them before it was hauled back by its driver. Lester thrust himself against Isabel to protect her but when the danger was past, he remained where he was, pressed close to her. Isabel, still aroused from her experience at the auction, returned his pressure. Scarcely noticing the hardness of the stone wall on her back, her body responded to his, cleaving to his chest, belly and thighs. Then his mouth was upon hers, seeking, driving, the whisky taste drowning hers. He smelt of camphor, hair-oil and sweat. Pulling away to take breath, she felt his desperation, his hunger for her.

'Charles!' She pushed his hands away from her breasts and attempted to smooth her hair. 'No, not here.' She felt him panting. 'Not yet.'

He straightened up, his eyes shining with moisture, and wiped his mouth with the back of his hand.

'Isabel. My love.' His voice was thick and husky.

Isabel slipped to one side.

'Come, Charles. You promised me some excitement.' She stepped forward, perfectly possessed, refastening her cloak which had slipped down round her hips. Lester seemed to stagger and to be breathing heavily. She grasped his arm and pulled him along with her.

Minutes later, they were at the gates of a tall house, all its windows blind with shutters. Lester rapped on the door, a curious double-knock. At the sound, the door opened a little and then wider, disclosing a grim-faced, thick-set man. He nodded to Lester like a man he knew well.

Once through the doorway, their cloaks were taken and they moved along a dark hall and down stone steps into an underground room, dim save for great golden circles of light over the gaming tables. Isabel was struck by the clash of colours – the men and women in black evening clothes, the green baize tops of the card tables, the red and black of the roulette wheel, spinning in the middle of the room.

Lester was already settled in what appeared to be his usual chair, columns of chips ranged in front of him, lips parted, eyes gleaming.

The croupier raked back the chips from the previous game.

'Faites vos jeux.'

As Lester and the other players round the table moved their chips onto the numbered squares, Isabel realised that she recognised two of the people there. The croupier was the ginger-haired young man she had seen on her first day in the city. Sitting across from her was the young woman, almost certainly his sister so alike were they. Her thinness was all the more evident in the low-necked dress she wore from which her bony white shoulders protruded. Her dress was black, trimmed with scarlet ruffles round the neckline. On her head she wore a rosette of the same scarlet material, vivid against her ginger hair. Her white face was heavily rouged, her lips scarlet as paint.

There were few other women in the room. An old one, raddled and wrinkled, her gnarled hands heavy with rings, sat hunched over the table. Like everyone else, she was in evening dress, the neckline revealing a deeply creased cleavage. Her eyes never left the roulette wheel. Next to her a younger woman stood behind a player, her fingertips resting on his shoulders. She threw a quick glance at Isabel, then at Lester, and resumed her role as escort, her grip tightening on the man's jacket. He paid her no attention, his hands curled round his stack of gambling chips.

The croupier's voice cut into the low murmur of conversation.

'Rien ne va plus!'

With a spread of his fingers, he set the wheel spinning. There was complete silence as all watched the small white ball tumbling, clicking on its way.

'19. Black.'

Some chips were pushed to the winner; most were dragged back by the croupier. The whole process began again.

After a slow start, Lester's luck began changing. Gradually, his pile of chips was growing, along with his excitement. Isabel saw that his face was very flushed and had become darker, with a purplish tinge, as the evening wore on. He drank steadily from a glass of whisky which was unobtrusively replenished by a waiter. He had forgotten all about Isabel, his gaze limited to the gaming table and the roulette wheel at its centre.

Now his pile of chips had reached a height unmatched by anyone else at the table. Isabel wondered if this was the moment he would stop. It seemed to represent a satisfyingly large amount of money. But she was wrong, utterly wrong.

As the next game began, Lester pushed every single one of his chips onto a red square, number 15. He did it very slowly and deliberately, evincing a gasp from the onlookers. The croupier and his observing sister betrayed no emotion.

The wheel began to spin. All eyes followed the ball. Isabel thought to touch Lester's hand but he was oblivious to everything, staring at the ball, following its cunning path. The wheel slowed. Isabel felt her heart thumping painfully. Total loss or total gain? Lester's eyes were bulging, his breath rasping, his forehead beaded with sweat.

The wheel stopped. The ball, as if bent on teasing, teetered between one number and the next, and then, as if exhausted, fell into number 15. Red. The crowd roared and Isabel turned to Lester, only to see him choking, gurgling, and falling head first onto the table, next moment, slithering to the floor with a crash.

'Charles! Charles!' she screamed, dropping to the floor beside him. Her fingers fumbled as she tried to loosen his collar. Seeing his eyeballs roll upwards, she shrieked, 'Get someone! A doctor! The manager!'

The ring of people parted and a tall figure stepped forward. It was Randolph Byrne.

CHAPTER FOUR

Sitting in the concert-hall, Charlotte experienced a wave of euphoria. The programme of Christmas music was all the more beautiful for being familiar. As Charlotte followed the rise and fall of the haunting phrases, she felt a sense of joy that was almost painful in its intensity. The music seemed to possess her utterly, carrying her with it, mind and heart. As it came to a close and the applause began, her awareness of where she was returned, together with the sweet consciousness of sitting next to Sam Armitage.

While the music was in progress, she rarely moved her head to look at him but could still see his firm hands, palms down, on his thighs. He kept very still throughout, which she liked, and drew a deep breath as the music stopped. He turned towards her.

'I thought that wa' champion!' His eyes shone, his lips quivering in a half-smile.

'Yes, yes. I thought so too. The Choral never let us down.'

A hubbub of voices arose as the applause faded away. Programmes rustled, heads turned. Attention focussed once more as the conductor stepped onto the rostrum and lifted his baton.

'And now, ladies and gentlemen, our final number. I ask you to stand and join the choir as we sing together *O Come All Ye Faithful*. You will find the words on the back of your programmes.'

Charlotte and Sam stood up, grasping the shared programme between them. Again, she was fascinated by the sight of his hand so close to hers until, embarrassed by her response, she fixed her attention on the words of the carol. As the descant took off on *Sing, choirs of angels*, she experienced once more the sense of soaring that held her in the grip of pleasure. Next to her, Sam's tenor voice rang out strong and clear amongst the wealth of sound that filled the hall.

The concert over, the audience stirred and began filing out. Charlotte nodded and smiled at a few people she recognised. One or two looked curiously at Sam who appeared not to notice. They stood outside on the pavement; carriages were drawing up along Queen Street. Charlotte shivered. Sam seemed uncomfortable for the first time that evening. But Charlotte did not want to let him go.

'You'll let us take you home in the carriage, Sam?'

Sam's quick rejoinder suggested that this was the source of his unease.

'Nay, but thank you. I'll walk – like I always do.'

'Very well but you will let us take you part of the way? We can put you down in Aspley – then you won't have so far to walk.'

Sam appeared to be struggling between principles and politeness. At last, he gave in. 'Thank you, Miss Charlotte. That is very kind.'

Charlotte's pleasure at the thought of having Sam in the carriage vanished. She didn't want this kind of respectfulness. But she understood how it was inevitable. And always would be – as long as she was the employer and he the employee.

'We need to walk down to the Beast Market. Henry will be waiting there. Perhaps, Sam, you would allow me to take your arm? It is somewhat slippery underfoot.'

Within seconds, Sam's awkwardness disappeared. Together they walked slowly along the street, Charlotte feeling the pleasant roughness of Sam's tweed jacket under her glove and enjoying his nearness. Like a young married couple, she thought.

'You have a fine tenor voice, Sam. Had you thought of joining the Choral yourself?'

'Nay. It's kind of you to say so but no, I hadn't thought of it. I'm busy most evenings. And I'm not sure they'd have me, anyroad.'

They both laughed. Charlotte tightened her grip on Sam's arm, pulling him closer. He made no resistance and they walked on in what felt like mutual contentment.

This mood was unfortunately disturbed when they reached the carriage. There were several men, all rough-looking, hanging around the Beast Market. As Sam opened the carriage door and helped Charlotte up the steps, they began jeering and catcalling. When he had climbed in after her, Charlotte saw that he had flushed red and was biting his lip.

'Never mind them,' she said gently.

'Aye, aye,' he replied. His colour slowly faded as he stared fixedly out of the window.

Charlotte had travelled in a carriage often with her father and sometimes with other gentlemen. They had all, she recalled, paid absolutely no attention to any abuse or comments such as they had just witnessed but had simply ignored the men as if they did not exist. She realised that Sam was unused to the situation, had perhaps not ridden in a carriage before.

'I don't think those men meant any harm,' she ventured.

'It's not that.' Sam's face flushed again. 'It's because I understand them doing it. I daresay I've felt like they did – when you see folk getting into carriages. Although I would never have shouted out.'

Charlotte considered his words.

'So is no-one to have carriages because some cannot afford them?'

Sam's sudden, transforming smile surprised her.

'I can see we're going to have some right good arguments, Charlotte!'

She laughed happily. 'By all means! I look forward to them!'

They both chuckled and she leant forward, daringly, and placed her hand over his.

'Come to supper next Friday – and bring your arguments with you. Along with the order-books.'

To her delight, he put his free hand on top of hers, without embarrassment, and spoke with more confidence that she had seen before.

'I shall look forward to it.' After a pause, he added 'All week.'

This time he blushed slightly. Charlotte's heart leapt and she felt her own cheeks grow warm. As the carriage slowed to a halt, she took refuge in etiquette.

'Good. And thank you so much for escorting me to the concert. I enjoyed it very much.'

He made some inarticulate reply and jumped down. When she looked out of the window, she saw him standing still, watching as the carriage drew away. She waved and saw him wave back in response. They held each other's gaze until darkness and distance made it impossible.

The good mood, brought about by the evening spent with Sam, lasted well into the next day. Even Isabel's letter was looked at more sympathetically. On first reading, Charlotte had bridled at Isabel's insolence – *'send me an advance, which I know you are well able to do.'* She felt an implied criticism of her father for failing to provide adequately for his second wife.

But now, as she re-read Isabel's letter in the library with the sun streaming in and the coal fire warming her feet, she saw that the expression was unarguably true. She *could* afford to send Isabel a considerable sum in advance of the sale of the family house. Better to maintain politeness in relations with her stepmother than to antagonise her needlessly. Isabel did have some right to a sense of grievance. She would make arrangements for a banker's draft to be sent without delay.

Once she had thought of sending the money, she could not settle to anything until she had put it into practice. She would go into town rightaway. The family solicitor had sent her a note asking her to call in so she could do that too. It took no more than a moment to find her cloak, bonnet and gloves and inform a startled maid that she was walking into town and would be back in a couple of hours.

She enjoyed the walk. It was a fine day though cold and she was glowing from the exercise by the time she approached the solicitor's office in Market Place. The solicitor, a Mr Crowther, was an elderly man who had handled the family affairs for more than forty years. He appeared to be in good humour as he sat behind his desk, his knotty, blue-veined hands resting on a pile of Blezard files. Mrs Schofield's solicitors had completed the paperwork necessary for the acquisition of the mill for which tenancies were already in place and solid buyers for the house in Wood Lane were waiting to hand over their money just as soon as Charlotte was ready to move out.

'I've seen a house on Sharp Lane, Mr Crowther, that I think will suit. I'm going to pay a second visit, just to make sure, but I liked it very much when I saw it. It's not as big as Wood Lane obviously, or as opulent, but an older house, with long, elegant windows. I think I shall like living there. I have friends in Almondbury already.'

'Good! I am glad to hear it!' said Mr Crowther, beaming at her over his spectacles. 'And I have some more good news for you.'

He began by going back in time, when her grandfather, her mother's father, Josiah Gledhill the mill-owner, was alive.

'He left the mill to his daughter, your mother, and his son-in-law, your father, as you know.'

'Yes. And Father left it to me in his will.'

'Yes. But your grandfather had considerable financial assets in addition.'

'And they came to me from Mother? I received those when she died.'

'Yes and no.' For the first time, Mr Crowther looked slightly ill-at-ease. 'Some of it did, certainly but – if I can explain, Charlotte, with as much delicacy as I can – '

Charlotte was puzzled. She couldn't imagine anything to do with her parents, upright and straightforward people as she knew them to be, that called for delicacy.

The solicitor looked her squarely in the face and seemed satisfied by what he saw there.

'The fact is, my dear, that although your grandfather did not doubt your father's motives in wanting to marry his beloved daughter Elizabeth Gledhill, there were others only too ready to advise caution.'

'You mean they thought Father was a fortune-hunter?' Charlotte was hot with indignation.

'I doubt it was as strong, as blatant as that, my dear. But fathers are usually very protective of their daughters – as you will know – especially perhaps when their daughters are set to inherit a good deal of money.'

Charlotte said nothing. She could not help but agree.

'So your grandfather left most of his assets in trust for any child or children of the marriage to be released when they reached twenty-one years of age. You are the only child of the marriage and I thought it wise to begin looking into the matter so the inheritance will be ready for you when the time comes. It is a little early to be precise on figures but my nephew, Silas, has been calculating for me.'

Here he gestured towards a young man who had come into the room silently and stood just behind Charlotte holding a box-file as if it were a Bible.

'Before very long, Charlotte, you will be a very wealthy young woman, very wealthy indeed.'

The solicitor smiled more broadly, revealing several missing teeth. Charlotte did not know what to say, although it was clear that both men expected her to say something. At last she managed 'Good! Good!' but immediately felt foolish.

'I wanted to tell you this now, Miss Charlotte, so that you could be thinking of how to use the money wisely when it comes. We will of course be happy to advise on investments, as will your bank manager.'

When Charlotte said nothing, he went on. 'I thought it would be helpful to know of the money in case you wanted to buy an expensive house and to ease your mind should the mill business slump a little in the future.'

Charlotte pulled herself together.

'Thank you, Mr Crowther, that was most thoughtful of you.'

The old man rose and held out a trembling hand.

'I will say goodbye now, Miss Charlotte. I've decided to retire from business at the end of the month. I leave you in the capable hands of my nephew, Silas Crowther.'

The young man in question stepped forward as Charlotte extended her hand to his. It was not a pleasant feeling. His hand was cold and clammy, his smile limited to a widening of his mouth. Still, this did not mean he would not be a perfectly adequate solicitor.

Minutes later, she was down the stone staircase and out into the fresh air. More money! She had to be grateful, whatever the planning behind it. She did not feel any great personal need for more money but Mr Crowther was right; if the mill business faltered, she would have enough to start up other business ventures.

As she stood on the steps of the building, half a dozen children suddenly appeared and gathered round her, each with a hand outstretched in begging position. They all looked dirty, ill-clad and half-starved.

Charlotte, like her father, did not approve of beggars. He had always maintained that a man could find some work if he put his mind to it. But this could not apply to these little children. Their poverty was not their fault, however one might argue.

Charlotte opened her purse and took out a handful of change.

'Here you are! Take this to your mothers. Or get something to eat.'

With some yelping and fighting, the children grabbed the coins and ran off. There would never be any lack of deserving causes if she wished to support them, she thought, as she walked forward into the space now full of market stalls and people.

Despite the coldness of the day, open stalls with tarpaulin covers rolled back were selling goods of all kinds, some still being unloaded from wagons and packs on horse-back behind them. To one side, a speaker on a rickety platform was shouting the praises of a patent medicine, listened to by a small crowd. Children darted between the stalls and underneath tables, sometimes dislodging wares and being cuffed round the head for it.

Two well-dressed men emerged from the bar-room of a hotel nearby and with a start, Charlotte recognised Seth Broomfield and James Hallas. Catching sight of her, they moved towards her, in Broomfield's case, unsteadily.

'Why, it's Miss Blezard! The business woman!' Broomfield's voice was loud, causing heads to turn. Charlotte caught James Hallas's eye. He looked embarrassed by his companion, especially when he lunged towards Charlotte. She stepped back but not before she had smelt the beer on his breath.

The expression on Broomfield's face was ugly.

'Tha mun be reet proud o' thisen,' he sneered, his dialect broadening with his temper. 'Tekking advantage of an old woman. An' bereaved.'

Now Charlotte understood. He had learnt of her arrangement to buy the mill from Mrs Schofield. Alerted by the promise of trouble, several bystanders stopped what they were doing and became attentive. James Hallas moved forward so that he stood between Charlotte and Broomfield.

'I'm very sorry, Miss Blezard,' he said in a low voice. 'I'm afraid Mr Broomfield has had a rather good dinner.'

'Wazzat?' The older man pushed Hallas's shoulder, causing him to stagger.

Charlotte was having none of it. She faced up to Seth Broomfield and spoke slowly and clearly to make sure he understood her.

'If you mean Mrs Schofield, then I think you are insulting her, Mr Broomfield. And me. If you remember, I said I thought we should approach her as soon as possible. As you did not see fit to include me in your business plans, I went ahead by myself.' She stopped, realising that Broomfield was too drunk to be taking in what she was saying.

Hallas took hold of her arm gently and turned her away.

'Please wait here for me, Miss Blezard. Mr Broomfield's coachman is over there. He'll take him home.'

Hooking his arm under Broomfield's shoulders, he steered him to where the carriage was waiting. A phlegmatic coachman helped him hoist the befuddled man up the steps where he fell with a crash through the open door of the carriage.

Onlookers who had watched with interest while there was some action began to drift away. Charlotte, for all her outward calm, felt exposed and vulnerable. She smoothed her cloak, adjusted her bonnet and pushed up her gloves, to seem in control of herself. James Hallas, returning without his drinking companion, looked relieved.

'I do apologise, Miss Charlotte. The fact is that Mr Broomfield has had a number of pieces of bad news just recently and hearing about Schofield's Mill was the last straw. Not that I blame you at all for your actions there – no indeed. I only learnt just now that you had declared yourself interested in joining us in the venture.'

Charlotte looked at him. He was quite a handsome man and now, at this moment, an engaging and likeable one. She was glad he was beside her. The noise and movement of the throng of people had become threatening. She was relieved to find her arm taken and tucked into Hallas's.

'I hope you will allow me to take you home, Miss Charlotte. Unless you have your own carriage in town.'

'No. I mean yes. Thank you, Mr Hallas. I should be very grateful to be taken home.'

It was an exceptionally fine carriage, much the finest Charlotte had ever travelled in. She could not help saying so.

Hallas seemed pleased. 'It is a good one, I must admit. Mrs Broomfield wishes to have one like it, now she has seen it.'

Charlotte leant back against the soft leather upholstery. The ride was much less jolting than in the old Blezard carriage. She could, of course, think of buying a new one now. It would really be quite easy to spend more money.

Almost at once, she felt guilty. Sensible spending was one thing; indulgence was another. The prudence she had absorbed from her parents would be hard to overcome. She came to, hearing Hallas talking about Christmas Eve.

They were both invited to spend the evening at the Broomfields. Hallas leant forward, the rhythmic swaying of the carriage bringing him close to her. His smile was beseeching and a little sad.

'I wonder if you would allow me to call for you in my carriage and accompany me for the evening.'

Charlotte remembered that his wife and child had fallen ill about a year ago. This was perhaps a time of painful memories for him.

'I expect there will be people you know there, the Thorpes, the Littlewoods. I don't think there will be any trouble from Seth. In my experience, he never remembers what he has said in his cups.'

He smiled as he uttered the last phrase and Charlotte did too. She thought he would have no difficulty in finding another wife before very long.

'Thank you, James. I should be honoured to accompany you.'

Some time later Charlotte was back in the library, composing her reply to Isabel. She had felt no ill effects after the encounter with Broomfield, in fact, she felt quite invigorated by the events of the day. And a social evening would be very nice at a time when she might have been prey to maudlin thoughts, remembering happier Christmas Eves in the past. She had the banker's draft. Now for the letter.

Wood Lane,
Newsome.
Huddersfield.
5 December 1867
Dear Isabel,

I was interested to hear you are now living in Bath and trust you are in good health. You must send me your new address when you have it. The house is not yet sold but we have a buyer waiting. In the meantime I enclose a banker's draft for £300.

Wishing you a happy Christmas, I remain,
Yours truly,
Charlotte

No sooner had Isabel registered the appearance of Randolph Byrne in the gaming club than she felt hands on her shoulders pulling her away, quite roughly, from the body of Charles Lester. A man in evening dress, possibly a doctor, was on his knees, ripping out Lester's collar stud and loosening his clothing. A gentler hand was pushing Isabel towards a chair, a glass of brandy guided into her hand. She became aware of the ginger-haired young woman close to her, of the heady smell of her cheap scent.

Randolph Byrne stood impassive as the man on the floor tried to find signs of life in the body. Isabel saw that Byrne's evening dress was beautifully cut, smooth across his broad shoulders, his shirt and cuffs immaculate. She continued to gaze at his profile, the thick blond hair, the luxuriant moustache. The rest of the gamblers had melted away. Only the croupier remained standing by his wheel and in the background, a couple of servants hovered, including the thick-set doorman who had let them in.

Charles Lester was a terrible sight – his face purple, his eyes rolled back, mouth gaping wide. It was no surprise when the man examining him looked up at Byrne and shook his head. Receiving the news calmly, Byrne turned to speak to Isabel. The look in his eyes and the twitch of his mouth revealed that he had recognised her as his recent travelling companion.

'My dear lady. Is it...Mrs Blezard?'

Isabel nodded. Although she felt no affection for Lester, his collapse was a shock. Her legs felt strangely weak. She was glad of the chair and the brandy. Byrne moved closer, putting his warm hand under her elbow.

'It would be better if we were to move to my office.'

She rose and, supported by his arm, allowed herself to be escorted to a nearby room containing a desk, two chairs and a large safe.

'I'm afraid your companion seems unlikely to recover. We will do all we can, certainly, to revive him but... ' Byrne looked grave and spread his hands, palms uppermost. 'Were you close, the gentleman and yourself?'

'Close? Oh no, not close. We were staying at the same hotel, that is all.'

As she spoke, Isabel realised that what she wanted, now, most of all, was to get away from the body of Charles Lester as quickly as she could. She began to stand up and then sat down again as Byrne went on.

'So, am I right in thinking you would wish to, how shall I put it, dissociate yourself from this unfortunate incident? If it can be done?'

Isabel felt a surge of relief akin to gratitude.

'Yes, indeed. I should be grateful if you could. What do you advise?'

Byrne stroked his moustache.

'I think it best if one of my men escorts you back to your hotel at once. As for the gentleman... ' His eyes narrowed. 'You can rest assured that we will do what we can for him. If there is nothing to be done – .'

'You will move the body?'

'Yes. To somewhere – to a more appropriate place.'

Byrne assumed a serious expression which did not quite convince. Isabel held back the words which sprang to her lips, that she didn't care a jot where they put him as long as it was as far away from her as possible. Instead she rose and extended a gracious hand.

'Thank you, Mr Byrne, for your assistance. In this delicate matter.' She was aware once more, as he took her hand, of his powerful attractiveness. Had Fate brought them together again? She was not going to lose him this time.

'Might I have words with you, Mr Byrne, perhaps in a few days' time, when this matter has blown over? To ask your advice about accommodation in Bath?'

Byrne remained silent. Desperate to bind him to her, Isabel said 'Mr Lester was about to advise me on investments. I am still awaiting a considerable sum from my late husband's estate.'

Immediately interest kindled in Byrne's eyes.

'I should be glad to do so, Mrs Blezard. Shall we say a week hence? Not here, I think. Seek directions to The Three Cups at Walcot. Not the most savoury establishment but I think we shall not be disturbed. At about 8.00.pm?'

Isabel was gratified but a moment later, still not satisfied. She needed to tighten her grip on this man, the first man she had ever met who had not succumbed to her allure and whom she wanted, badly. Although no mention had been made of the gaming club, she knew that it did not rank as a respectable profession, that its secrets were kept for safety in the shadows. Looking up at him, she smiled her agreement and added, 'And we must not forget that Mr Lester had just won a handsome sum at the roulette wheel.' She held his gaze, without flinching. 'He was, of course, playing with my money.'

Byrne's smile tightened. Then it relaxed and he brought his mouth so close to hers that she felt his warm breath.

'I understand, Mrs Blezard. Perfectly. Until next week then?'

The night air was cold against her face. Isabel pulled her cloak up tight about her neck and followed the servant, disdaining his offer of an arm. As she picked her way along the uneven paving-stones, she took careful note of where she was, which corners they turned, which landmarks they passed on the way back to the hotel. She might need to find the gaming club again if Byrne did not turn up.

The servant disappeared as soon as they were within sight of the railway station. A night porter was on duty in the lobby as she went into the hotel. As he gave her the room key, she could see him noticing the fact that she was alone. All to the good.

'Good evening, Matthew. Thank you. Yes, Mr Lester and I have enjoyed a good dinner but I'm afraid I lack his stamina for further amusements.' She glanced at the clock, pointedly. 'Eleven o'clock is late enough for me. I wish you good-night.'

'Good night to you, Mrs Blezard. Thank you.'

The young man blushed slightly as Isabel swept past him and mounted the stairs. He'd be sure to remember that conversation, should any questioning arise.

It was two days before it did. The next morning, Isabel repeated her account of the mutually enjoyed dinner to Ada Cleaver and then made sure she was out all day on the pretext of visiting an old friend in Bradford-on-Avon.

It was at breakfast time on the following day that a constable appeared at the desk and was ushered into the manager's office. As Isabel expected, she was called into the room to be questioned. The manager was clearly worried. Deaths were not good for business.

'My dear Mrs Blezard. Pray sit down. I'm afraid I have some distressing news for you. About Mr Lester.'

'Oh dear! Nothing serious, I hope. I was looking forward to seeing him today. After my absence yesterday.'

'Indeed. I'm sorry to say, Mrs Blezard, that Mr Lester's body has been found in – well, never mind where, not in the best part of town, shall we say. It has taken the constable some time to trace this hotel. Mr Lester had little in his pockets to identify him.'

'Oh my goodness!' Isabel did her best to look shocked. 'Not killed? Not murdered?'

'No, Madam.' The constable spoke. 'Our doctor tells us it was some kind of fit.' His voice softened. 'It would have been very quick.'

The manager poured Isabel a glass of water as she fumbled for her handkerchief. The constable continued, almost apologetically.

'Could you perhaps tell us when you last saw Mr Lester, Madam?'

Isabel obliged, from the dinner to the stroll around the city to her return to the hotel by herself.

'About eleven o'clock I think it would have been.'

The constable and manager appeared well satisfied with all that she could tell them, including the information that Mr Lester had a son living in London whose address might possibly be found in his hotel room. They thanked her profusely and helped her out of the office.

The week passed very pleasantly for Isabel, especially with the arrival of the cheque from Charlotte. It had not taken her long to discover which parts of the city were best avoided with their noise, dirt, mean lodging-houses and beer shops and which afforded her means of amusement and profitable window-gazing.

With some of the money from the auction sale at her disposal, she visited Mathers' to be measured for a new pair of boots, chose a new bonnet from Rodway's in the Abbey Churchyard and returned again and again to Milsom Street with its fashionable shops and elegant clientele. She was particularly taken by Finigan's and made an appointment to have her hair washed, perfumed and dressed on the day of her assignation with Randolph Byrne.

There was the slightly uncomfortable meeting with Lester's son from London which she knew she was bound to undergo. But she repeated her story to the young man and his wife, with appropriate expressions of sorrow and appreciation of the man she had known, and respected, for such a short time. She felt that the young man's grief was on the way to being alleviated by the thought of what he was to inherit once the formalities had been completed.

She dressed with particular care on the night she was to meet Byrne, carrying very little money and enveloping her low-cut gown with a black, voluminous cloak. Walcot was heaving with people as she pushed her way through them, the smell of the beer-houses overlaid with an unfamiliar stench emerging, she supposed, from the slaughterhouses on the riverside. The Three Cups looked slightly more respectable than the other premises alongside and she was pleased to find Byrne already at a table in a dark corner when she entered.

She answered his questioning look with satisfying news. The body had been found, identified and taken to Weymouth for the funeral. The constable and the son had accepted everything.

'Good! Good! What will you have to drink?'

Byrne was at his most expansive. As they talked and Isabel sipped her brandy, she relished the closeness and warmth of his legs under the table, just touching hers. After the second brandy, they were on first name terms and looking into each other's eyes in a promising way delicious to Isabel. Byrne could not have been more helpful.

'The money won at the roulette wheel amounted to some £200, which would be very sensibly invested in the gaming club. The shares would provide a good return. You would of course always be welcome to attend. A handsome well-gowned woman will add brilliance to any gathering.'

Isabel felt deliriously happy. She saw Byrne's gaze dropping to her low neckline which she knew exposed the creamy line of her breasts. She leant forward, accentuating them still further.

'It is good of you to say so, Randolph. All I need from you now,' she said, running her tongue over her lips, 'is your help in finding some suitable accommodation in this beautiful city of yours.'

Byrne became business-like.

'This is most propitious. My two young employees, Michael and Kitty Nolan, who are brother and sister, are seeking the same. I suggest renting a small house in a central and inexpensive part of the city where you might take the superior rooms and sub-let the others to the young couple.'

'That sounds satisfactory. May I leave that to you to arrange, you with your local knowledge?'

He nodded.

'And perhaps you – ?'

He understood her at once.

'Ah. I have suitable quarters at the club. But I shall enjoy – visiting.'

The last word was heavy with suggestiveness.

As they walked down from Walcot towards the Abbey, with Isabel's arm snugly crooked in Byrne's, though all around them people were milling about, shouting, laughing and avoiding the horses and carriages in the street, she felt a contented satisfaction such as she had not experienced for a very long time, so long ago, in fact, that it took her a while to recall it.

When she did remember, it was not wholly pleasurable. She was walking along the promenade on the South Cliff in Scarborough, a young girl proud to be holding her father's arm, overjoyed at having him all to herself. The moment had been exquisite, all the more so for being so short-lived.

Isabel shook herself. Recollection was not profitable; the past was gone. The future was what mattered. It was amazing how things worked out! When, as a girl, she had nearly died of peritonitis after a burst appendix, her mother had lamented when the doctor told them that she would almost certainly be unable to have children.

It had mattered little to Isabel then. Now it seemed a positive advantage. No squalling brats to fear when her relationship with Randolph Byrne ripened into what she intended it to be. Marriage? Unlikely, but who cared?

During her final weeks at the Royal Hotel, Isabel explored Bath more thoroughly. She was already beginning to see the city with the eyes of a resident rather than those of a visitor, moreover a resident with a commercial interest in the population.

She understood that it was a city of well-to-do residents and of tradespeople whose shops filled the streets – food and drink suppliers, tailors, dressmakers, milliners, furniture makers, bootmakers as well as all manner of services from hairdressing, dancing and painting lessons to the chemical cleaning and purifying of feather beds.

To the south, beyond the river, stood the engineering works and woollen mills that gave employment to hundreds; to the north, builders were at work on Bathwick Hill erecting ornate mansions for the well-off seeking the purer air above the bowl in which the city lay.

On Sundays she saw large congregations spilling out of the many places of worship of all denominations – bewhiskered men and well-upholstered wives with their broods of children. These displays of morality did not daunt her. On the contrary, she was sure that from this population, outwardly conventional, would come customers seeking the thrill of gaming to bring excitement into their restricted lives.

At last there came what she had been waiting for – a note from Randolph Byrne. He had found a house he thought would suffice, furnished, in Old

King Street, just off Queen's Square. Could she meet him there at ten o'clock next morning?

The house, in a short Georgian terrace, was small but the rooms on the ground and first floors were charming, with pretty fireplaces and long sash windows. It had been left in decent condition, the wooden floors and stone stairs swept, the rubbish removed.

'The rent is reasonable for its location,' said Byrne, ducking his head under the lintel. 'And the Nolans' contribution will reduce it further.'

It took very little time to arrange for the conveying of Isabel's belongings to the house – valises, trunks and tea-chests, the latter now fewer in number following the auction sale, and the painting, still wrapped in its protective cover. Two brawny-armed locals carried everything up the narrow winding stairs without difficulty.

Nor did it take her long to unpack for she left many of her clothes in their portmanteaux and the silver cutlery set locked in its box. However, she delighted in shaking out the fine bed-linen she had brought with her. When she had managed to position the looking-glasses in her bedroom so that she could see all views of herself, she sat down, well satisfied.

The Nolans arrived that same afternoon. Without her garish face-paint, Kitty Nolan looked young and frail, with the pale skin of the redhead. But her cheekbones were good, her retroussé nose and wide-set eyes appealing.

Her brother Michael resembled her but with poorer skin and a long, thin top lip which gave him a sardonic expression. Both of them were thin and below average height. They each carried a piece of battered luggage which they put down in the tiny hallway.

'I understand you are looking for lodgings,' said Isabel.

Kitty nodded. Her brother remained silent.

'Did Mr Byrne explain that the top floor would be available for you?' Isabel was relishing her position of power.

'Yes, we've seen it,' cut in the young woman.

Isabel drew herself up.

'I believe Mr Byrne has told you about the rent?'

Michael said nothing. Again, his sister spoke for them both.

'We were thinking we might be of service, Mrs Blezard. Cooking, cleaning, laundry, seeing to fires and the like.'

Isabel had not expected this. She had already noted the name of Miss Archbell in Chapel Row who would supply domestic help as required but this would certainly be a more convenient arrangement. A young man in the house would be useful carrying coal and ashes up and down the stairs. Kitty, with her cheap hat and cloak trimmed with gaudy feathers, did not look like an ideal housekeeper but it was worth a try.

'Mm.'

Isabel pretended to be considering the matter. The Nolans waited, impassive.

'Very well. I will give you a month's trial. We will see how things are then. Mind!' she said, seeing their faces relax, 'I shall want accounts, detailed, of all provisions bought.'

'Of course,' said Kitty. 'And as we shall be working for you, then our rent should be less. In lieu of wages.'

Isabel's eyes narrowed. Wages for domestic servants were low but if they lived in, you had to pay for their food and the wretches commonly ate like horses.

'We'll see about that,' she said coolly. 'When – ?'

'We could come right now,' said Kitty.

'Do you not have more luggage to collect from your present lodgings?'

'It's here,' said Kitty, gesturing towards the two bags. When she saw Isabel's look, she added, 'If we need anything else, we can get it in the market. Now what about a nice meat pie for your supper?'

'Very well, yes,' Isabel replied.

The couple vanished, one upstairs, one downstairs.

'And don't forget, I want accounts!' Isabel shouted to the empty hallway. She was going to have to watch these two.

CHAPTER FIVE

Charlotte was always excited when she was expecting Sam for supper but this time, there was something else, something stronger. She put down her hairbrush and gazed at herself in the mirror. Could a man, or rather Sam in particular, love that face? Was that how it worked? What made people fall in love? When you thought of some couples you knew, it wasn't difficult to answer that. Her recently-married friends, John and Anne Brook, were both extremely handsome; it was easy to understand why they should love each other. But most people weren't and yet married each other and seemed, for the most part, happy enough.

It wasn't just physical appearance that counted although it undoubtedly played a part. She loved the way Sam looked – his distinctive ginger hair, the clear fair skin, the way his mouth moved when he spoke. Although slim, he was strong and could walk for miles without getting tired. She admired too his strength of mind and independence of spirit.

But these separate qualities still didn't explain love – the way she felt when she was near him, the sense of loss when he went away, the joy of his return. There were differences between them of wealth and social position but if he really loved her as she loved him, surely these would be overcome, as they had been by her own parents?

Yet when he stepped over the threshold that evening, a sense of foreboding overcame her. The maid stood quietly by, waiting to receive his overcoat and Charlotte sensed he was embarrassed by the situation. He mumbled something to the maid, with his head down, and then allowed himself to be drawn into the parlour by his hostess.

Charlotte poured him a glass of sherry which he looked at suspiciously before drinking it down. She thought she would seek safe ground.

'The concert was splendid, last week, wasn't it?'

'Aye. Grand.'

'And will you be going to the Carol Service at All Hallows?' As soon as she had mentioned it, Charlotte wished she hadn't. Sam made no secret of his lack of Christian belief.

'No. I don't think so.'

He gave her a penetrating look as if he was wondering whether to give his reasons for not doing so. Fortunately, he said nothing.

Charlotte quickly changed the subject.

'Have you any plans for Christmas?'

'No. It isn't that important to me. I shall have my Christmas dinner with my parents and then likely go for a walk somewhere – unless it's siling down.'

Charlotte didn't know what to say. If Sam hadn't been invited to the Haighs on Christmas Day, it would be tactless to tell him about it. So she said nothing about her Christmas invitations, particularly not about going to the Broomfields with James Hallas on Christmas Eve.

There followed a period of silence. Charlotte waited for Sam to introduce a topic of conversation but he didn't. She kept thinking of something to say and then censoring it in case it led to an area of potential disagreement. It was a relief when the maid called them to the dining-room.

Here at least were matters to occupy them although the absence of conversation made the drinking of soup embarrassingly audible. Charlotte could not help remembering how happy she had been when Sam first dined with her, how the pleasure of each other's company had enhanced the evening. She would try again.

'I'm going to buy that house in Sharp Lane, Sam,' she said, helping herself to cabbage.

'Oh aye.'

'It will be grand to live in Almondbury. I've always liked it. The Brooks won't be far away. Or the Haighs.' After a slight pause, she dared to say, 'Or you.'

Sam gave a hollow laugh.

'Right enough. Although I can't see you having much to do wi' Town End.'

Charlotte thought this unfair and opened her mouth to say so. But Sam's expression stopped her. He had gone red and looked both upset and annoyed. Because of what he had just said?

The meal continued in silence. Sam cheered up slightly at the appearance of the treacle tart but it became increasingly clear that something was interfering with his ability to enjoy Charlotte's company. Had people been gossiping, talking about his paying social calls to his employer? It was the kind of thing people would do and exactly what would make Sam angry.

Nevertheless he was here and she wouldn't give up her attempt to draw him closer to her. She would try again to speak of things they had in common. She knew of his social conscience which she, to some extent, shared.

'I've been thinking, Sam, of how I might do some good. In the town. With my money.'

Sam's lip curled. Oh dear, had she said the wrong thing again, unthinkingly?

'Well, you won't find any shortage of deserving causes.'

'No, no, I realise that,' she said hastily. 'When I was last in town, there were children –'

'Yes, no doubt there were – ill-fed, ill-housed and with no schooling as well.'

Charlotte nodded and began to agree but Sam carried on without a break, his voice thick with emotion.

'The children suffer most because they can't help theirselves. The conditions they live in are worse than pigsties. In some of the courts I've seen in town, there's a dozen families sharing a tap wi' bad water. And as for sanitation – ! Disease spreads like wildfire. And who cares? Not the landlords who collect the rents on these middens.'

'I know.' Charlotte broke in. 'I know from what Rachel tells me. She says the Infirmary does what it can but it's mainly just giving medicine from the dispensary.'

'Well, it would be, wouldn't it?' Sam's voice was almost a snarl. 'Th'Infirmary wa' set up to cater for injuries to t'workers – so they can patch 'em up and get 'em back to work as fast as possible.'

His face was flushed, his eyes burning with anger. Charlotte tried to speak but he could not be stopped.

'Th'employers think only of their profits. They don't see t' workers as human beings like theirsen, they don't care owt about their welfare.'

'But it's better than it used to be, surely? In what they call the bad old days. When little children were forced to go down the pit or into the mill. And sometimes were terribly injured or killed?'

Charlotte recollected past horrors, of children trapped and maimed by machinery or burnt to death like they were in a mill in Kirkheaton, locked in and unable to escape.

'Mebbe,' said Sam. 'But not a lot. There's still mills where people work till they drop – where all that matters is the machine and the brass it makes for the mill-owner.' He stopped, as if realising he had gone too far.

Charlotte stood up, gripping her hands together. Although he had probably not intended it, Sam's words had cut her to the quick. While his words might apply to some mill-owners, they could never be said to be true of her father, George Blezard, who had cared about his workers, if only because he had been one himself in his youth. To suggest she was herself such a mill-owner was an insult beyond any she had ever met before.

Now Sam was also on his feet, the look on his face suggesting he knew he had overstepped the mark. They stood facing one another in the parlour, the coffee pot and cups on the table beside them ignored. Charlotte wanted to speak but feared she might sob if she mentioned her father. She stood mute while Sam stared at her in misery.

There came a slight tap at the door. It was the maid, bearing a small jug.

'I'm sorry, Miss Charlotte. I forgot to bring the milk just now.'

'Thank you, Bella.' Charlotte spoke automatically, her eyes never leaving Sam's face. When she began to offer him some coffee, he shook his head.

'Thank you, Miss Charlotte. I think I'd best be going.'

Charlotte knew there were polite things she could say to try and persuade him to stay a little longer but she could not bring herself to utter them. Out in the hallway, Sam shrugged himself into his overcoat while she watched. Straightening up, his expression changed. His eyes seemed to grow softer and beg for forgiveness. Charlotte knew it was up to her, to lay a gentle hand on his arm, to smile and speak kindly and the barriers would come down. But she could not make herself do it.

The next moment, she had opened the front door and Sam had gone down the stone steps. When he reached the gravel drive, he turned and looked at her, the gas lamp illuminating his beseeching face. But it was too late. Charlotte moved her mouth into a half-smile, stepped back and shut the door. Behind her came the sound of light, scurrying footsteps.

'I'm sorry, Miss Charlotte. I didn't know your guest was going.'

'Never mind, Bella. Neither did I. You may clear the parlour. I shall not be wanting any coffee.'

'Very well, Miss.' Bella made a slight bob and disappeared into the room.

Charlotte climbed the stairs slowly, gripping the banister every few steps. The heaviness in her heart seemed to have spread throughout her body. Once in her room, she had to sit down before embarking on the effort of undressing.

She could not remember having felt so wounded before. True, the grief she had felt at the sudden loss of her father was the greatest pain she had ever suffered but this time, it felt as if a knife had, without warning, been plunged into her heart. And it was a heart, she knew, that had been open to Sam Armitage and was ready to love him without reserve.

The tears began to come. Pressing her face into her handkerchief, she sobbed. He could not love her or he would not have spoken as he did. All the daydreams she had fashioned around him, the imagined life together she had pictured, were utterly foolish.

Sitting up, she caught sight of her red-eyed, blotched face in the mirror. It seemed to confirm all she feared about herself; she was a plain young woman who would find it hard to find any young man to love her enough to want to marry her.

The following week seemed to go by very slowly. There were some outings to divert her: church services, two tea parties, one female and frivolous, the other more serious and attended by people who shared Charlotte's wish to start some charitable work in the town.

Her attitude to Sam Armitage underwent a change. For the first few days, she struggled to reconcile herself to the fact that their relationship could never be other than a professional one between mill-owner and mill-manager. His intemperate remarks, easily recalled, still hurt her. She was stupid to think they might ever have made a love match.

But as the week drew on, she found herself thinking of him more and more and hoping he might appear on Friday evening as he had done before. There was always some mill business which could provide him with a credible excuse for calling.

She sat as long as she could in the library reading *The Examiner*, as afternoon darkened into evening, until she could delay dinner no longer without causing consternation in the kitchen. He did not come. She had only half-expected it.

Somehow she found herself thinking of his side of the situation. How could he come, without invitation, if he was at all sensitive to how he had behaved? The more she thought about it, the more she felt sure he would have suffered some degree of mortification. She recalled the look on his face as he was leaving. She had given him no opportunity to say he was sorry, no opportunity whatsoever. He might really be in some pain which only she could relieve.

By Monday, she became fired with resolve to take the first step towards reconciliation. She would visit the mill, catch him at his work, talk about mill business and find a way of smoothing things out between them.

But when she arrived there, she learnt that Mr Armitage had gone to Bradford to look at some machinery and no, there had been no message of any sort for her. The shock of finding him absent left Charlotte feeling deflated. She returned home with a sensation of gloom she found difficult to shift.

Even the prospect of Christmas Eve failed to cheer her. But she made an effort, if only because Bella was so excited by it on her mistress' behalf.

'Oh Miss, it'll be grand next year when you'll be properly out of mourning – when you can wear a bright gown.'

She was brushing Charlotte's long hair very gently, smoothing the light brown waves with her other hand as it rippled over her shoulders.

'I'm fair glad you're out of your black.'

Charlotte said nothing. Her parents had always said nine months was long enough for any daughter to remain in deep mourning, never mind what the custom was for widows. But it had felt strange to lay aside the black clothes entirely. She thought she would continue to wear them on public outings for a while longer, certainly until the spring.

Bella was holding up the new gown, ready to button her mistress into it.

'It's a beautiful gown, Miss Charlotte!' she breathed. It was true. It was a beautiful gown, dark purple, as was appropriate, and of a rich silk which rustled softly and felt very pleasing against the skin.

'And the amethysts, Miss Charlotte. They look just right with it.'

Charlotte touched them gently. They had belonged to her grandmother and being old-fashioned in style, had fortunately escaped Isabel's clutches. These, and the purple dress, suddenly brought an image of her stepmother into her mind. If she had still been living in Huddersfield, she would have been preparing for this evening as Charlotte was. Perhaps she would have been awaiting the arrival of James Hallas? Handsome, widowed, of similar age, they would have made a pretty pair. The thought did little for Charlotte's confidence.

But it was too late for such foolish fancies. When Bella had finished dressing her hair, she wrapped her mother's fur cape around her shoulders and went downstairs to await James and his carriage.

The Broomfields' house looked even more impressive than Charlotte remembered it. All the windows were ablaze with light, upstairs and down, illuminating the gravel drive as bright as day. A giant Christmas tree dominated the entrance hall while the sitting-room was festooned with holly wreaths interspersed with huge, looped bows of red satin.

It was a pity that Seth Broomfield was unable to convey an air of much jollity himself but he was doing his best, grinning and encouraging his guests to make themselves at home. Jemima, with half the effort, was playing the part of the welcoming hostess very well. It helped that she looked festive herself in a silk dress of red tartan, her shiny, dark ringlets and pink cheeks making her as pretty as a doll.

Charlotte moved easily among the guests with James at her elbow, introducing him where necessary and fielding several compliments on her new gown. He proved to be a diligent escort, finding her a comfortable seat and fetching her as much food and drink as she could possibly want.

'No more, James, really!' she protested.

'Come, you need to keep your strength up!' he joked. 'First to hear the musicians and then to take part in something afterwards.'

'What, what?' enquired Grace Littlewood who was hovering close by. 'I've not been told what's to do. Tell me!'

'Ah, Miss Littlewood! I don't want to spoil the surprise. You must wait and see.' James disappeared into the throng.

Grace shook her fan vigorously.

'I suppose he thinks he's very clever. I think it's very bad manners, not to tell a lady what she asks.'

'Don't be too harsh, Grace,' said Charlotte. 'We shall know soon enough. Just enjoy yourself. I see we are to have some music.'

A space was cleared for the musicians and the guests eventually fell silent and still, except for a few gentlemen who disappeared, glasses in hand. Charlotte was pleased to see James return and sit beside her where, to all appearances, he enjoyed listening to the selection of Christmas music. Grace was mollified by the attentions of Frederick Thorpe who had no difficulty in dividing them between her and his wife. Seth Broomfield stood leaning against the mantelpiece, his eyes fixed on the slim figure of his wife as she moved amongst her guests and then sank down into a low armchair to listen to the music.

When it was over, she led the polite applause and held up her hand for attention.

'Thank you. We hope you have enjoyed the music. After a few minutes, when the musicians have refreshed themselves, we hope you will move with us to the drawing-room which we have turned, just for this evening, into – a ballroom!'

There were gasps of surprise and pleasure from the guests, some of whom settled themselves more firmly into the armchairs they were occupying. But the keener folk were up on their feet and moving about already with excitement, Frederick Thorpe among them, his wife watching indulgently from a sofa.

James turned to Charlotte.

'What do you think, Charlotte? Would you like to dance?'

Charlotte considered. She already felt a little exposed, dispensing with her mourning black.

'I think not, James. Not tonight. But thank you, I will in future.' She saw him looking slightly crestfallen. 'But you must dance with the other ladies, you must. Come, I shall enjoy watching at any rate.'

Taking his proffered arm, she rose and they followed the would-be dancers into the drawing-room which had been cleared, its rugs removed, the pine floorboards gleaming with fresh polish. After a few minutes, the musicians struck up and dancing began.

'Well, I think we might have been warned,' said Grace crossly. 'I call that ill-mannered, not being told there was going to be dancing.' However, a moment later, James had turned to her and asked 'Will you do me the honour?' and soon they were circling the floor in a waltz, Grace's pinched features momentarily relaxed.

Charlotte did not expect to see their host dancing but Jemima soon waltzed by in the comfortable embrace of Frederick Thorpe. They looked well together, both graceful and at ease with themselves and the music. Instinctively she turned to look at Seth and then wished she hadn't. His displeasure was obvious, his body rigid, his black eyebrows drawn down over eyes glowering with fury.

Charlotte was not the only one to observe him. Mrs Littlewood, who had come to sit beside her, made a tut-tutting sound.

'It distresses me to see Seth Broomfield so. He must realise his wife, as hostess, is free to dance with their guests. He does himself no good by acting in that way.'

'Perhaps he can't help it,' ventured Charlotte. 'He does seem very much in love with her. She is very pretty.'

'And very young,' added Mrs Littlewood. 'He knew that when he courted her. He shouldn't have married her if he couldn't cope with the attention she was bound to attract. I'm afraid it's a familiar tale. A rich, older man making a fool of himself over a pretty young woman.'

'I don't think he has anything to fear from Frederick Thorpe. He is charming to all the women, not just Jemima.'

Mrs Littlewood sighed.

'I'm afraid that won't be much consolation to him. Jealousy finds its own reasons.'

During the rest of the evening, Charlotte kept away from their host as much as possible, finding his displeasure and barely-concealed frustration very wearing to witness. But as the time for departure approached, she could not avoid him. She had joined some of the other guests in the entrance hall where Broomfield stood amongst a group of men, a wreath of cigar smoke above their heads. His voice was loud and thickened by drink.

'A friend to t'poor! To hissen, more like!'

Charlotte recognised the quotation immediately. It was from a letter to the Editor of *The Examiner* which had appeared a couple of weeks previously, signed 'A Friend to the Poor'. The writer had suggested it was the duty of all Christians to make some sacrifice and relieve the suffering of the poor, the first step being to give up Christmas parties and spend it on the relief of those in need. The letter had caused Charlotte a pang of guilt. Not so Broomfield and his listeners.

'What dusta think, Jed?' Broomfield lurched forward, jabbing his cigar towards one of the men. 'Dusta fancy being on 'is committee, then? *'To receive donations and visit the abodes of want and misery'* He exploded in a coughing gust of laughter, echoed by the others. 'He said – he said – he'd be glad to contribute his 'mite'!' The final word set him off again.

Charlotte drew back, repelled, and was glad to see Jemima glide up behind her husband and pull him away from his cronies.

'Seth! Seth! Our guests are ready to leave!'

Still spluttering and unsteady on his feet, Broomfield made a futile attempt to appear in control of himself.

'Aye, aye,' he said, mopping his mouth with a handkerchief.

Coats, cloaks and hats were brought, farewells and Christmas greetings exchanged. There was a general move towards the handsome front door but as it was opened, the visitors halted. Instead of the usual drivers waiting at a respectful distance, a group of working men stood at the bottom of the steps, a lantern lighting up their thin faces.

'Merry Christmas, Sir, Madam.' A young man at the front spoke up. Unsure, the visitors fell silent. 'Mr and Mrs Broomfield, is it? We're collecting for the family – wife and children – of Joseph Smith. Of Rose and Crown Yard, Almondbury.' A pause. 'The weaver. Who wa' drowned in Mr Shaw's mill dam.'

The guests, about to leave, warmly wrapped up to meet the cold air, stood still in surprise, those behind them coming to a halt as they found their exit blocked. Only Seth Broomfield pushed forward, scowling and flinging his arm up.

'Na' then, folk are wanting to leave. Get out o' t' road!'

One or two of the workmen shifted their feet but held their ground. None of the guests moved but began to mutter amongst themselves, unsure what to do next.

Charlotte felt ashamed. She wanted to give the speaker some money but had brought none with her. She was just about to ask James to lend her some when Jemima Broomfield took charge, sensing the mood of the moment.

'Will you just wait a minute?' she said to the young man, placing herself in front of her husband. 'Mr Broomfield and I will of course give something for the Smith family but we should like our guests to be allowed to leave first.'

This suited most of the guests who scurried to their waiting carriages, heads down. A few, Charlotte was pleased to see, stopped and fished inside their wallets for money which they put into the collector's box. At Charlotte's bidding, James Hallas donated a ten pound note before steering her towards his carriage.

'I heard about that fellow,' he said, tucking a woollen rug around her. 'Sad case. Took his own life almost certainly. Out of work for months. In despair, no doubt.'

He stopped when he saw that Charlotte's face was white with shock. As they had crossed the courtyard, she had recognised one of the men in the group – Sam Armitage. As their eyes met, the expression on his face, already grim, had hardened as he looked from her to her companion, warm and prosperous in his silk hat and wool overcoat. Any kind of explanation was impossible, not just at that moment but perhaps, forever.

Isabel soon found out that the meat pie, hot from the baker's oven, was the first of many. Kitty was no cook but she knew all the food suppliers in Bath. Meat pies, faggots, saveloys, tripe and onions, hotpot – she or Michael would rush in with dishes still hot to be washed down with ale. She knew when every baker's shop or stall-holder sold off the day's produce at half-price and was at the street door smiling, jug in hand, whenever a certain susceptible milkman went past.

For his part, Michael lost no time in filling the coal hole with firewood and sacks of coal. Where it came from, Isabel did not ask. It was certainly a lot cheaper than that advertised in *The Chronicle*. He continued to be a young man with little to say for himself. Isabel wondered whether the French words he spoke as a croupier were the most he spoke all day.

The understanding between him and his sister was close and seemed to need very little language to sustain it. Kitty, on the other hand, was never silent for long. Isabel would hear her singing in the room below her sitting-room, sometimes popular songs, sometimes haunting ballads which were perhaps learnt as a child from their Irish parents.

Despite Isabel's initial worries, the pair did not seem to be fleecing her. True, she paid for their meals but they had agreed a reduced rent for their services to their mutual satisfaction. Isabel did not know how much they earned at Byrne's gaming club or whether Kitty did well from tips. She knew customers were always more ready to buy girls a drink than to give them money. Kitty knew this too.

'I go to the bar with the money. Paddy gives me a glass of water and puts the money in a pot for me. I tell the customer I'm drinkin' gin!'

A pleasing consequence of the Nolans' employment was that, arriving back well after midnight, they slept late in the morning. This suited Isabel who hated early rising. The shutters across her windows kept out the light and much of the noise of the Bath streets until she chose to open them. The first noise in the house was the sound of Michael padding downstairs. Isabel would hear him raking the grate and then building a fire to boil water for the tea they all drank in the morning.

It was, she thought, sipping hers, a poor life compared to the well-heeled comfort she had enjoyed as the wife of George Blezard, mill-owner, in Huddersfield. She remembered how she had furnished their brand new house in style and how a week never went by without her buying something new to wear, a gown, a bonnet, or gloves.

There had been a constant round of tea-parties and dinner parties to pass the time but in truth, she had been bored by most of the people in their social circle. Most of all, she had been bored by her husband. She had also had to endure his sickening affection for his daughter Charlotte who was as boring as he was, with her books and her serious interest in her father's business.

Still, she did not count the marriage a complete failure. It had enabled her to get away from her parents' hotel where she had worked as a virtually unpaid receptionist and transport her to a more moneyed existence. Blezard, unfortunately, had not been as rich as she had hoped – the dratted textile trade going through a 'bad patch' as he called it – but it had afforded her a wealth of possessions, many of which she had managed to bring with her.

She was sure Bath would suit her very well. She had just enough money to live on at the moment and when her full share of the Blezard estate came through, she would be secure. But was that enough for happiness? Isabel did not need to think twice. No, she relished insecurity, danger even, and she wanted it with Randolph Byrne.

There had been no sign of him at Old King Street. Isabel decided to take the initiative.

That evening she dressed herself elegantly, as she always did, and applied the rouge to full effect. There was no problem gaining entrance to the gaming club. The doorman recognised her at once.

Moving out of the gloom into the bright light over the roulette wheel, she came upon the familiar scene: the gamblers sitting round the table in various poses, some hunched jealously over their stakes, some slumped as if tired or drunk, some leaning back as if they attached little importance to what they were doing, chatting to their companions or the club hostesses. Kitty turned her head as Isabel approached but showed no sign of recognition. Isabel admired her for it.

Byrne looked up in surprise when Isabel knocked and walked straight into his office. He did not seem particularly pleased to see her. With a pang, Isabel thought he looked more handsome than ever before. He had taken off his jacket and had loosened the collar of his white dress shirt revealing the base of his throat which glistened in the lamplight. His cuffs were pushed back, his wrists and hands strong and shapely. Isabel felt a leap of desire inside her. When he spoke, she found herself fascinated by his mouth beneath the blond moustache.

'Isabel! What a pleasant surprise!' His expression belied his words of welcome.

'Good evening, Randolph. I hope you are well?'

'Yes, indeed. And you?'

'Yes, thank you. I thought you might like to know that I am well settled. I thank you for your help in finding the house for me.'

'Good, good! And your tenants? I believe they are well settled too.'

'Yes, they seem so. I have been grateful for their knowledge of Bath.'

'Oh yes, they can tell you all you need to know about living in Bath. Perhaps I should say 'surviving'. They have known hard times.'

Isabel was not interested in hearing the life story of the Nolans but disguised the fact.

'Dear me! Is that so? Then they are lucky to have found such a considerate employer.'

Her smile and the flattery achieved the effect she wanted. Byrne smiled back.

'And lucky to have found you, Isabel.'

Isabel tossed her head. 'I shall count myself lucky when you favour me with a visit.' When Byrne did not reply, she could not help herself. 'Perhaps tomorrow evening? About nine o'clock? I cannot think the club needs your continual presence.'

Byrne's expression was inscrutable but after a moment, his face relaxed into acquiescence.

'Very well, Isabel. We will say nine. And now if you will excuse me...' His actions – the arm around her shoulders, his hand on her arm – were friendly but it was clear that he wanted her to leave.

As they left the office, Isabel almost stumbled over two men locked in some kind of struggle. The customer, red-faced and drunk, was protesting about being cheated. Byrne's man was restraining him and gradually pushing him towards the exit. The appearance of the doorman ended the incident. A swift punch at the back of the customer's neck made him go limp whereupon the doorman hauled him off as easily as he might have lifted a small child. Byrne merely raised an eyebrow.

'Good evening, Isabel. Till tomorrow.'

Isabel experienced difficulty getting to sleep that night. Ever since she had left Byrne, her mind had been filled with images of their lovemaking; now, in bed, they were inescapable. She found herself writhing in frustration, pressing her face into the pillows, inhaling Byrne's imaginary scent. She fell asleep at long last and awoke heavy-eyed.

As the time for his visit grew closer, she completed her preparations. She built up good fires in both the sitting-room and bedroom, feeding them both in turn to ensure glowing warmth, and lit shaded lamps which cast a rosy light. His favourite drink, brandy, awaited him. She washed and perfumed herself and put on a gown which was easy to remove.

Nine o'clock came and went. There was no sign of Byrne. Isabel understood that events at the club might prevent his leaving. By ten o'clock, she had exhausted all possible reasons. She stood by the window with one shutter open for a long time, watching the street until she became thoroughly chilled. By eleven o'clock, her patience had run out and was replaced by anger shot through with worry. Where was he? Why had he not sent a message? Was this a deliberate insult? Perhaps he had met with an accident or been attacked by a street robber?

She could wait no longer. Snatching up her cloak, she went out into the street where the gaslights flickered and the paving-stones glistened with damp. Without thinking, she hurried along and then, as she calmed down, realised she had arrived at the entrance to the gaming club. For a moment she hesitated in front of its forbidding door. To her left, a drably dressed woman was offering her services to a passing gentleman. She caught the low tones of their conversation and saw them disappear into the night. Isabel realised what she was doing, coming running after Byrne a second time. It would not do!

Turning on her heel, she walked quickly away and found she could not stop. On and on she went, along dark narrow streets and out into the light outside the Theatre Royal, still illuminated although closed, where passers-by were stopping and reading the posters. Some of them turned and looked at her with curiosity as she hurried past until she reached the quieter space of Queen's Square where the trees cast strange shadows on the lawns beneath. Some ragamuffin children were clambering on the railings. A small one lay on the kerbstone, apparently asleep.

She was now close to home but her mood drove her onward, up Gay Street, through the King's Circus and along Brock Street until she reached the beginning of the Royal Crescent which stretched out in front of her, its great curve of houses mainly in darkness. Here and there upper-floor windows were lit and in a few houses, light blazed from the grand first-floor rooms where people could be seen standing, moving, chatting, drinking. Carriages were waiting outside, their drivers huddled in greatcoats on the box or walking up and down, slapping their arms around them and stamping their feet to keep warm.

Isabel was surprised to find herself at the far end of the Crescent and sweating from her fast pace. She looked out across the lawn and the green sweep beyond. She was no nearer attaining this kind of life now than she had been when she first arrived. Was she foolish to think that Byrne was the man who could give her the life she wanted? Should she break away and look for a safer, and richer, bet?

To her horror, Isabel knew the answer to this even as she was asking it. She had done something utterly stupid. She had made Randolph Byrne indispensable to her happiness. She could not contemplate intimacy with another man. Somehow Byrne occupied that place in her mind, perhaps in her heart.

For the first time in her life, she had put herself in a man's power and it appalled her. The face that flashed into her mind at that moment was not Byrne's but that of her father, Maxwell Rowe, the darkly handsome hotelier whom she resembled in appearance. As a girl, she had swelled with pride when people remarked upon the fact – the same dark curling hair and long-lashed brown eyes, the same large white teeth and dazzling smile. More memories flooded in.

She must have been about fourteen. Something unusual had happened and the girls had been sent home early from school. The hotel was deserted as she entered the porch. The only sound was the loud ticking of the long-case clock in the hall. None of the gas lamps had been lit.

As she turned to climb the final flight of stairs to her room, she heard an unfamiliar noise. The bedroom door next to her was not quite shut. She put her hand on the doorknob and pulled.

There were two people on the bed, a man and a woman. She did not know the naked woman who looked at her wildly. But the man was her father, sweaty, dishevelled, wearing only his shirt, supported on his elbows over the woman.

Isabel stepped back in shock and willed herself upstairs, away from the scene. Once in her room, she poured some water into the bowl on the washstand and bathed her burning face. What made her feel sick was not the couple on the bed. It was what she had seen when she looked down through the stair well to the ground floor – the upturned face of her mother, miserable but resigned.

Isabel started. She did not know how long she had been standing outside the end house of the Crescent, only that she was wet through. It was raining heavily and water was running down her neck and off her skirt into her sodden boots. With an effort, she shook herself and began walking back along the Crescent, the houses now mostly in darkness and the carriages gone.

A cold wind swept across the grassy expanse. Shivering uncontrollably, she reached Old King Street. She was glad to see a light from the lower ground floor which meant Kitty and Michael were in and not yet gone to bed. She hoped they had lit a fire.

Her reception by Kitty was gratifying.

'Mrs Blezard! Isabel! Thank God you're back! And wet through! Let me help you get those wet things off at once!'

Kitty fussed over her like a mother hen. Isabel, who usually scorned such treatment, gave way to the weakness she felt and allowed herself to be rid of the wet clothes and helped into dry ones.

Sure enough, the Nolans had lit a fire and before long, all three were sitting with their stockinged feet in the hearth, drinking brandy and hot water. Isabel suspected it was her brandy from upstairs but said nothing. She was grateful that no questions were asked about where she had been and why. Feeling some kind of appreciation was called for, she praised the well-made fire. Kitty and Michael exchanged glances.

'Michael knows all about firewood, eh?' Kitty winked at her brother. At Isabel's bemused look, she went on. 'When we were children, after our parents died, we were sent to orphanages – not that they called them that. Mine was the Industrial Home for Girls and Michael's –'

Michael spoke, for almost the first time.

'Sutcliffe Industrial School.'

His sister nodded encouragingly but he had said as much as he wanted.

'We were taught all sorts.' She pulled a face. 'Laundering, cooking, cleaning, sewing. I hated it. Michael was taught some trades – tailoring and shoe-making, weren't you?' A faint sneer flitted across the young man's face. 'But the firewood was best. The boys had to cut it up and then deliver it around Bath so they got to go out, especially in the winter. He used to come to my place on Fridays. I used to watch out for him and then run down to the back door and speak to him.'

'And did they allow that?' asked Isabel.

'Oh no!' said Kitty cheerfully. 'I got my ears boxed many a time. So when I knew they were watching me, I would put a note for him under the door-knocker. Although if they read it, I got punished all the more. For what I said about them.'

Isabel was suddenly seized with a fit of coughing.

'You best get to bed,' said Kitty.

As they parted on the stairs, Isabel said, as casually as possible, 'Mr Byrne away tonight?'

'Yes. Away on business, I suppose. He goes away a lot.'

It was not much but was enough to satisfy Isabel. She spent a bad night, shivering and sweating by turns, waking frequently with a dry throat, and then fell into troubled sleep again, riven by bizarre dreams featuring Byrne, her parents and girls she had known at school.

The next day she slept late. Kitty brought her a boiled egg and some tea in the afternoon before she went out. Michael lit a fire in her bedroom and brought up plenty of coal.

By the evening, she was feeling better and thinking she should get up, if only so she could go to bed again. Disinclined to dress properly, she put on a clean nightgown and a robe of rose-pink chenille, one George had bought her as part of her trousseau. She sat languidly at her wash-stand, looking at herself and brushing her hair rhythmically over and over until it lay on her shoulders, shiny and falling into ringlets.

There came a knock at the door, firm but not hostile. Isabel went down the stairs and opened the front door very slightly. Randolph Byrne stood there, his thick fair hair shining in the lamplight. The shock was intense and pleasurable. Isabel gasped, could do nothing but stand back to let him in.

'My dear girl. I am so sorry to have let you down yesterday. Urgent business.'

Isabel didn't care, hardly heard what he was saying, simply looked into his eyes and felt her legs going weak. He came close and put one arm round her waist. With his other arm around her shoulders, he brought his mouth down to hers, pressing lightly at first and then, as she responded, more deeply. They stood kissing behind the door until she felt she could barely stand.

Soon they were in her bedroom and he was clasping her hips so that she could feel his hardness thrusting against her. Then he was undressing her with practised ease while she fumbled with his shirt buttons and cuff-links until she could run her hands over his chest and back. His body was firmly muscled, his skin satiny-smooth, his nipples hard, the male smell of him wonderful. Before she was swept away by sensation, she was aware of one thought – that this man was an expert lover. In no time at all, she had achieved ecstasy.

They rolled apart and she fell back on the pillows in a state of peaceful joy. Turning back towards Byrne, brimming with words of love, she was dismayed to find he was already standing up and dressing hurriedly.

'Randolph?'

She sat up, wrapped in the sheet, her damp hair framing her flushed face. Fiddling with his collar stud, he gave her a tight smile.

'That was very nice, Isabel, very nice indeed. I hope you found it worth waiting for. I have to go, I'm afraid. I have an appointment in a few minutes.'

Running his fingers through his hair and his moustache, he smiled again and moved swiftly out of the room and down the stairs. His slamming of the door shook the house.

Isabel lay on her back and pulled the blankets up around her. What she had longed for had come to pass. She had not foreseen it would be over so soon.

CHAPTER SIX

When Charlotte awoke next morning, it was a minute before she remembered that it was Christmas Day. Her mind was still full of the last moments of her visit to the Broomfields the night before. The faces would not go away – Seth Broomfield's, heavy-jowled, sneering and snarling at the men on the doorstep whose faces, ghostly yellow under the lantern, were tense with their mission – and finally, the worst recollection of all, Sam's face, serious and still until it twisted with scorn at the sight of James Hallas.

On the way home last night, she had sunk back into the luxurious depths of James's carriage and tried to block out what he was telling her and what she did not wish to hear – the details of Joseph Smith's suicide, the cap found on the dyehouse dam bank, the fetching of a hooked iron rod (kept for the purpose? she wondered with a shudder), the retrieval of the body and its transport back to Rose and Crown Yard. What kind of Christmas would that family be having?

Heavy-hearted, she pushed back the bedclothes and sat up. This would be the first Christmas without her father who was always as excited as a child and could hardly wait to watch her open her presents. I have been adored and indulged, she thought, and I never knew it till now.

But it was Christmas morning, a time for rejoicing. She must make an effort. Downstairs, she greeted the cook as cheerfully as she could.

'Good morning, Mrs Burton! And a happy Christmas!'

'Good morning, Miss Charlotte. And a happy Christmas to you. I thank you for your gift. We all do.'

Charlotte had given all the servants a gift of money as well as a personal present. By now, she knew exactly what they liked, whether it was a fine lawn handkerchief, a cake of scented soap or a leg of pork. Mrs Burton's choice was the latter. She was taking it home to cook for her family's Christmas dinner.

'It feels bad, leaving you all on your own, Miss Charlotte.' Mrs Burton sounded genuinely sorry. 'I've left a light lunch for you in the kitchen for when you get back from church.'

'Thank you, Mrs Burton. I assure you that is all I shall need. Don't forget I am going to the Haighs for my tea. I shall be in no danger of starving.'

This drew laughter from both women, Hannah Haigh's generous hospitality being well-known in the village.

Hannah and Eli Haigh lived on a farm in Almondbury high above the town, not far from Castle Hill, and had three sons and a daughter, all married apart from the youngest, Ben. Charlotte's mother had been friendly with Hannah since they were young and Charlotte had happy memories of her childhood visits to the farm.

Although the daughter, Rachel, was nearer to her in age, she had always felt closest to Ben, who was five years older than her. She recalled vividly how he had once held her hand and taken her to see a new-born calf, letting her stroke its soft ears and feel its velvety jaw.

Later, after her mother had died, she had come up to the farm to escape the atmosphere of the house of mourning for a few hours, returning better able to support her father in his grief.

Ben was not much of a talker but his presence was comforting. Like all the Haigh men, he was big and strongly-built, his fair skin ruddy with the outdoor life, his blue eyes crinkling into creases when he smiled.

He was smiling now as he let her in.

'Charlotte! It's grand to see you! Happy Christmas!'

'Happy Christmas, Ben! Is all the family here?'

The question was unnecessary. The big farmhouse kitchen, decorated with boughs of greenery, was crammed full with three generations of Haighs. Matthew and Joe sat with their wives and four young children each, who played, jumped about, crawled under the table or sat on the laps of grandparents, parents, aunts and uncles as vacancies arose.

It was a happy, noisy scene and cheered Charlotte instantly. Hannah hugged her, bringing with her the scent of nutmeg and cloves.

'Charlotte! You're just in time for your tea. Walking up that hill, I expect you're ready for it.'

Her words provoked a burst of laughter from those who heard her. It was a family joke that Hannah never stopped believing that people who had walked up a hill to visit her (as almost everyone did) would collapse unless immediately nourished by food, usually bread, scones, tarts or some kind of sweetcake baked by her.

At Christmas-time, she excelled herself. A long wooden table groaned with food, the centrepiece a huge pork pie which everyone knew would have to be eaten before they left.

But before the feast began, silence was called for and heads bent for grace, said by Eli as head of the family. Then everyone helped themselves with much clinking of plates, knives and forks, the noise gradually dying down as the eaters concentrated on the Christmas fare.

Charlotte knew there would be no alcoholic drink, the Haighs being devout Methodists, but it seemed to her a much merrier occasion, in the true sense of the word, than the one she had attended on Christmas Eve.

The happy atmosphere was infectious. Charlotte felt herself drawn into the warmth of the Haigh family circle and not just accepted but valued. She chatted to Rachel and her new husband, a doctor at the Infirmary, enquired after the farms of Matthew and Joe and dandled any infant that came to her knee.

Ben remained close to her most of the time except when he was tossing children up into the air and catching them as they begged him to in their turn, until the more cautious mothers, fearing injury or too much excitement, told them to stop bothering their uncle. It was Ben who walked her home in the cold crisp night air, carrying a lantern until they reached a gas-lit street.

'I'll say good night then, Charlotte,' he said as they reached her front door. He paused, as if waiting for something, and looked down at her affectionately.

'Good night, Ben. Thank you for bringing me home. It has been a lovely Christmas day.'

She put her hand forward for him to shake, suddenly feeling that he might have been on the point of giving her a friendly kiss. Sure enough, he shook her hand gently with a slight air of disappointment about him. She watched him as he walked away. It would perhaps have been nice to be kissed by Ben but cruel to encourage him when she knew her heart was given elsewhere. But how long could she go on like this, loving Sam without hope of a return?

Sam did not appear at the house on that Friday but sent a package containing statements and details of orders taken and cloth produced. The mill was working short time, like others in the district, having delivered most of their spring orders but with few for next winter's goods. Buyers in the Cloth Hall, including several from London and Canada, were showing some interest in fancy trousering but there weren't many of them.

Charlotte looked over the figures listlessly. They seemed blank without Sam there to share her interest. She already knew that the mill was not working to full capacity when she compared them with the annual statements her father had kept in his bureau.

In preparing for her move to a smaller house, she was busy clearing out cupboards and deciding what to keep. Opening a stout cardboard box, she came upon the wedding photographs of her father and Isabel, carefully posed and taken in a studio in town. She gazed at them, the sight of her father striking her to the heart.

The age difference between the couple was more marked here than in real life. Charlotte could see now that her father, for all his smiles, looked tired and not in the best of health next to the blooming Isabel in her wedding finery. She decided to keep the photographs because of her father but would not have them on show.

She wanted no extra reminder of Isabel. A letter would come from her soon enough claiming some more money. Presumably she would have left the hotel by now. Perhaps then the woman would be out of her life for good.

Meanwhile there was all the business of removal to take her mind off grieving about Sam Armitage. She was surprised how much there was to do but was glad to apply her mind to it. The house she had bought in Almondbury was smaller than the one in Wood Lane, built earlier in the century and to her mind was more elegant.

Fortunately the weather remained fine for the actual removal and now, a week later, the house was almost set to rights. Charlotte was deciding whether to put books on the shelves in alphabetical order or according to size when Bella knocked and came in. 'Excuse me, Miss Charlotte. Mr Hallas has called to see you but quite understands if you are not yet ready for visitors and will call later if that is more convenient.'

'No, not at all, Bella. Show Mr Hallas into the parlour and bring tea for us, please. Tell him I will be with him directly.'

Upstairs, Charlotte removed the pinafore she had been wearing and washed her hands and face. It would be good to talk to James. She had not had any company all week.

When she entered the parlour, he sprang to his feet. He was holding a large bunch of daffodils which he offered her rather shyly.

'I thought these would brighten a room. They're the first to arrive in the market.'

'Oh James, they are lovely!' Charlotte bent her head. 'I love the smell, fresh and green, like spring.' She held the bunch in her arms until Bella arrived with the tea-tray and relieved her of them.

'And how are you, James?' she asked, when she had answered his polite enquiries about the removal to her new home.

As he replied, mentioning his involvement with his business, meetings in town and the like, Charlotte noticed that he was not at ease. She could not decide whether it was caused by anxiety or excitement. There was a light, a softness in his eye which seemed to stem from some kind of new feeling which had taken him over. She did not understand it and steered the conversation onto familiar ground.

'And what of our friends, the Broomfields, the Thorpes, the Littlewoods? Have you seen them lately?'

He seemed happy to follow her lead.

'Yes, indeed. I saw Frederick Thorpe at a board meeting last week. The Littlewoods, no. The Broomfields...' He hesitated. 'Truth to tell, Seth Broomfield has had some bad luck recently. Some disappointments in business, ventures that have failed and so on. And his chemical factory has been in trouble with the Rivers Pollution Commission. Perhaps I should not say so but it seems he may have over-reached himself with the big house in Dalton. Very grand, of course. I know he has spent a lot on it. It must take some keeping up.'

'I'm sorry to hear that,' said Charlotte. 'It will be a worry for Jemima too.'

'Yes,' he replied, looking down and pulling at his cuffs.

Charlotte did not want him to speak further. He was definitely ill at ease.

'It's been so kind of you to call, James,' she said, rising and putting out her hand, signalling the end of the visit. 'And thank you again for the flowers. They are beautiful.'

And cheering, she thought, as she watched James walk away from the house. A sign of new life, of good things to come. She must try hard to sustain this mood. But it would not be easy. Thoughts about Sam, and visions of him, would keep returning.

They were reinforced later the next day when Bella brought her a slip of paper which had come through the door. The circular was couched in general terms to all Almondbury residents and referred to plans for the new road into town. There was some concern that its construction might interfere with the valuable springs of water that supplied the village. Those interested were invited to attend a meeting the next evening at eight o'clock to discuss the matter.

Charlotte's interest was caught, especially when she saw the address and the name of the writer – Samuel Armitage. She would go, no matter what it looked like. In any case, she cared about the water supply for the villagers of Almondbury.

The next evening she set out, walking up into Westgate, turning left past the church and continuing along Northgate until she reached the Old Bank.

The Armitages lived in a three-storey weaver's cottage set at right angles to the road just before it plunged steeply down into Moldgreen. Other people, mostly men, were approaching the house from all directions. All climbed the two flights of stairs to the top floor with its long, open space, rows of windows on either side and at the far end, an empty hand-loom.

Sam positioned himself behind a small table as people came in and stood around. Charlotte found a place at the back and kept the hood of her cloak up. She did not want to chance embarrassing Sam in any way.

By a quarter past, the room was almost full of people, mostly men in their working-clothes with a few better-dressed amongst them. Sam spoke clearly and simply. He had seen the plans for the road and feared they might threaten the water supply, there being no other waterworks in the district.

His words were met with a thoughtful silence. Charlotte sensed that he was well-known and respected. A few men spoke, the last a very old man who began reminiscing about his childhood playing in the local streams until he was cut short by someone asking the important question – 'What dusta think we mun do about it, Sam?'

Sam was obviously ready for this.

'I think we should contact Colonel Graham, Sir John Ramsden's agent, and tell him about danger to t'water. Very like th'*Examiner* will report the matter. The more people hear about it, the better.'

There were nods and mutters of agreement. Sam suggested that a small deputation might be a good idea whereupon three others proposed themselves and were accepted. With the business done, the assembly filed out, the deputed men staying behind to confer with Sam.

Charlotte was one of the last to leave. As she reached the doorway, Sam suddenly broke away from the group and hurried towards her. What he said was nothing out of the ordinary but the look on his face was anything but. His eyes were aglow, his lips quivering, his expression beseeching in the extreme.

Charlotte felt the blood rushing to her face as he came close. She felt unable to speak. Instead she put her hand forward and at once Sam took it between both of his. The warm pressure made her heart race and they stood for a moment, oblivious of all others, until someone came up and spoke to Sam.

Charlotte's step was light as she walked home. Even the grey stone buildings of the village seemed sturdy and friendly instead of stern and forbidding. When she reached the house, she found it hard to calm down and settle to her book for the rest of the evening.

Her lightened mood returned on waking. He must love her, he wouldn't have looked and acted in that way if he did not. Surely he would speak soon?

It was a Saturday and she knew he would be free of his work by late afternoon. Expecting him to call, she deliberately stayed in, although she had accepted a dinner invitation for that evening. With a stab of guilt, she sent a note via Henry, with her apologies, claiming she was indisposed.

But Sam did not come. All that evening her emotions were in turmoil. Every sound from the road sent her to the window but he did not appear. Had she mistaken his behaviour yesterday? Had she seen what she wanted to see?

By bedtime she was in despair and lay in bed, hearing the clock tick and watching the moonlight through the gap in the curtains, unable to sleep until the early hours.

On Sunday morning she attended church as usual. Outwardly she was the same, greeting friends and acquaintances, enquiring after the poorly, exclaiming at the progress of the infants and commiserating with the bereaved. But the words of the General Confession had never seemed so just.

'We have followed too much the devices and desires of our own hearts and there is no health in us.'

It was true. What was the dishonest note of the evening before but a device, a cunning lie, in pursuit of her desire for Sam? There seemed no way forward except to hope and pray.

The rest of the service passed in a blur. She left the church less tranquil than she had entered it, hurrying away to avoid conversation.

It was a fine clear morning. When Charlotte reached her house in Sharp Lane, she felt too restless to go indoors and continued walking down to Lumb Lane and along the valley.

The scene was enough to cheer anyone. Cattle were grazing peacefully in the fields where cottages and farmhouses nestled and beyond them, the rising slope was crowned with trees bordering Farnley Line, the whole brightened by the noonday sun. Now the lane began to rise as it approached the great earthwork of Castle Hill. Charlotte struck out to the right. Without consciously choosing, she was making for the Haighs' farm for comfort and advice as she had done when her mother had died, and again, just over two years ago, when her father had told her he was going to take a second wife. Hannah Haigh would be kind and understanding, as she always was.

Charlotte opened the farm gate but had barely taken two steps when she realised there was no-one about. Of course, they would all have gone to chapel. How foolish of her not to think of this! Feeling stupid now as well as miserable, she hesitated. Should she simply turn round and walk back home?

Instead, she stepped forward and surveyed the scene from this high vantage point. In front of her, hundreds of feet below on the wide plain of the valley bottom, lay the town of Huddersfield, its mills and factories silent, its looms and engines still, on this day of rest. Behind her were open fields and beyond them, the long dark shape of Penny Spring Wood and beyond that, though unseen, Old Bank and Sam's home. Realising this, she turned and began walking in that direction.

At this height, the wind was strong. Soon it had whipped off her bonnet so that it hung down her back by its strings. Charlotte paid no heed and feeling her hairpins come loose, shook her hair so that it flowed out behind her.

Whether it was the fresh air, the exercise or her own mental state, she did not know but as she walked, her determination grew strong to find Sam and tell him what was in her heart. If he rebuffed her, she would bear it and set about recovery. If he did not – her mind could not contemplate it clearly but dissolved into joyous confusion.

It was not long before she came to the border of the wood and left the open landscape for the shade of the trees, now bare of leaves. She slowed down and began to pick her way carefully amongst the stones and exposed tree roots. As she began to descend the steep bank to the stream below, her boots slid on the wet leaves underfoot and she caught hold of a tree trunk to steady herself.

A sound made her look down. There, at the bottom of the ravine, stood Sam, his eyes wide with surprise. Charlotte did not think twice. She simply let herself go, arms flung wide and feet rushing downhill.

In an instant she was in Sam's arms, their bodies pressed firmly together. Their cool faces touched and then their lips. She could feel his heart thudding through the thick cloth of his jacket. They separated to draw breath and then returned to their kissing, moving their heads from one side to another for a fresh, and delightful, sensation.

'I was going to see Hannah,' Sam said, when they had calmed down enough to speak. He did not loosen his hold on her.

'So was I,' laughed Charlotte. 'No need, no need.'

When he could speak again, Sam was contrite.

'It was all my fault. Me and my cussed pride.'

'No, no,' said Charlotte, putting a finger on his lips. She knew he was right but was not going to agree.

'It was,' insisted Sam. 'Because you own the mill and have money and position. I didn't like what people would say.'

'What do other people matter? We are the only ones it concerns.' And she kissed him again to emphasise her point.

'Are you sure, Charlotte, really sure this is what you want? When you could take your pick – James Hallas for one?'

Charlotte laughed. 'He's a pleasant enough man but not the one for me.

I went to the Broomfield's party with him because he had no partner. And his wife died the Christmas before.'

Sam's face was contorted with emotion. It was some time before he could express himself.

'So you are sure – you want to be my wife?'

'I can't think of anything I would like better,' said Charlotte with conviction.

It was several minutes before they were composed enough to think of practical matters. Charlotte was to meet Sam's parents as soon as possible.

'Have they any idea?' she asked.

'Well, I haven't said owt but they've likely seen what a black mood I've been in since Christmas. I should think they'll be right glad.'

They agreed to part for the moment, though the prospect inspired another bout of kissing. Sam insisted on escorting her back through the wood towards Broken Cross from where she could walk home easily. It would not do to be seen walking together yet. He would call for her at six o'clock that evening and they would take the carriage back to his house to meet his parents. He thought a few hours' notice would be all they needed. Charlotte wondered if that were so but was too happy to think of disagreeing.

Back home, she could not keep still. She ran up and down the stairs several times, thought about an extra wardrobe and, blushingly, a double bed. The small bedroom could be Sam's study if he wanted. It simply needed bookshelves and a desk.

Every now and again she would stop and look at herself in a convenient mirror. Her hazel eyes sparkled and looked larger somehow. It was hard to stop smiling. All the miseries of the recent past had disappeared. Nothing mattered now except Sam, not other people, not Isabel, particularly not Isabel. There might be some unpleasantness – she thought of Grace Littlewood's sneer and Seth Broomfield's coarseness but she would weather it all.

As she stepped out of the carriage outside Sam's house, she felt a prick of doubt. But his parents welcomed her warmly, without a trace of obsequiousness or a sense of being patronised. It was clear that they adored Sam, their only child, whose cleverness had amazed them since he was a child. It was no surprise to them that Charlotte should value him so highly.

They sat down to tea and sweetcake in the neat sitting-room. Mr Armitage apologized for the occasional smokiness of the fire. Charlotte suspected it had not been lit for some time. She would have been just as happy to have been received in the snug kitchen but knew such familiarity would come later.

The marriage was approved and the wedding agreed upon a few months hence. Mrs Armitage hoped that would give Charlotte sufficient time to prepare. Charlotte was sure it would. She had little idea of how much was involved but didn't really care.

The carriage drive back to Sharp Lane gave the lovers a few precious minutes of intimacy. They alighted with faces glowing.

'The carriage can take you back again if you like, Sam!' called Charlotte as Sam began to stride away.

'No thank you, Charlotte! I prefer to walk!'

Charlotte understood. She continued smiling until he disappeared from sight.

Old King Street
Bath
28 December 1867
Dear Charlotte

You will see from the above address that I have now found permanent accommodation in Bath. The house is situated in a good area off Queens Square, near to the houses of quality. I have the services of a maid, cook and handyman and look forward to paying and receiving many social calls. The shops are beyond belief, far superior to anything you will have seen. I am sure Ellen Thorpe would be delighted with them. Please give me her new address and be so good as to give her mine. It would be delightful if she and Frederick were able to visit me during one of their visits to London. The train from Paddington takes no more than an hour and a half.

I look forward to receiving what is owing to me from the sale of the house.

Yours truly,
Isabel Blezard

Isabel signed her name with a flourish as she always did and addressed the letter to the family solicitor in case Charlotte had already moved. An image of the house in Wood Lane went through her mind – the handsome hallway with its blue and ochre tiles, the ruby velvet of the chairs in the parlour, the pretty piano with its marquetry and brass candlesticks. But there was no point dwelling on the past; it was over and the money the house would fetch was all that mattered. Yet the memory of what she had been forced to leave behind nagged at her. After a minute, she broke open the sealing-wax and added a postscript.

P.S. Charlotte, it seems to me I should also receive my share of the proceeds of the furniture which you will be obliged to sell on moving to a smaller house. I trust you will see your way to complying with my request without recourse to the solicitor. You will remember that the piano was a particular gift to me from my husband on the occasion of our anniversary so I think you should reimburse me with the full cost. (The receipt is inside the lid.) Naturally I would rather have the piano but regret I have no room for it here so, as you can see, I should have its value added to what is already owing to me.

Isabel re-sealed the letter, pleased that she had thought of this in time. How remiss of her not to think of it before! A pity about the dining-table and chairs but it couldn't be helped. Feeling well pleased with herself, she tied on her bonnet and went out to post the letter and then on to her favourite trip, walking along Milsom Street and looking in the shop windows to see if any new fashions had arrived.

It was a fine afternoon and as she left the shade cast by the tall buildings, she felt the sun on her back as she joined the throng of people in the city's smartest shopping area. The window display of a shop selling silks and furs drew her in. The door she opened led her into the haberdashery department. Trimmings of all kinds – satin, silk, velvet, grosgrain, lace – as well as trays of buttons and hair combs of jet and tortoiseshell were all beautifully set out on the counter-tops. Nearby, a plain, earnest-looking assistant was showing a customer some leather gloves, a customer she recognised at once as Kitty.

'These are very nice – very supple as you see,' said the assistant, smoothing them onto the young woman's fingers. Kitty said nothing but moved her hands daintily back and forth. 'Madam has very pretty hands, very slender,' ventured the assistant and then coloured slightly as she saw Isabel listening.

'I'm not sure,' said Kitty. 'Have you any with a longer cuff?'

The assistant turned round, took some more gloves from a glass-fronted drawer behind her and laid them out on the counter. Isabel strolled further down the shop to look at some handkerchiefs and over her shoulder, saw that Kitty was leaving, a small, neatly-wrapped parcel in her hand. The assistant, smiling happily, made it to the door just ahead of her customer and opened it for her.

'Good day, Madam. Thank you. I hope we can be of service again.'

Kitty swept out, leaving the assistant to gather up the scattered gloves. Isabel, still watching, saw her meet her brother Michael on the pavement outside, lean towards him for a moment and then set off down the street on her own. Meanwhile Michael crossed the road with controlled haste and strode off in the opposite direction.

In the shop, the assistant had become flustered and sought the help of a superior who came over and began counting the pairs of gloves.

'You're sure you only put one pair of gloves in the parcel?'

She spoke sharply to the assistant whose face was now flushed with distress. A moment later, the two of them went out onto the pavement, scanned Milsom Street in both directions and then came back inside, the superior tight-lipped, the assistant close to tears.

Isabel got out of the shop as fast as she could. She was finding it hard to breathe. Her first reaction to what she had witnessed had been a grudging admiration for the sleight of hand practised by the Nolans but it was instantly replaced by anger and then a mounting fury. These two, who had pretended to be so pleasant, were nothing more than common thieves! And she had given them free run of the house!

Her gorge rising, she turned on her heel and almost ran from the scene, her heart thudding, her face reddening. Twice she banged into other walkers who started back and stared at her as she blundered past.

When she reached the house, her hand was shaking so much she had difficulty getting the key in the lock. She burst into the sitting-room, frantically checking its contents. It seemed intact but she could not be sure. Then she thought of the bedroom. The bedroom! Of course!

Bounding up the stairs, she threw open the door and darted over to the locked cupboard in the corner where her valuables were locked. Thank God, it was still locked and the key where it should be, on a ribbon round her stays. No, it must be her clothes Kitty would be after.

Isabel began pulling the drawers out of the chest, banging them with her fist when they stuck, and rifling through the clothes press. Where was the short woollen cape trimmed with grey fur, one of her favourite pieces? Kitty had admired it only the other day. It was a beautiful, expensive piece which she had bought in Bond Street when she accompanied Ellen Thorpe on a trip to London. Ellen herself had envied it.

She flipped through the garments again. Wool, worsted, velvet, silk, bombazine, – but no sign of the cape. She felt her temper rising and at the sound of the front door opening, her rage exploded and sent her hurtling down the stairs. She flew at Kitty who stood in the hall, her back flattened against the door.

'Where is it, you thieving bitch?'

The slap across Kitty's face slammed the girl against a side wall so that she staggered. Isabel threw herself forward and gripped the young woman's shoulders with both hands. The bones were as thin as a child's.

'What have you done with it? I know what you get up to, I've seen you – in Milsom Street, shop-lifting.'

Kitty's face was white save for the red mark of Isabel's hand on her cheek but she drew herself up and faced the older woman, a flash in her green eyes. She said nothing as Isabel raged on.

'My short cape! The one with grey fur! You've stolen it, haven't you? Admit it!' Isabel swung her fist towards the other but this time Kitty dodged and avoided the blow. Her hat had slipped to one side, her cheek already swelling. Isabel's bloodshot eyes were bolting out of her head, her teeth bared.

'Where is it?'

Kitty edged herself along the wall.

'Let me show you,' she said quietly. Gathering up her skirts with both hands, she descended the stairs to the lower ground floor. Isabel followed her, disbelievingly. There, draped round a chair, was the grey cape. Kitty positioned herself behind it, as if for protection.

'I brought it here. To press it.'

Isabel peered at it. It did look better than the last time she had seen it, crumpled up on the floor where she had dropped it. Then she saw the two flat-irons left to cool in the hearth and a thin cloth folded beside them. Kitty saw the direction of Isabel's gaze. She spoke now with an air of injured dignity.

'The gloves I bought are for you.' She held out the slim parcel. 'Go on. Open it.'

Isabel did so. The gloves, inside the tissue paper, were of the softest leather of a light grey colour exactly like the woollen cloth of her cape. Isabel could not think of anything to say. Kitty spoke in a low voice.

'It's true I took another pair. They were so beautiful. I-I wanted some for myself. It was wrong, I know.'

Isabel was knocked off balance by this mixture of dishonesty and truth. She could not deny that the gift was thoughtful – and extremely elegant. Knowing that she herself had not been robbed made all the difference. She stroked the gloves.

'Put them on, do, Isabel.'

She did so, easing her fingers into the silk lining and flexing them gently against the supple leather.

'They are very nice.' With an effort, 'Thank you, Kitty.'

The tension eased.

'Let's have some tea,' said Kitty, stirring the fire into life. Isabel, finding herself shivering, was agreeable and sank into a fireside chair.

'I've always loved beautiful things,' murmured Kitty, staring into the flames.

'So have I,' said Isabel.

'I always used to look in the shop windows when I was a child – at the dresses and jewellery and fans. Michael used to look at the food shops. Then we'd go back home, to Avon Street.' Kitty's nostrils flared at the recollection. 'Stinking, over-crowded, noisy. And probably get thumped by our father – if he was sober enough to catch us.'

Isabel was silent. Her childhood had been privileged compared to Kitty's. An only child, she had had her own small room in the attic of the hotel with a distant view, if she stood on a chair, of Scarborough's South Bay. She could not remember either of her parents laying a finger on her.

Kitty was lost in reminiscence.

'When I was little, my mother got a few hours cleaning at the Theatre Royal, the one that burnt down. I loved going with her. It was my job to crawl under the seats and pick up anything left there. Nasty, some of it, but sometimes there was a fan or an earring. Once I found a brooch. One Christmas – ' Kitty's face registered excited recollection and pain at the same time. Isabel had never seen such an expressive face before. She prided herself on having more self-control – and the ability to make her face express or conceal what she wanted it to.

Kitty took a deep breath. She went on, the memory mixing joy and pain.

'Once, the theatre manager invited children from poor families to see '*Jack and the Beanstalk*'. Free! I remember my mother got me a clean dress and a neighbour brought me a ribbon for my hair. They both cried and kissed me and said I was a picture.'

Kitty's eyes filled with tears.

'When we got to the theatre, with lots of other children, they turned us away. Said the show was cancelled. I cried all the way home. My mother had to let me go to bed in my dress and hair-ribbon. I wouldn't let her take them off.'

Isabel felt herself drawn, in spite of herself, into the tale.

'Why was it cancelled?'

Kitty's lip twisted.

'It was one of them interfering group of busybodies. Worrying about our morals. So they said.' She looked as if she was about to spit in the fire but remembered herself in time. 'I think it's made me want to work in the theatre all the more. Oh, I don't mean cleaning!' she said hastily. 'I mean, on the stage, acting, singing. It's what I want to do.'

'But would it be regular work, enough to live on?'

Kitty's face fell.

'I doubt it. That's why I'm working at the club – to get some money behind me.' Isabel said nothing. In truth, she was impressed by the other's drive and ambition. Admiration did not come readily to Isabel, certainly not for another woman. To feel it, without envy, was foreign to her.

Kitty's face was lit up once again.

'When they rebuilt the theatre, Ellen Terry came down from London to play Titania in Shakespeare. It was wonderful! And last year, Henry Irving! Michael and I went to see him in '*The Rivals*'. It was sixpence in the gallery. We went on our birthday.'

Isabel had not realised the couple were twins.

'And is Michael as fond of the theatre as you are?'

'Not as much. But he loves music as I do. You should see him dance, especially after he's had a drink! We did that in the streets for a while, me singing and him dancing, after Mother died. We used to do it outside the theatre at night when people were coming out. People would throw pennies, sometimes more. Then we'd see the constable coming, pick up the money and run.'

'When did you begin working at Mr Byrne's?' The name felt strange in her mouth.

'After we left our schools, we had to go into service at big houses in the country. I was a kitchen-maid, Michael a bootboy. But they wouldn't let us work in the same house so we ran away and came back to Bath.'

'And is Mr Byrne a good employer?'

'He's all right. He tells us what to do and leaves us alone. I have to get the men to spend money, on betting, drink and so on.'

Isabel wondered how far encouragement went, whether Kitty provided further pleasures or simply access to them. But she would not enquire. It was none of her business. Yet the desire to keep talking about this man drove her on.

'Did I tell you how I met Mr Byrne? It was on a train when I was leaving Yorkshire. He was very helpful.'

'Oh, he would be. He gets on very well with women. There's usually someone hanging about him.'

The words struck Isabel painfully. She tried to make light of them.

'Well, I suppose he's a good catch. Handsome, and successful in business.'

'Yes. Michael says he's got clubs in other places. That's why he goes away a lot. Brighton, London, I think. Perhaps more.'

'And no wife?'

'Not as far as we know. I think he likes his freedom.'

Isabel stood up abruptly to avoid Kitty's gaze. She moved to the window but there was nothing to see but a stone wall. She was caught between two opposing feelings – despair that this man was and perhaps always would be unattainable, and an excited determination that this elusive man would one day be hers. Surely Fate had sent him to her? She turned to look at Kitty who was tactfully folding laundry.

'Kitty! Would you like to go to the theatre next week? With me?'

The young woman needed no further invitation. Taking Isabel's threepence, she ran out and returned with a copy of *The Chronicle.*

'It's nothing special. A melodrama, then some ballet and a farce.'

'Never mind. I fancy an outing.'

At that moment, Michael returned. He showed no interest in accompanying them but was willing to go out and buy the tickets for them.

'What shall I get? Gallery? Pit? Dress circle?' The latter were three shillings a seat, the pit one shilling.

'We'll have two in the pit,' said Isabel. The dress circle could wait.

The night of the theatre trip arrived and the two women set out together, Kitty in a state of high excitement, Isabel less so but curious nevertheless to see the interior of the building. It did not disappoint.

A great chandelier hung from the centre of the painted ceiling, highlighting the gilding of the richly decorated auditorium. She could see that the dress circle seats were upholstered in scarlet plush. Those in the pit were of similar colour but in a cheaper fabric. Fashionably dressed people were taking their places in the stage boxes where they made themselves at ease. They were soon resting their arms on the scarlet rail and training their opera glasses on the assembled crowd.

From higher up in the gallery came a buzz of chatter. Kitty was alight with joy, provoking a stab of envy in Isabel. When the musicians in the orchestra pit began tuning up, she pressed her hands together with pleasure.

Isabel was mildly entertained by the performance although not moved to laughter by the comedy nor to sympathy by the sickly melodrama. Kitty remained rapt throughout, only returning to reality during the interval.

This was the part Isabel enjoyed most because it gave her the chance to observe a section of Bath society as closely as she could. She was particularly taken by the look of a beautifully dressed woman in one of the stage boxes. She wore an elegant black dress topped by a shimmering diamond necklace which sparkled in the light.

Her other distinctive feature was her silvery blonde hair which was elegantly coiffed and held in place by jewelled combs. Waving a black lace fan, she turned, with a charming smile, to speak to a man, obviously an admirer, who appeared in the box behind her and engaged her in conversation.

'Do you know that woman?' she asked Kitty.

'No. Very fine. And wealthy by the look of the jewels.'

The performance began again with more music from the orchestra, giving Isabel time to study the woman queening it in the box. One day, she, Isabel Blezard, would sit there in her finery and enjoy the attention her person and position deserved.

CHAPTER SEVEN

The coals in the parlour fireplace shifted and settled into a comforting red glow. Sam, who was sitting on the hearth-rug with his back against the sofa, made as if to move and put more coal on the fire but Charlotte laid a hand on his shoulder.

'Don't bother, Sam. The room's plenty warm.'

It was indeed. From outside came the sound of rain lashing against the window-panes and the low roar of the wind off the Pennines but no draught disturbed the room's thick velour curtains. A tray with two empty coffee cups stood on a low table. A sheaf of papers lay scattered on the far side of the rug.

Charlotte ran her fingers through Sam's springy red hair. He responded by catching her hand and drawing her wrist towards him so he could press his lips to it. She gave a sigh of contentment.

'I'm not sorry it's raining. It's grand to be indoors.'

Sam turned and smiled his agreement.

'I wish we could always be like this, Sam. Just the two of us, together. And no-one else to bother us.' Charlotte had been reclining on the cushions at one end of the sofa but now she sat up and smoothed her rumpled hair. 'But I know we can't. I know we have to tell people.'

Sam turned round to face her.

'You're not afraid, are you, Charlotte? Or – ashamed?' He looked doubtful.

'No, of course not! It's just that – I know I have to, because we live in a society and other people have a right to know. But it would be so nice if we could live – I don't know how, in our own little private world – at least, for a while.'

Sam got up and came close to her by kneeling on the sofa.

'It would be nice, right enough,' he said, kissing the tip of her nose, 'but I doubt we'd sell much cloth.'

Charlotte laughed and threw her arms round him.

'You're right, Sam – as you usually are.'

Sam's face softened, his voice growing huskier.

'And you are beautiful – as you always are.' He bent towards her and kissed her. They remained together while time and place were suspended. Moving apart, they gazed at one another and began kissing again, their bodies gradually slipping down onto the sofa. After a few moments, Sam pulled away, stood up and moved towards the mantelpiece. When he had regained his composure, he spoke.

'I reckon you'd better tell your friends soon.'

'I will, Sam, I will.'

At that moment, the clock struck ten. Charlotte looked at it ruefully.

'I suppose you'd best be going, Sam,' she said, turning up the gas lamp and ringing the bell for the maid. In the entrance hall, Charlotte could not resist helping Sam on with his overcoat and wrapping the scarf round his throat. Bella disappeared discreetly into the kitchen with the tray.

When he had gone, Charlotte climbed the stairs dreamily. She undressed slowly and sank back against the feather pillows. Since the day of their meeting in Penny Spring Wood, she had known happiness she had never imagined possible. Every moment she spent with Sam was precious and he became dearer to her at every meeting.

Their discussions about mill business became absorbing, their shared responses quickening their interest. Their walks were not yet as extensive as they both hoped they would be. They were still shy of the public gaze, at least until their betrothal was made known. In any case, the weather had not been fit, keeping them indoors. She smiled to herself as she thought of the evening they had just spent together. If all went as she hoped, they had a lifetime of such moments to look forward to.

It ought to be easy, thought Charlotte, as she sat balancing a cup of tea on her lap in Mrs Littlewood's drawing-room. All I have to say is that Sam and I are betrothed. Grace Littlewood will no doubt have something sour to say, Ellen Thorpe and a few others will probably think I could do better for myself but it won't matter. Nothing matters, except the feelings Sam and I have for each other. I must tell them if there is to be a wedding because this is how our society arranges itself. For the moment, however, she was content to sit in silence amidst the unbroken buzz of conversation.

There were four women in the room besides Charlotte. She knew Ellen Thorpe, Jemima Broomfield and Grace Littlewood well. The other woman was Maud Crowther, the new wife of Silas Crowther who had recently taken over as their family solicitor. Charlotte thought the two couples looked odd as they bent their well-dressed heads towards each other, their full skirts ballooning out around them so that each pair created a strange, double-headed human form. Ellen and Jemima, beautifully dressed in pale blue and dark blue respectively, looked as if they were talking about fashion, judging by their gestures. Grace, in an unfortunate shade of green, was speaking rapidly and quietly to Maud Crowther, a sallow, thin-faced woman who appeared to be avidly drinking in all the gossip the other was passing on. Charlotte would have been quite happy to sit and observe the others had not Mrs Littlewood, their hostess, entered the room and with a smile, positioned herself next to her.

Mrs Littlewood was a pleasant woman in her fifties who took a benevolent interest in people. Charlotte also admired her for the forbearance she displayed in the company of her sharp-tongued daughter and her unattractive husband. It was common knowledge that Dr Littlewood drank more than was good for him and as his medical skills were not highly regarded, his practice had few patients. Fortunately Mrs Littlewood's private income enabled them to live in more style than might have been expected. Charlotte's father had told her this. He said he kept up the acquaintance because Mrs Littlewood had been a friend of his wife since childhood.

'Charlotte! My dear! How good to see you! Forgive my absence. We have a new parlourmaid who needs a little reminding on the serving of tea.' Mrs Littlewood leaned closer. 'You're looking very well, my dear. It's good to see you out of your black. That light mauve suits you. It was a colour your mother was also fond of, I remember.'

Charlotte smiled and found her heart beating a little faster as she prepared to announce her news.

'Thank you very much, Mrs Littlewood. Yes, I am feeling very well at the moment – that is to say, I expect it is because I'm very happy too.'

This admission of personal feeling, with the expectation of more to come, reached the ears of the women who simultaneously fell silent and turned their heads towards Charlotte.

'I would like you all to know that Mr Armitage, Mr Samuel Armitage, has asked me to marry him and I have accepted his proposal. We hope to be married later this year.'

There was a general cry of pleasure and good will, although Charlotte would have been happier not to see Grace's sidelong smirk at her new friend and her lips move with what looked like the words 'her mill manager'.

'My dear Charlotte,' said Ellen, kissing her and bringing a wave of fragrance with her. 'I'm so happy for you and I know Frederick will be too.'

She was followed by Jemima, rustling in her silk gown.

'Many felicitations, dear Charlotte.'

Mrs Littlewood's good wishes bore the sincerity of someone who had known Charlotte since she was a baby.

'My dear girl! I am so glad you have found happiness as your dear parents did.' She embraced Charlotte who felt a surge of emotion threaten to overcome her.

Grace had not spoken so far but now did so with a gleam in her eye.

'And is there a ring for us to admire, Charlotte? No proper betrothal should be without one.'

Charlotte was prepared for this and held out her left hand for her companions to see the antique opal ring in its elaborate gold setting. It was her grandmother's ring, a fact she was certainly not going to reveal. Sam had needed a little persuasion to approve the ploy but had seen sense as Charlotte knew he would.

The responses were pleasing .

'Oh, it's beautiful!' 'Most charming!' 'A favourite with the Queen, I believe.'

Grace sniffed, with what sounded like satisfaction.

'Opal! Said to be unlucky!'

Her mother gave her a reproving look and said, 'Now, Grace! Perhaps you would call the maid to bring in the cakes. I'm sure our guests are ready for a little more refreshment.'

'There's no need to be nervous,' said Charlotte, laying her hand on Sam's wrist. He flinched slightly.

'I'm not nervous. It's just – the clothes. They feel right strange. But I'll get used to 'em,' he said, turning to her in the carriage as it rolled through the town centre.

It was true that the clothes had almost been a sticking-point. When the invitation to dinner with the Thorpes arrived, Charlotte had been pleased but a little apprehensive. 'It's understandable – and right, Sam. They want to meet you.' Sam raised his eyebrows. 'The thing is, we always wear evening dress on these occasions.'

Sam scowled as Charlotte hurried on.

'You're going to need evening dress in the future so we might as well get you fitted up now. When there's a special musical evening, for example, or a formal gathering of business people.'

She had chosen her words carefully, knowing that the mention of music and business would help persuade Sam of the need for clothing he saw as representative of a class system he despised.

So he had relented and had been measured by the best tailors in town. Charlotte could see that, although he would not admit it, he was impressed by his appearance in the well-fitting black coat and trousers with the crisp white shirt which showed his neat build and fair skin to advantage. As he looked at his reflection in the pier-glass, he brushed the sleeve with his hand and said 'Nice bit o'cloth.'

Sam did not know any of the dinner party guests personally but knew as much about them as most local people.

'The Thorpes? Didn't they rent Dartmouth Hall before buying this new house in Edgerton? Gives herself airs, Mrs Thorpe, eh? From London? Thinks we're all savages up here. Frederick Thorpe sounds decent enough. Local magistrate. Bit more enlightened than some of the old 'uns. Broomfield's a bit of a thug according to them as knows 'im. Dr Littlewood – well, we all know what's said about him.'

Charlotte was amused, especially as Sam claimed to disdain gossip.

'You seem to have a pretty good idea of my father's friends. What else can I tell you? Oh, that Jemima Broomfield is the Littlewoods' niece? No? Well, the only one there you don't know will be James Hallas.' She paused, expecting, and receiving, a sharp glance from Sam. 'Don't say anything you might regret, Sam. As I told you, a young widower with a machine-making business down Leeds Road and a business colleague of Frederick's. Very pleasant. We'd all be happy to see him find a new wife.'

Sam chuckled and squeezed her hand. 'So would I – as long as it's not mine.'

Charlotte sensed Sam was in a good mood when she drew up in the carriage outside his house. As he came out, his parents stood framed in the doorway, looking proudly at their finely-dressed son. She hoped this mood would continue during a social occasion which could well be decisive for their future acceptance. She knew that if Sam disagreed strongly with some of the opinions expressed, he would find it hard to stay silent. On the other hand, his passionate commitment to social justice was one of the things she loved about him.

When they arrived at the Thorpes, she was pleased to see how gracefully he performed his social duties – handing her down from the carriage, giving her his arm along the drive, removing his hat as they entered, doffing his cape and handing it to the maid without any trace of embarrassment.

As they went towards the drawing-room, he gave her a sly wink. Charlotte lifted her chin, put her arm through his and entered the room with more confidence than she had ever felt before. She felt almost beautiful in her rich purple gown, the amethysts warm at her throat, the opal ring gleaming on the hand that rested on Sam's arm.

Soon they were standing, sherry glass in hand, with the other guests. There was a hint of tension in Ellen's demeanour, understandable in view of her reputation for first-class 'cuisine'. Charlotte realised it would not be long before it was her turn to give dinner parties. Frederick Thorpe was as poised and handsome as ever. He was talking to James Hallas, who was similarly good-looking but shorter in stature. Charlotte bowed to James and was glad to see him respond with a relaxed smile.

By contrast, Seth Broomfield was his usual black-browed, glowering self. Although his clothes were always expensive, he wore them gracelessly and would have distressed his tailor if he could have seen how crumpled and uneven he always made them look. At the moment, he was at peace. His wife Jemima was engrossed in talking to her aunt, Mrs Littlewood, about the gas supply that had only recently been installed at All Hallows' Church, Almondbury.

'I find it so much easier now to follow the service in the prayer book,' said Mrs Littlewood.

There was gentle disagreement from Jemima who favoured oil lamps and candles. The discussion of the merits of both kinds of lighting was extended to those on either side. Charlotte was glad that Sam was not drawn into the conversation, knowing his attitude to religion. She could hear him telling Ellen about the second delivery of letters, after the one at half-past eight in the morning, that Almondbury now enjoyed. He held his face straight as Ellen described the vastly superior postal service in London and told her he hoped to pay a visit to the capital one day.

'And how are things progressing with the new road into town? And the water sources?' asked Frederick. 'I hear you made representations to Ramsden's agent.'

'Yes, we did,' Sam replied. 'We had a good meeting, presented some geological diagrams for the road builders to make it clear what needed protecting.'

'Good man!' said Frederick, patting Sam on the shoulder. 'Now friends, my dear wife tells me she would like us to take our places in the dining-room.'

The guests filed out and entered a spacious room where a long oval table was laid with an ecru linen tablecloth, fine silver and glassware. Ellen was politely suggesting that the guests should sit alternately lady and gentleman.

Suddenly Seth Broomfield, on seeing his wife about to sit next to Frederick, pushed forward and steered her, none too gently, two places further on so that she sat between James Hallas and Dr Littlewood.

'Here y'are, lass,' he boomed. 'Sit next to thi uncle – he'll be glad to 'ave such a pretty lass next to 'im.'

Charlotte was sure she could not be the only person who thought him very rude, particularly to the other ladies in the room. He was obviously jealous of their host's charming manner towards Jemima. However, she seemed not to mind being manipulated in this way. Charlotte found herself between Frederick and Seth and was quite happy because she faced Sam across the table.

As the delicate beef consommé was served, the conversation turned, as conversation will, to the weather. The week before, there had been two days of non-stop wind and rain. Several mills in Lockwood and Honley, according to Seth, had been flooded. In the space of four hours, Bilberry reservoir in Holmfirth had risen twenty-one feet.

'Oh, don't mention that name!' cried Mrs Littlewood with a shudder. 'I lost good friends in that tragedy.'

James, the only newcomer, was curious.

'It was in 1852,' said Sam, 'about this time of year. There was heavy rainfall for days on end which the Bilberry embankment couldn't cope with. It burst outward and more than eighty million gallons of water escaped, travelling three miles in twenty minutes down to Thongsbridge, Honley and Armitage Bridge. A four-storey mill was thrown down and boilers tossed about like corks.' His voice dropped. 'There was considerable loss of life.'

The listeners who knew the general facts about the dam burst fell silent in the face of Sam's authoritative and vivid account.

'And why did it happen?' asked James. There was a pause which nobody filled. All looked to Sam to answer, which he did.

'A combination of bad engineering and penny-pinching,' he replied.

Any further discussion was halted by the arrival of the fish which Ellen informed them had come from the east coast that very day. As it was being served, Charlotte heard James Hallas tell Sam he would like to talk about engineering with him later when the ladies retired. Though listening to Frederick telling her about his work as a magistrate, she kept one eye on Sam who was now discussing social matters with Mrs Littlewood. When Grace's high-pitched voice cut across the conversation, she was all attention.

'I wonder, Mr Armitage, whether you find time for other pursuits. I mean, you must find much of your time and energy taken up by your employment.'

The room became silent. Ellen's eyes registered a flicker of alarm. Sam spoke calmly.

'You are quite right, Miss Littlewood. I am very absorbed in my work but I might call it partly a labour of love.' The look he directed towards Charlotte filled her with joy. 'But I try to make time for other interests. Miss Charlotte and I are looking forward to the Choral's performance of *Judas Maccabeus* later this month and we also plan to go to Leeds and Manchester for concerts.'

'Leeds and Manchester! Dear me! I had no idea you travelled so widely!'

Grace Littlewood spoke with a sneer. Charlotte felt, rather than saw, Sam's temper rise. Outwardly he appeared unmoved.

'Yes indeed, Miss Littlewood. I must confess I have only passed through London once on my way to Paris last year for the Exhibition.'

Charlotte felt like applauding. She knew, if Sam didn't, that Grace had not been to either city. Ellen joined in with animation.

'Of course, Sam, you went to Paris last year when we did, Isabel and I! But I'm ashamed to say we went merely for pleasure. You, I am sure, had a more serious purpose.'

'You are right, Mrs Thorpe. I was very interested in all I could learn about the textile trade and our competitors abroad.'

'You do right,' growled Seth.

'I have to say I was impressed, and worried, by the high level of technical education shown by the continentals. If I may say so, –. '

'Do, Sam, do!' said Frederick.

'I think we mustn't lag behind. We've a strong engineering tradition in this country but we must pay attention to the other sciences, particularly chemistry, which can help the textile trade.'

'You're right again,' said Seth. 'Chemicals, dye-stuffs – all important in my way of business.'

Charlotte felt she had been silent for long enough.

'Sam will be too modest to tell you so I will. As a member of Mr Jarmain's chemistry classes, he passed the exam set by the Society of Arts in London two years ago and was top of the list!'

There was a murmur of praise which caused Sam to blush. It serves Grace right, thought Charlotte. She should not have spoken to Sam as she did.

'I didn't know about this,' said Frederick, 'that people could take those exams up here.'

'Yes indeed,' said Sam. 'And when the Society did a trial run, our Mechanics' Institution was the only centre outside London to take part.'

Amidst the general approval, James spoke up.

'Well, I'd heard tell that Huddersfield was a proud town. Now I can see it has much to be proud of.'

This proved to be a very popular sentiment. Frederick clapped his hands, Jemima rewarded James with a dazzling smile and Ellen gave a polite nod of recognition. Even Grace looked less sour than usual.

Charlotte looked at Sam's pursed lips and caught his eye. She knew his impulse was to continue the conversation, to stress how many social issues the town still needed to address but she admired his obvious restraint. She could almost hear what he was thinking – 'I've probably said enough on this first meeting so I'll keep quiet for now.' She gave him a glowing look which she hoped he could interpret. When he returned her look, she was sure he had done so.

The rest of the evening passed pleasantly. Charlotte gave Ellen Isabel's new address in Bath and a polite summary of her news. Mrs Littlewood told her how impressed she was with Sam and how she was sure they would be happy together. Jemima concurred but seemed strangely absent as if she was in some dream of her own.

Eventually Charlotte and Sam were able to escape into the private world of the Blezard carriage.

'I was so proud of you, Sam,' she said as he took her in his arms and kissed her.

'And I was of you,' he replied. 'None of those other women could hold a candle to you.'

Charlotte laughed. She had heard the saying 'Love is blind'. She felt it must be, at least, a little short-sighted.

As Isabel came downstairs in her dressing-gown, her hair hanging loose on her shoulders, she was pleased to see not one but two letters awaiting her. She was able to recognise the hand-writing on both; one was from Charlotte and the other from Ellen Thorpe. There was no doubt which one carried the more important news. She made herself comfortable in the warm kitchen and opened Charlotte's.

Sharp Lane
Almondbury
10th January 1868
Dear Isabel

I am glad to hear you are well settled in Bath. I have given your address to Ellen Thorpe as you asked. I have also arranged for the sum of seven hundred pounds to be transferred to your bank which I trust you will agree is a fair sum. I now regard this matter as closed.

You may be interested to know that I am betrothed to Mr Samuel Armitage. We hope to marry later in the year.

Yours truly,
Charlotte

Seven hundred pounds! A good sum, thought Isabel, but only what I deserve. Samuel Armitage! One of the mill workers! Well, well, not exactly calculated to raise her position in society. Foolish girl! She remembered Armitage as a red-haired young man whom George thought highly of. A good choice if you wanted a husband who understood boilers. Yawning, she made herself some toast and put her feet up against the kitchen range while she read what she was sure would be a more interesting, if less productive, letter.

New North Rd,
Edgerton,
Huddersfield
10th January 1868
Dear Isabel,

I was delighted to hear from Charlotte that you have found congenial accommodation in Bath. I shall certainly come and visit you when I am next in London.

We too are well satisfied with our new house in Edgerton, a handsome one of fine stonework standing in extensive grounds. Frederick knows the builders and made sure we had one of the most select. I am happy to say that the children are in good health and enjoying their schooldays. I am still troubled by my headaches but suppose they are a cross I have to bear.

You will no doubt be hearing from your step-daughter that she is betrothed to her mill manager, Samuel Armitage. I was not impressed when I heard this and thought she could have done much better for herself. There are several eligible young men in the area to whom Frederick and I could have introduced her. We were particularly hoping she might form an attachment to James Hallas, a business colleague of Frederick's, who is very agreeable and not long widowed.

However, when we met Mr Armitage at our dinner party recently, we were pleasantly surprised by him. He spoke well on a variety of subjects and bore himself almost like a gentleman. There does seem to be a real attachment between them.

Things continue very much the same here as when you were with us. Jemima still has to cope with Seth's over-bearing jealousy. I do not know how she manages to live with it. We hear that his temper has not been improved by some unfortunate business decisions of late. Frederick and I think he may have over-reached himself when he bought that great house at Dalton – its upkeep must cost a fortune. Jemima does not seem too worried about it, however.

Last but not least, I have heard that the full hooped skirt may be going out of fashion. Can you let me know if you are of the same opinion? I would not wish to place an order for several new gowns in this style if I thought this was the case. There has been nothing about it in my magazines but a London friend of mine has just returned from Paris and has told me this in confidence. Let me know what you think.

I remain,
Your friend,
Ellen Thorpe

Isabel stretched her limbs in pleasure. She found herself almost on the point of purring. There was undoubtedly a hint of envy in Ellen's letter that she, Isabel, was now living much nearer to the heart of the fashion world than Ellen was. True, Isabel was not certain that Bath was really that close to it although assuredly closer than Huddersfield. She dressed herself languidly in front of the looking-glass, changing her clothes three times before she was satisfied. Those boots had lost their sparkle of newness. Why, she could afford several new pairs if she wanted now! Finally satisfied with a dark blue walking costume and matching hat, she sallied forth with the prospect of a happy afternoon of shopping ahead of her, after an equally cheering visit to the bank.

It was a fine day with a feeling of early spring already in the air. As she strolled along, Isabel regarded her surroundings with complacency. How good it would be to introduce Ellen to the sights of the city!

The weather and her energy drew her to walk away from Milsom Street and the lure of its merchandise. After a few minutes, she found herself on South Parade with the façade of the railway station in the near distance. It seemed a long time since she had arrived there on that wet night, escorted by Randolph Byrne before he disappeared into the darkness.

She remembered their last meeting. The memory of its abrupt ending had faded. All she recalled was the thrill of their encounter, the strength of his body against hers, the sensation of his touch. It would, it must happen again! She simply needed the chance to re-awaken his interest and his passion. The thought of the money in the bank raised her spirits still further.

Turning back to Pierrepont Street, she saw a procession of wheel-chairs, like giant perambulators, being slowly pushed along by menservants. She caught a glimpse of a sickly face beneath a creased leather hood and quickened her step. That Bath attracted invalids among its visitors repelled her. It was a feature she would not bring to the attention of Ellen Thorpe.

As she skirted the railings around the flower-bed in the centre of Orange Grove, she was delighted to see Randolph emerging from a nearby hotel. He had not seen her. He stood still waiting for a drayman and his cart to pass by. Isabel quickened her step so that she could meet him as if by accident. When he caught sight of her, she was gratified to see a look of pleasure cross his face.

'My dear Isabel! How good to see you on this fine morning!'

'Randolph! Yes, indeed.' Isabel smiled as he bent over her gloved hand and bestowed a token kiss on it.

'How splendid the abbey looks and how fortunate we are to have this magnificent building in our midst!' he exclaimed.

'What? Oh yes,' said Isabel, looking at the abbey over her shoulder. 'Yes, indeed. Very fine.'

'You are looking very fine yourself this morning, Isabel. A most handsome costume!'

'Thank you, Randolph. How kind of you to say so!' Isabel beamed and gave him what she felt was her most beguiling smile. 'True, I am feeling very well today. I have just received some good news.' As she said this, Isabel was aware of the need for caution. It would not do to be too candid. 'I wonder – if you are not engaged this evening, if you would allow me to entertain you to dinner.' As he seemed to hesitate, she went on. 'To celebrate my good fortune.'

'Of course, that would be delightful. Although I need to be at the club before ten o'clock.'

'I understand. I should like to pay it a visit also.'

A time and a likely hotel were decided upon and Isabel went on her way with a spring in her step. She had not really had the chance to talk to Byrne for any length of time, not since their meeting in Walcot.

Her reception at the bank in Abbey Churchyard was most pleasing. From the moment she entered the mahogany-panelled hall, she was treated with a courtesy which increased to the point of obsequiousness when she was invited into the Manager's office.

'Most happy to receive you as a valued customer, Mrs Blezard,' said the man, his domed bald head contrasting oddly with his bushy grey whiskers.

After their discussion about interest rates, Isabel felt slightly less sanguine. To live in the style she wished for called for a larger sum on deposit. And she had been so looking forward to spending lavishly on new clothes.

'You will perhaps be able to invest a further sum in the future,' said the Manager. It was not clear if this was a statement or a question.

'Oh, undoubtedly!' replied Isabel. 'I expect more funds before very long.'

'Very good, very good! It has been a pleasure to meet you, Mrs Blezard.'

He rose and taking her hand, held it longer than was customary. Isabel felt its heat through her glove and smiled at him. He let go of her hand with apparent reluctance.

'Good morning! Thank you for your help, Mr Etchells. I'm sure we shall meet again.'

'I truly hope so,' he said, now looking decidedly foolish.

Isabel escaped onto the street, hiding her amusement. But why not? Any influence with a bank manager could only be a good thing.

The bank-notes in her bag produced their own brand of warmth. Perhaps just a new pair of boots? Minutes later, she was seated in Mather's in Princes Buildings, revelling in the sight of the footwear on display – leather, morocco, kid, satin, and even some from Paris. But it would not do to be too extravagant.

Her feet were measured by a personable young man (how delightful!) and she ordered a pair similar to those she was wearing. A quarter of tea from Theobald's completed her shopping and she returned home, eager to remind herself of what she still had in her possession which might raise money.

She did not wish to sell the French clock which looked so splendid on the mantelpiece and she was certainly not going to dispose of the linen or silver cutlery. No, the obvious choice was the Blezard picture which she had brought with her to Bath, still wrapped in its covering. She untied the string round it and removed the hessian so she could see it properly.

It was an oil painting and looked quite old. The subject was the Virgin Mary and the baby Jesus, not a subject to appeal to her but no doubt it would to the religious. She personally thought Mary looked very miserable and the baby unnecessarily naked. The colours were however attractive and there were pretty scenes in the background with hills, towers and thin, dark green trees. Best of all, in her view, was the handsome gold frame, not solid gold obviously, but beautifully carved. She would seek Byrne's advice about how best to sell it.

When he arrived to collect her that evening, Isabel had the picture propped up on a chair for him to look at. He glanced at it, peered at the bottom of the painting, looked at the back and with a sigh, replaced it on the chair.

'What is it, Randolph? Has it some value?'

'Well,' he said. 'Its subject matter, the Madonna and Child, will always find a buyer. We live in a Christian country after all.'

'And the frame? The frame is very handsome, is it not?'

'Oh yes. Very handsome.'

'So shall we take it to an art dealer in Bath?'

Byrne appeared to be giving the matter some thought.

'I think perhaps an auction house might be a better idea and in London rather than here in Bath.'

'Why is that?'

'Because at an auction there is the chance that bidders will become excited by the presence of competitors and pay more highly for a work if they sense that others are keen to possess it. And in London you are likely to have a greater number of interested customers than in Bath.' When Isabel said nothing, he continued. 'An art dealer may pay you less for a picture because he must make a profit when, and if, he sells it while the auctioneer will take a smaller, agreed percentage.'

Isabel was persuaded by the good sense of this and agreed to have the picture ready for collection by one of Byrne's men the next day.

Soon they were comfortably and privately seated in the corner of a dining-room, cushioned by burgundy upholstery.

'So,' said Byrne, his spoon suspended over the turtle soup, 'what is this good news we are celebrating?'

'I have at last received the money owing to me from the sale of my late husband's estate. Needless to say, it is less than I deserve. The major portion went to his daughter.' Isabel was watching Byrne for his reaction but it was hard to gauge what he was thinking.

'Still, it is not negligible, especially when I add the sum raised by the picture you are so kind as to dispose of for me.'

'What is she like, this step-daughter? A sour-faced spinster of uncertain years?'

'Oh no, not at all. She is about nineteen or twenty, I think. Plain, I agree. She tells me she is to marry her mill manager later in the year.'

Byrne raised his eyebrows.

'Exactly', said Isabel. 'Socially beneath her. *His* motives are not hard to understand. She owns the mill where he works and has other business interests as well. I imagine they will be very comfortably off.' She could not prevent a note of bitterness creeping into her voice.

'And has she told you all this?'

'Oh no! I have received another, much more informative letter from a dear friend, Ellen Thorpe, who I hope will visit me before long. She is a particular friend of mine.' Byrne seemed to have lost interest and had turned his gaze towards a young woman who was taking her place at a nearby table.

'And what of your plans, Randolph? Are you content with the gaming club here in Bath or do you intend to extend your business?'

His interest was caught.

'I already have an interest, a part-share, in a club in London but yes, I do have plans for this one. It seems to me...'

He rested his elbows on the table and spoke intently, his face inches from Isabel's.

'It seems to me that the club would benefit from improvements – re-painting, refurnishing, new lighting. We do not, fortunately, attract the riff-raff. There are plenty of low gambling-dens in the city to cater for them, generally in the back-rooms of the beer-houses. No, we attract a better class of people, gentlemen, and some ladies, of course.'

'Who have more money to spend.'

'Exactly. I think we would attract even more clientele if a degree of elegance could be added to the surroundings.'

'And your staff?' Isabel was thinking of the Nolans and prepared to speak in their defence, if only to ensure they remained able to pay the rent.

'Some small changes. The Nolans do a good job as does Pickwick the door-man but I shall lay off Paddy, the bar-man. He would be out of place in the new bar I have in mind to instal, more stylish, with a greater range of drinks on sale.'

'And at higher prices.' They exchanged smiles of agreement.

'As a newcomer to our fair city, Isabel, you may not know its history. Sixty, seventy years ago, it was highly fashionable and famed for its many pleasures – balls, card-parties, assemblies, concerts – the Georgians threw themselves into enjoyment with more gusto and in greater numbers than you may see today. Bath has become a more residential, more sedate place, rather than a gay holiday destination. There were many more gaming clubs, for example.'

'But that, surely, is to your advantage?'

'Perhaps so. And I believe that those who attend regularly do so more seriously than the more capricious players of the past. There are several gentlemen, I know, only too happy to throw off the restraints, one might say the burdens, laid on their respectable shoulders.'

Isabel looked at him admiringly. She had not heard him speak at such length before. He was certainly a fascinating man.

'I am impressed by your grasp of the business opportunities, Randolph.'

For a moment, he looked embarrassed and applied himself attentively to his roast mutton.

By the time they were drinking coffee and liqueurs, Isabel felt she had grown closer to Byrne in just such a manner as she had hoped. He had revealed something of himself, although he had said little of his origins, and they had found common interests which she felt boded well for their future relationship. And he had made no attempt to move his legs when she had gently inserted one prettily-shod foot between his at a later stage of the meal.

It was a cool star-lit night as they left the hotel. Isabel tucked her arm into Byrne's as they walked along the street towards the club. She did not want to let him go. The fresh air did not clear her head; it seemed rather to strengthen the effect of the alcohol she had drunk in the course of the evening. She felt possessed by lust, every part of her body aroused and longing for close contact with his. She hoped he might suggest calling in at Old King Street on their way but he did not. Never mind, he must have rooms at the club.

Descending to the gaming-room, they entered an atmosphere thick with cigar smoke and the smells of strong drink, hair oil and cheap scent. Kitty was one of three young women encouraging the gamblers to spend their money by whatever means they could. By the look of it, they were succeeding. Voices fell as Michael called for last bets and set the roulette wheel spinning, sending the ball on its clicking way.

Isabel, sitting in a chair against the wall, witnessed the occasional burst of elation, some groans of despair but more usually a stony-faced reaction to repeated loss. She saw that some of the players seemed unable to move from the table but went on placing losing bets again and again like automatons.

Then someone moved and she was able to see that the woman sitting with her back to her was the striking blonde woman she had seen at the theatre. Again she wore black but this time her silvery hair was threaded with jet beads. A black feather boa lay across her slim shoulders.

As Isabel watched, she saw the woman rise, adjust the boa and walk over to Byrne who had come out of his office and was leaning against the bar, smoking a cigar. Their greeting was cordial and they made a handsome pair as they stood close to one another, their fair hair distinctive against their black clothing. Isabel could not hear what they were saying and was dismayed to see them disappear into Byrne's office.

Jealousy streaked through her like a hot knife. Impelled by the emotion, she found herself pushing open the office door without any recollection of crossing the room. Inside, the pair looked innocent enough. Randolph had opened his safe and was exchanging a large bank-note for several smaller ones. His surprise was evident.

'Isabel? Do come in. May I present Mrs Amelia Ford? Mrs Ford. Mrs Blezard.'

The two women nodded to each other. Close to, Isabel saw a woman of about her own age, with a creamy complexion and green eyes beneath immaculately-drawn eyebrows. She was wearing diamonds again but this time, less lavish than before. She was very slender and lacked Isabel's voluptuous curves.

'Good evening, Mrs Blezard. It is a pleasure to meet you.' The voice was high and silvery like her hair. It was also, Isabel was mortified to notice, an unmistakeably high-class voice.

'Good evening, Mrs Ford. I trust you are meeting with some luck tonight.'

The woman laughed.

'No, unfortunately not. But perhaps I should say fortunately from Mr Byrne's point of view.'

She gave a pretty laugh and twinkled at Byrne who looked visibly pleased. Isabel felt a strong desire to kick her. The woman raised her hand with its sheaf of bank-notes. 'Thank you for these, Randolph. I intend to spend only some of them. But I know I have said that before, to my cost.' She turned and swept elegantly out of the office, the jet beads on her skirt swishing against the door-jambs.

Isabel lowered her eyes, concealing her motive for being there. But Byrne seemed unaware of any tension.

'Do you wish to leave, Isabel? I can send someone with you. The streets become more dangerous as it grows late.'

'No, not yet, I think,' she said, forcing a bright smile. 'I will stay until the gaming finishes, if you have no objection.'

'Of course. Just as you wish. Though it may be near two hours.'

Isabel returned to her seat, fortified by another drink served by the said Paddy. He was efficient but one-eyed and ugly – eminently in need of replacement.

The time passed in a smoky blur. Michael continued as croupier as long as there was someone left who wanted to bet. Isabel was pleased to see Amelia Ford leave. She was accompanied by a female chaperone. Was there a husband? There was no way of telling – as yet.

The staff busied themselves clearing up. Michael and Kitty left together, followed by Paddy when he had finished drinking the dregs left in the customers' glasses before rinsing them in a stone sink in the back room. Pickwick was nowhere to be seen.

Isabel opened the office door. Byrne was sitting at his desk, shirt open, hair ruffled, counting bank-notes and coins. When he saw her, he swept the money together with the side of his hand and dropped it into a cash box. The door of a wall safe behind him hung open. He got up and pushed the cash box deep inside, clanging the door shut.

'Isabel! I did not realise you were still here.'

Isabel went towards him. She felt drugged by drink and tiredness but her desire was as strong as ever. Without speaking, she came close and pressed herself against him and drawing his head down, kissed him full on the lips. At once she felt him respond. Now their tongues explored each other's mouth. Isabel was running with moisture. She parted her legs and felt his hand reach under her skirts. Moaning now, she pulled his head down towards her breasts. Then he jerked his head up as she knew he would.

'What is this? Isabel?'

He had found what she had secreted there – a rolled bank-note between her breasts. Playfully she pulled away from him..

'It's yours, Randoph – if you can get it!'

Now she was on the far side of the desk, her hair dishevelled, her face flushed. As he came at her, she darted away to the other side, keeping it between them. But he was too fast for her and too strong. He hurled the desk aside and rushed at her. Now she flung the desk chair between them. He lunged at it but it spun round, evading his grasp.

With a shriek of laughter, she tried to escape him but he threw himself at her, pinning her against the wall safe. Throwing up her skirts, he found her body, plunged and then hooked himself inside her, thrusting her up and down so that the metal lock of the safe dug agonisingly into her spine. Groaning, screaming, they were locked in wild, convulsive passion until climax. Noise, movement, desperation – all faded.

Byrne released himself and pulled back. Isabel went limp and attempted to smooth herself and her clothing. They were both sweating and breathing heavily.

'My God, Isabel! You –'

He could not find any more words. Shakily he poured a glass of water from a carafe and handed it to her. She gulped some down and gave it back to share. The bank-note had fallen out. He picked it up and offered it to her.

'Here!'

'No. You keep it.' It was a fifty pound note. 'Towards the refurbishment.'

Shrugging, he took it and pushed it into his trouser pocket. Finding his jacket, he put it on and smoothed his hair. By this time, Isabel had almost restored her appearance to normality.

'Here.' He lifted her cloak and draped it round her shoulders. 'I must lock up. Pickwick will see you home.'

Isabel wanted to refuse the offer, wanted him to say he would escort her but was overcome by a sense of weakness. Moments later she was out in the street, picking her way over the cobbles while the silent Pickwick kept a respectful distance. By the time they reached Old King Street, her legs were almost giving way. She opened the door and just managed to mount the flight of stairs before collapsing on the bed in complete exhaustion.

CHAPTER EIGHT

'Well, I'll be beggar'd!'

Sam looked completely stunned. When he realised what he'd said, he turned to Charlotte and burst out laughing. A moment later, still laughing, he seized her round the waist and whirled her round the parlour in an impromptu polka.

Charlotte laughed too, as much with relief as anything else. She had not known how Sam would react when he discovered the full extent of her wealth. She was aware that some might have cautioned her not to reveal such important information until they were married but the knowledge of it burdened her. It felt dishonest, as if she was hiding something from him and that she could not bear.

She had to admit she had enjoyed watching his face as he read through the large number of documents she had laid out for him on the table. There were the mill accounts, which he was already familiar with: the list of rentals at Schofield's Mill, which he had heard about and then a number of assets he knew nothing of – stocks and shares in the railways, in the engineering and chemicals industries, British government annuities as well as investments in property, textile machinery and several other commodities. Finally there was a list of cash deposits in various banks, both capital and accrued interest, written out in Silas Crowther's small spiky hand.

'I never knew your father had all this,' said Sam when they sat down, out of breath.

'He didn't! This is nearly all from my mother's father, Josiah Gledhill. He was always full of energy, always wanting to be doing something, something new and profitable. My mother told me that when he heard about gas first coming to the town, he couldn't rest until he'd invested some money in the company. He had a good idea about what folk would use and want in the future. Look at how much railway stock he bought early on!'

But Sam declined. Protesting that his head was spinning from all this talk of money, he wanted nothing more than a pot of tea which was soon brought. Eventually they both calmed down from the excitable mood that had captured them both.

'So what do you want to do with all this brass?' asked Sam, looking not at her but out of the window. 'Big house, lots of servants, travels to the continent and such like?'

'Oh no! Not at all! I'm not saying I might not like a bigger house one day –' She stopped shyly for a moment. 'No, I mean to do some good with it. For those who deserve more than they get in life, especially children. So – finding ways where poor families can get a decent place to live which they can afford. Or where they can have free treatment for their children when they are poorly, perhaps even seaside holidays for them. We live so far inland that most folk never get to see the sea. When I was a child, I got taken to Scarborough regularly. Sometimes Southport or Blackpool or Morecambe as well, at least until my mother became poorly. And then my father would take me on day trips – some of the happiest days of my life!' She grew flushed and animated as she spoke and found Sam looking at her tenderly.

'I'm right glad to hear you say that, about doing good. It's just what I would like to see myself.' As one, they looked towards the door, saw that it was securely shut then ventured to come close and exchange a kiss. Soon afterwards, Sam left, having confirmed arrangements for their next meeting later that week.

When he had disappeared down the lane, Charlotte felt too excited to settle to anything. Remembering that she had not passed on the news of her betrothal to Hannah Haigh, she set off for their farm at the top of Kaye Lane. The demanding walk – up the hill to Broken Cross, the long sweep downhill and then the lengthy pull up to the farm – was just what she needed to calm her restlessness. In any case, it was always a pleasure to see Hannah.

As she opened the farm gate, she saw Ben preparing for milking, his sleeves rolled up, revealing his strong, tanned arms. He smiled broadly as she approached. 'Na then, Charlotte! It's a while sin' we saw thee.'

'I know it is, Ben. I'm sorry but I've been busy moving into my new house on Sharp Lane.'

He grinned. 'Grand! I'm glad to hear it. Moved to Almondbury, best part!'

Like most of the locals, he pronounced the name of the village 'Aim-bry.'

'Is Hannah at home?'

'She should be.'

Ben indicated she should go into the farmhouse. He would not follow her in his muddy boots. She found Hannah sitting by the window, darning socks. The kitchen was just the same as ever – rag rugs on clean-swept stone flags, a fire steadily burning in the range and a smell of recent baking in the air. Soon she found Hannah's plump arms around her and after refreshments, in this case, two cups of strong tea and a currant scone, she told her of her betrothal to Sam. Hannah was delighted as Charlotte knew she would be.

'Ben! Have you heard Charlotte's news?'

Ben had come into the kitchen in his stockinged feet and now stood near the door, his head skimming the dark wooden beams of the ceiling.

'She and Sam are betrothed! You know Sam Armitage? You went to school together, you, Sam and John Brook.'

'Well now. I wish you both every happiness,' said Ben, his voice sounding flat. Charlotte could not meet his eyes. She found herself thinking of that moment in the byre, all those years ago. His mother did not appear to have noticed anything but continued to smile happily.

'I'm right glad you've found someone, Charlotte!'

Too choked to say more, she hugged Charlotte again. When Charlotte emerged from her aproned embrace, Ben had gone.

The Huddersfield Literary and Scientific Society met in a small museum they rented in South Street. Charlotte had already visited one of the society's meetings with Sam and as they entered, they were greeted or nodded to by several of the other members. They were, on the whole, a serious-looking group but it was pleasing that there appeared to be a good mix of people from all walks of life.

The subject of tonight's talk was of particular interest. It was about the history of Castle Hill, the great grassy mound which stood nearly a thousand feet up at the tip of Almondbury, overlooking the town of Huddersfield.

'A walk up Castle Hill' was a local treat although in bad weather it felt more like a punishment. The incline was long and steep, the higher banks sliced by ditches and hollows which were a delight to children.

At the top were two flattened areas which were used for recreation and occasional meetings. A public-house stood on one; the other carried a beacon which could be lit as a warning visible for miles.

Once the summit was reached, walkers enjoyed impressive views of the surrounding countryside, the sharp ridge of the Pennines to the west and the town lying in the valley. The one constant on the hill-top was the wind which sometimes blew so strongly that it could knock the very young or very frail off their feet.

The speaker was a local historian called Dr Raven, although no-one knew what he was a doctor of. He wore sombre clothing, sported a full set of black whiskers and had a somewhat lordly air which Charlotte soon realised Sam disliked. He caused a stir immediately by inviting the audience to gather round a table on which he spread a large, beautifully drawn map of Castle Hill. Raven stood aloof for a few minutes while people bent over the map, exclaiming as they recognised familiar landmarks.

He began his talk by referring to the myths and legends associated with the hill, the tales of secret tunnels, the devil, and a dragon guarding a treasure-hoard. But he, Tobias Raven, was only interested in the truth. Sam gave an audible sniff. Questions, said Raven with a lofty air, would be welcome. Charlotte doubted it.

'It is clear,' he began, 'that ancient tribes occupied the hill hundreds of years before the birth of Christ.' Sam raised a finger. Raven deigned to give him a nod.

'Do we know how many hundreds of years? Two, three? Or are we looking at a thousand or two?'

Raven answered patiently. 'It is very difficult to give an exact date. Our theories are based on the discovery of tools and other artefacts in the ground. In general, the depth of the layer where they are found suggests the age. Here, for example, is a flint, a primitive tool, I found while digging on the hill.' He took a sharp-edged piece of quartz from a cloth bag and held it up like a magician producing a rabbit from a hat.

'May we be allowed to see it at close quarters?' asked a man at the back.

'Of course,' replied Raven and handed the object to the member at the end of the front row. When it reached Sam, he looked at it and then spoke.

'I see this is not local stone, Dr Raven.'

Raven looked annoyed. 'Yes and no, Mr –?'

'Armitage. Samuel Armitage.'

'It was found locally but you are right, Mr Armitage, in surmising that it comes from further afield.' Before Sam could say any more, the speaker hurried on. 'We know from documents that the hill was used by the de Laci family in the twelfth century. However, my special interest is the period of the Roman invasion, about the time of the birth of Christ, when the disciplined legions of Julius Caesar marched into this area and into conflict with the wild and hardy natives, the Brigantes. How easy it is to imagine the local tribes clustering for safety on the hill fort with their women, children and their animals to withstand the onslaught of the greatest military force the world had ever seen!'

Charlotte could hear Sam breathing heavily and sensed his irritation. Facts, Sam said, were what science was based on, provable facts. She knew this imagining of a scene would not be to his liking.

Raven continued fantasising. The audience were asked to imagine the brave locals withstanding a siege by the fearsomely efficient Roman army until they reached the point of starvation and were forced to eat the captive birds and dogs they had brought with them. As evidence of siege, he unrolled a piece of linen, revealing the skulls of the aforesaid creatures.

There was an appreciative murmur and several members came up for a closer look. Sam, who counted natural history as one of his many interests, was not convinced. 'I'm afraid, Dr Raven, that I doubt your hypothesis.'

There was a shocked silence. Raven looked furious. Sam explained.

'These skulls, fair enough, come from hunting dogs. But these' – he picked up two tiny bird skulls –'unless I'm much mistaken, belong to a partridge and a goshawk. In other words, they're signs of hawking, not half-starved natives eating owt they can lay their hands on.' Sam's dialect became stronger as he became more excited. 'So, these, to me, look like signs of later folk, like the de Lacis, wi' time on their 'ands, spending it 'awking and 'unting.'

Raven looked stunned. But Sam had not finished. 'And what you say about layers is right. It depends whereabouts in t'soil you found 'em. Did they come from t' Roman layer? Or from t' time o' t' de Lacis?'

The chatter began as a buzz and built to near-uproar. The chairman felt impelled to call for silence. Several members were obviously bursting to have their say.

Raven looked grim. With something like desperation, he held up a mis-shapen lump of blackened stone.

'This, I maintain, is further evidence of siege. When the Romans could not starve the Brigantes out, they set fire to their ramparts and burnt them out!'

It was a thrilling speech but it failed to impress a white-headed old man in the front row. Leaning forward, he put out a gnarled hand for the piece of evidence and turned it over a couple of times. There was total silence. Everyone waited to hear him speak. When he did, his words bore the stamp of experience.

'I mun say, Dr Raven, tha knows nowt about it. This stone's bin 'eated up far past what any Roman could do. I've seen stuff like this down t' pit, after it's set light to itsen. Sithee, this is nature's doing, not man's!'

No-one dared contradict him, least of all Raven who looked baffled and beaten. In response to the growing sounds of argument, the chairman stood up and brought the meeting to a hasty close, thanking the speaker and assuring him he had given them all 'something to think about.'

People got to their feet and carried on arguing amongst themselves. Charlotte had felt uncomfortable at the disagreements so forcefully expressed but she could see that Sam and the other men had enjoyed them.

'That was more like!' Sam exclaimed, his face animated. 'A right good evening!' They made their way out slowly amongst the crush of people. Raven was seen leaving the room hastily by the back door.

It was a frosty dark night with moon and stars masked by cloud. A gas lamp glimmered in the distance. The members of the Society seemed unwilling to move, in spite of the cold, and stood in a dense crowd outside the door.

Sam, his arm around Charlotte, eased his way through until they reached the edge of the kerb. Then he stepped forward into the road, looking for the Blezard carriage. At that moment, a horseback rider came up from behind, going at speed.

Charlotte had a glimpse of a tall-hatted, cloaked figure with a whip as the horse careered dangerously close. With a shout of warning, Sam threw up his arm and pushed Charlotte behind him. The horse reared, squealing, hooves flailing.

Whether it struck Sam or not she could not see but she saw him fall back with a sickening thud against a kerbstone. Throwing herself down beside him, she found him apparently lifeless.

'Sam! Sam!' she cried, touching his face with her fingertips. Someone came forward and pushed the other bystanders back. It was the chairman.

'What has happened?'

'Sam has cracked his head on the stone! I'm sure of it!'

Sam's eyes were shut. He did not move. Another man came forward and gently lifted his wrist. He turned and spoke kindly to Charlotte who was beside herself with anxiety.

'He has a pulse. He may just be unconscious – from the blow. Here. Wrap his cloak round him. He will go cold from shock.'

Hurriedly Charlotte did as she was told. Someone who recognised her had the foresight to fetch the carriage alongside.

'Is it all right to move him?' she asked wildly. If only she knew what to do! Another voice spoke.

'I don't see as how you can leave him there – he'd freeze to death. Best get him home and into bed. Rest cures most things.'

With the help of bystanders, Sam was lifted gently into the carriage where he lay cradled in Charlotte's arms. Even in the dim light, she could see his ghostly pallor. There was almost no blood apart from a swelling cut on the side of his head. As the carriage rolled very slowly through the town, Sam gave a slight moan. Charlotte bent over him, tears of relief falling on his face.

The carriage went even more slowly as it began to ascend Old Bank on the way to Sam's home. Charlotte had directed Henry, the driver, to take them there, judging that a mother's right came before hers. Now she regretted the decision but it was too late to alter. Sam was lifted down and carried indoors. Getting him up the narrow stairs was difficult but at last it was done. Charlotte was relieved to see that Sam's mother was calm and in control herself. She could not have borne to leave him otherwise.

'Now you get home, my dear, and get to bed. I will stay up and attend to him.'

'I will come down tomorrow early,' said Charlotte, 'to see how he is going on. Unless you think I should get a doctor now?'

'I don't see it would do much good,' said his mother. 'I think they'd say, see how he goes on with some rest. But yes, come tomorrow and we'll see how he is then.'

There was nothing else Charlotte could do but leave, after a lingering look and a kiss on Sam's pale brow.

She spent a sleepless night, going over and over what exactly had happened. She watched dawn break and counted the minutes until she could show herself at the Armitage home. It was just after six o'clock when she was shown in. One look at Mrs Armitage's gaunt face told her all she needed to know.

'He's been unconscious nearly all night, or perhaps he slept. I don't rightly know. Then, about an hour ago, he was sick. I think we had best get a doctor.'

Charlotte was off at once. There was only one doctor she trusted – Rachel Haigh's husband, a newly-qualified young Scotsman. The Haighs would know where to find him.

Rushing back to her carriage which Henry had just managed to turn round in the road, she told him to drive her up to the farm near Castle Hill as fast as he could. But the horses, old, set in their ways, could not be hurried. Charlotte sat in an agony of tension on the edge of the seat, her mind racing with dreadful images, frantic to go faster.

As the carriage rolled ever more slowly up towards Broken Cross, she felt a wild desire to get out and run the rest of the way. But common-sense held her back. The final steep stretch to the farm would have defeated her. Instead, she forced herself to endure the steady clip-clopping of the horses' hooves while her mind was silently screaming 'Faster! For God's sake, go faster!'

She was opening the door of the carriage while it was still moving and running into the farmyard. Hannah appeared at the door, followed by Ben. He needed no urging but was on horseback immediately and away to Rachel and Donald's house.

With Hannah's arm round her shoulders, Charlotte stumbled inside. Her panic had given way to violent shivering. Hannah wrapped her in a shawl, set her close to the fire and gave her a hot drink. Taking Charlotte's trembling hands, she held them between her own warm ones.

'We can only wait – and pray,' she said.

For the next hour, she sat with Charlotte, putting a blanket over her knees, her feet on a stone hot-water bottle, all the while talking of things pleasant. At last came the sound they were waiting for, Ben's return. They were at the door at once.

'I found him at home! Donald. He's on his way to Sam now.'

Out in the farmyard, the Blezard carriage horses were contentedly chomping hay in their nosebags. Charlotte looked at Ben. He understood her immediately.

'Come with me, Charlotte! If you're not afraid.'

Afraid! At that moment Charlotte would have dared to do anything if it would have helped Sam. Only when she had been lifted onto the saddle did she remember her childhood fear of the height of a big horse. But Ben got up before her and told her to hang on to him tight as they set off down the hill towards the village. All the way she kept her arms wrapped round Ben's middle, her face pressed against his back, inhaling the scent of leather mingled with the smell of horse and fresh air.

When she entered Sam's bedroom, the doctor was examining him very gently. He felt his arms and legs and brought a light close to his eyes. Finally, he moved the young man's head very slightly on the pillow and saw the evidence of a blood-flecked yellow fluid on the pillow. With a grave face, he beckoned Charlotte and Sam's parents away from the bed where Sam lay silent and un-moving.

'I'm afraid that there are signs of skull fracture and of bleeding to the brain.'

'What can we do?' cried Charlotte. 'Anything? Whatever can be done. I will pay anything.'

The doctor shook his head. 'I do not know any surgeon who would attempt such an operation. We can do nothing but wait and see how he responds. The body can heal itself and if there is no fever...' He turned and looked at the body on the bed. 'He is strong and healthy. He may recover if the injury inside the head is not too serious. I will give him a draught that will help him to sleep.'

Days and nights passed. Charlotte and Mrs Armitage sat by the bedside in turn. Charlotte was so tired she lost track of the hours, even of the days. At last, Mrs Armitage suggested she went back home for a night in her own bed. Sam had been very hot all day but had now apparently fallen into a deep sleep. Charlotte dragged herself home and up to bed and fell exhausted into it.

The birds were singing in the near-dawn when she heard knocking at the front door. She ran downstairs to open it. A young boy stood hesitantly on the step with a note. It had to be from Mrs Armitage. Automatically Charlotte went to her purse and gave the child a sixpence. Overcome with dread, she opened it while the boy ran and skipped down the drive.

Flinging on her cloak, she ran up into the village and along Northgate towards the Armitages' house. Her boots sounded loud in the empty street, matched only by her gasping breaths. When she neared the house, Mrs Armitage was already waiting for her, the strain etched on her face. In the background Mr Armitage moved back and forth as if motion could disperse his grief.

Upstairs Sam lay dead. His mother had already washed him and laid him out. He looked incredibly young, like a boy asleep in a pure white bed who would at any moment awake and be up and at play. Mrs Armitage had folded his arms across his chest as was the custom. A sob rose and fell in Charlotte's throat when she saw the purple fingernail he had bruised at the mill. It seemed an age since she had put her lips to it and kissed it.

'I must have fallen asleep in the chair,' said Mrs Armitage. 'When I woke up, he had gone. I don't think he suffered at the end.' Her face was white, anguished. She looked as if she had aged overnight.

Charlotte could think of nothing to say, nothing that would not be foolish or unnecessary. The two women stood for a while in silence and then Mrs Armitage put her hand on Charlotte's arm and said 'I'll go downstairs. Come down when you're ready.'

As Charlotte stood looking at Sam, a wave of unbearable sadness engulfed her. But she could not cry; grief seemed knotted somewhere in her chest. For a brief moment, she thought about snipping a lock of Sam's red-gold hair as a keepsake but instantly dismissed the idea. To disturb him in any way seemed like sacrilege. She bent over and kissed his forehead so lightly she scarcely touched him.

Downstairs she found Mr Armitage with his head in his hands, his wife attempting to comfort him. Mrs Armitage's eyes were bloodshot from crying but she struggled to remain calm.

'Shall we arrange the funeral, Miss Charlotte? And will you let the doctor know?'

'Thank you. Yes, I will do that. And let me know of any expenses.'

It sounded so cold but she did not mean it that way. She turned away and began to trudge home. Did the Armitages blame her at all for what had happened? If only they hadn't gone to that meeting! But it had been Sam's choice.

She tormented herself with thinking of all the things she might have done – fetched a doctor sooner, had Sam brought to her more comfortable and airy home, asked for another medical opinion, looked harder, perhaps in Leeds or Bradford, for a surgeon. But all this was futile. It did not alter the fact that Sam was dead and the happy life she had envisaged with him had gone for ever.

By the time she reached home, she felt like an old, weak woman. Somehow she managed to drag herself upstairs and take off her outdoor clothes. Only then did she realise she still had Mrs Armitage's note crushed in her hand. She looked at it again. It read '*Come at once. Sam failing.*' As the piece of paper fluttered to the floor, the tears came gushing forth. Charlotte threw herself on the bed and buried her face in the pillow. Perhaps she would sleep and escape her heartache for a few hours at least.

She awoke next morning weighed down with grief and heavy-eyed from a restless night. Getting up and getting dressed seemed to sap what little energy she had. Her cook and maid came to see her, expressed their deepest sympathy and went about their work in respectful silence. How she got through the day she did not know.

The next day she was surprised to have a visitor – George Smeeton, the chairman of the Literary and Scientific Society. Bella showed him into the parlour where he offered his condolences and then fell silent, looking unsure of himself.

'Miss Blezard. I took the liberty of questioning as many witnesses of Mr Armitage's accident as I could. I thought therefore that I should inform you of my findings.'

Charlotte said nothing. She did not want to hear this but knew she should show some appreciation of Smeeton's motives and efforts. She nodded.

'It seems clear that, although it was an accident, it was precipitated by the man on horseback who came so close that he caused Mr Armitage to fall. Several people recognised the rider as Dr Raven, our speaker that evening. They are of the opinion, an opinion I share, that there is a basis here for a criminal charge of assault. That being the case, we thought we should inform you of this. I need hardly say that all the witnesses would be prepared to testify in court.'

In court? Charlotte was stunned. She walked to the other side of the room to compose her feelings and think of what this meant. She had suspected from the start that the horseback rider had been Raven from the split-second she had glimpsed him over Sam's shoulder. The man deserved to be charged and punished. Desire for vengeance was strong – for the moment. But as time ticked by, while George Smeeton was twisting his hat in his hands, Charlotte came to feel that to have the whole incident repeated and re-lived in court was the last thing she wanted. She felt sure that Sam's parents would feel the same. What good would it do? Nothing could bring Sam back. Whatever punishment were meted out to Raven – a caution, a fine, even imprisonment – it would bear no relation to the evil that had been done and could never be undone.

'Mr Smeeton. It is very good of you to come. And I appreciate the enquiries you have made. However, I do not think we should pursue this matter and I am sure Mr Armitage's parents would agree. To have the whole incident repeated in court – no, it would be too dreadful, too painful, for Mr Armitage's parents as well as myself.' Her composure left her as she fought the impulse to weep.

George Smeeton was visibly affected. 'My dear Miss Blezard! I am very sorry to have distressed you but our members felt –'

'I am sure they did,' said Charlotte, now in control of herself again. 'Please tell them I am grateful for their concern but hope they will understand that I would prefer to let the matter rest.'

Smeeton seemed to be struggling between relief and uncertainty.

'If you are sure, Miss Blezard?'

'I am, Mr Smeeton.'

'You may be assured that news of Raven's conduct will travel fast around these parts, Miss Blezard. I think it safe to say that his reputation is destroyed, probably for ever.'

'It may be so, Mr Smeeton. And that will be justice of a kind, a real kind, I should think.'

Smeeton bowed his head in agreement and soon took his leave. When he had gone, Charlotte sat down and drank a glass of sherry, something she never did on her own. She was glad this meeting had happened and was over.

The funeral was brief, simple and well-attended. Charlotte's friends were there, close behind the family pews. But behind them were scores of people she did not know. Talking to some of them later, she discovered they were friends and colleagues who shared Sam's interests in music, chemistry, engineering, natural history, politics and geology. It emphasised just what a remarkable man she had lost.

For the next few days Charlotte could take no interest in anything. Everything seemed pointless, not worth bothering about. She had no appetite and without the attentions of her domestic staff, she would have eaten nothing. But when a meal was served, she struggled to eat it in order to avoid the pressure of their concern.

When she felt able, she went down to Blezard's mill. As she pushed on the heavy door, she remembered how she had come to see Sam in his new position as mill manager and how sensitive he had been to the occasion, feeling how the setting would bring back memories of her father. Now, as she climbed the wooden stairs to the office, she thought how this spot would always serve to remind her, all too strongly, of the two men she had loved and who had loved her in return.

Sam's desk was just as he left it. Invoices, rough paper dotted with calculations, a calendar – all laid out on his blotter. She opened a ledger. There, in his neat handwriting, were the accounts of the mill, the columns of figures immaculately regular and sharply marked in black ink. The last column was unfinished, lacking its totals, awaiting the attention of a successor.

The only thing she took away was his work jacket that hung on the back of the door. It smelt, not of him, but of oil and wool, as she expected. There was nothing in the pockets. Charlotte folded it up gently and carried it downstairs where some of the mill girls came up to her to offer their condolences.

In her bedroom she draped the jacket round a chair. When she went to bed, she lay looking at it for a long time, with a deepening sense of a future forever lost. At last the sobs broke painfully from her and she drifted into an uneasy sleep.

As time passed, she cried less, partly because she came from stock who believed that too much weeping was a sign of weakness and self-indulgence. She had also been taught that concentrating on other people was helpful in coping with bereavement and forced herself to do this. She did not have to wait long before she could put it into practice.

Three months into her mourning, the local newspaper carried notice of the forthcoming Annual General Meeting of the Female Educational Institution. It was a charity which Charlotte's parents had long supported by contributing an annual sum but they had never, as far as she knew, attended any meetings in person. She would begin, right now, to involve herself in charitable work. If it helped to lessen the pain of loss, it was an added bonus, one that did not need too much apology.

The Institution had been set up to provide education for girls who worked in dress-making or in service but mostly in the weaving trade as piecers, winders and feeders. They could study reading, writing, arithmetic, grammar, geography, history, plain sewing and vocal music. It was administered by a committee who were seated around a long table when Charlotte arrived, comprising the President, a Mr Laycock, the Secretary, the Treasurer, a vicar and his wife and a Mrs Field who represented the teaching staff.

The minutes of last year's meeting largely went over Charlotte's head but she began to listen more closely to the Treasurer's report.

'Annual subscriptions amounted to £112.18s.6d, leaving us with a deficit of £10.19s.5d.'

The word 'deficit' clanged in Charlotte's ears as it would have done in her grandfather's. A balance sheet was passed round. Charlotte raised her hand.

'May I ask how much the girls pay?'

'The fees are threepence a week but some of the girls are subsidised by their employers.' The Treasurer was a little flustered; he was not used to questions.

'And there are 146 pupils?'

'Correct. Although it does vary a little, of course.'

'So the income they bring in is less than £2 per week?'

'Correct.'

'May I ask how much you pay your teachers? How many are there?'

The Treasurer began to shuffle his papers in search of information but was saved by Mrs Field, a grey-haired woman who spoke with dignity.

'Perhaps I could reply? There are fourteen teachers, eight of whom give their services free.'

'That is very good to hear,' said Charlotte. 'Would those eight ladies prefer to be paid if it were possible?'

'I do not think so. If payment were offered, I think they would donate it to the Institution for the benefit of the girls, by buying books, materials and so on. The music teacher would like to take her pupils to a concert or two. She is very dedicated.'

'I am delighted to hear it. Mr Laycock, may I speak plainly?'

'Please do, Miss Blezard.'

'I should like to put this very worthwhile institution on to a firm financial footing by means of a lump sum to clear debts and also make a guaranteed annual subscription. I would willingly pay the girls' fees as well if you thought that appropriate. Or you may think that if they were to pay, say, a penny a week, it would please them and also make them feel they were still responsible for their own self-improvement.'

She stood up and as she did so, the others did the same, pleasure mixed with relief on their faces. Charlotte went on.

'I will leave it to the Treasurer to let me have details on paper which we can agree upon. I believe you have my address.'

The Treasurer nodded. The President spoke warmly.

'Miss Blezard! We are most grateful for your interest. We shall be informing all our subscribers of your generosity.'

'Thank you, Mr Laycock. May I add one thing? I should like my contribution to be known as 'The Samuel Armitage Bequest.'

The President smiled.

'It shall be done.'

Charlotte's step was less heavy than it had been for some time. It seemed to confirm the hope she had always had, that cheering other people up would make you feel more cheerful yourself. It was the right thing to do, for more than one reason.

It was too nice to stay inside on this beautiful spring day. The sky was blue and the breeze milder than it had been for months. She started walking without quite knowing where she was bound. Her mind was still full of the meeting she had just attended and how it was, perhaps, just a beginning but a very promising one.

She made her way along the valley bottom and then struck up along a footpath which brought her out on Wheatroyd Lane. All around her, trees were coming into leaf; even the air felt fresher and cleaner. Turning, she found herself at Broken Cross. In front of her was the field path which led to Penny Spring Wood where she and Sam had first declared their love. Would it be foolish to revisit the scene? Would the tears she was doing so well to control come flooding back? It was a chance she had to face. She could not keep away from the spot for ever.

She came to the border of the wood. Tiny, pink-tipped white buds were showing on the hawthorn hedge while above her, the sycamores were unfurling their young foliage. What took her by surprise and delight were the bluebells, pushing their green spears up through the leaf-mould.

When she neared the spot where she had let herself fall into Sam's arms, she hesitated. This was far enough. Not cowardice, she told herself, just caution. Later she would climb down the ravine to where the stream was now in spate and think of Sam when she could do so without crying. For now, it was enough to feel her heart lift at the signs of new life and the renewal of purpose.

CHAPTER NINE

The bruise on Isabel's spine soon disappeared. Unfortunately, so did Randolph Byrne. She had learnt, however, to reconcile herself to this happening. Randolph was an occasional feast, not a regular event. She told herself this did not worry her. Life had convinced her of the horror of sameness – the inevitable consequence of domesticity. The trouble was that, in between the exciting encounters she enjoyed with him, there were long stretches of boredom for which she was ill-equipped.

For Isabel, a major problem was money, or rather the lack of it. She received an income from her bank deposits which was adequate for her needs but insufficient for her wants. With the passing of each month, the shops in Milsom Street displayed ever more enticing goods which were a pleasure to see but a torment to ignore.

Isabel was not good at self-denial. Her brief marriage to George Blezard had spoiled her. His open heart, and purse, allowed her to buy whatever she fancied – and she had fancied a great deal. True, he had begun to criticise her lavish spending but she found it easy to pay little attention to him. She was sure businessmen always pretended they were worse off than they really were. Everyone knew that. In any case, she deserved her rewards.

The hopes she had pinned on the sale of the Blezard painting were completely dashed. She had awaited Randoph's return from the auction sale with great excitement. When he arrived, however, his expression did not bode well. It was raining heavily and he was thoroughly drenched on his walk from the railway station to Old King Street. When Isabel had removed his wet cloak and put a glass of port in his hand, he appeared slightly more cheerful. But his words were not.

'I'm afraid, Isabel, that the news is not very encouraging. There was no great interest in the painting.'

'Oh dear! How much?'

'A hundred pounds. So – not a negligible sum but perhaps not as much as you were hoping.'

Isabel pursed her lips.

'No matter. The money is more use to me than the painting. Here.' She withdrew a ten pound note from the wad he had given her and handed it to him. 'I am grateful for your trouble.'

He nodded his thanks and drained his glass, holding it towards Isabel for a re-fill. He stayed that night but then disappeared again, this time to Northern France. It was several weeks before she saw him again.

To make matters worse, the weather had been particularly depressing. Cool, overcast spring days had been followed by a brief period of warmth and sun but now the rain had returned, with most days grey and showery.

This was just such a day. To make it worse, it was wet, cold and altogether dismal. The muddy, swollen river Avon was running high between its banks and the gutters were flooded and choked with debris. It was not a day to be out walking. Isabel took rain as a personal insult. How could one enjoy a stroll window-shopping in such conditions? Added to this was the knowledge that she had spent as much of her capital as she ought to.

Isabel did not read, play the piano, sketch or sew. This left few diversions for the long empty hours. She had looked through her fashion magazines till she was bored with all of them. Sighing heavily, she looked out of the window but could see no-one passing. Michael was out but she could hear Kitty moving about downstairs. It was worth spending threepence if it would help to pass the time.

Leaning over the banisters, she called out, 'Kitty!'

Kitty poked her head round the kitchen door.

'Kitty! Would you go out and buy a newspaper? Then we could have some tea.'

'Shall I buy some biscuits?'

'Yes, do.' Isabel shut the door. Tea and biscuits! Still, they would help to relieve the boredom.

Later the two women sat in the kitchen drinking tea. Isabel had been able to categorise Kitty as a 'lady's companion' in her mind rather than a servant. One did not drink tea with a servant in the kitchen even if it was the only warm place in the house. Kitty was engrossed in reading the newspaper long after Isabel had glanced through it. Isabel watched her idly, surprised that she should find so much of interest in it. After five minutes, she felt she had endured the silence long enough.

'Kitty! What are you reading? Is there anything entertaining or amusing happening in Bath?'

'There's opera at the Theatre Royal.'

Isabel pulled a face.

'Or a pianoforte recital at the Assembly Rooms.'

'Oh no! You know I find listening to music very tedious. I do not understand how people can sit for hours. And opera is so silly and drags on so long.'

Kitty continued turning the pages. 'Aha!' she said. 'Here is something to interest you. Next week. A fancy dress ball at the Assembly Rooms. Tickets half-a-guinea each.'

Isabel sat bolt upright. 'A fancy dress ball! Exactly what I should like! Mr Byrne should be back by then too.'

'I think I heard Mrs Ford talking about it at the club last night. She was certainly discussing fancy dress with another lady.'

This strengthened Isabel's resolve. 'Then I shall certainly go!'

'There may be a snag,' said Kitty.

'What? How?' Isabel did not tolerate being thwarted.

'It says "*No tickets are issued except through the Committee nor can they be obtained unless the Applicants are known by, or introduced to the Committee.*" '

'Why should it say that? Isn't anyone's money good enough?'

'Apparently not,' said Kitty drily. 'It's a way of keeping the company select – exclusive.'

Isabel's colour rose. 'Who's on this committee then?'

'I don't know any of them,' Kitty said, after reading through the names. 'There's a colonel, a general and four captains. They're all men. A Mr England, a Mr Etchells – '

'Etchells. Did you say Etchells?'

'Yes. Why? Do you know him?'

Isabel's eyes sparkled. 'If it's the same man. He's my bank manager. An odd-looking man. Bald head and bushy grey whiskers.'

Kitty was pondering. 'I think I've seen him. At the club.'

'What? Gambling?'

'Yes. And laying heavy bets, I seem to recall. Michael would know.'

'Where does one go for tickets?'

'The Assembly Rooms. Between 2.00 and 4.00 pm. It says the tickets are selling fast.'

Isabel was up two flights of stairs, dressed in outdoor clothes and out of the house in fifteen minutes. It did not take her long to reach the bank. Shaking her umbrella, she stepped into the entrance. Yes, Mr Etchells could see her now.

The look on the man's face suggested he had not forgotten her and there was a hint of embarrassment in his manner as he showed her to a chair.

'Mrs Blezard! To what do I owe the honour ?'

'Mr Etchells. I hope you will forgive me approaching you on a personal matter.' She paused. The man gave a nervous smile.

'Of course, Mrs Blezard.'

'You know that I have not been in Bath very long – a mere matter of months, and so I have not had time, exactly, to establish myself in society.'

Etchells made no response.

'It really is very frivolous of me, Mr Etchells, I confess, but I have a mind to attend the fancy dress ball next week. You will understand. Having been widowed... I wondered therefore if you could give me a brief note of introduction to the committee which I might produce this afternoon when I call in to buy my tickets.'

Etchells still said nothing. Isabel played her trump card.

'I believe we have already met socially, Mr Etchells. At the gaming club owned by Mr Randolph Byrne.'

Etchells went pale. He seemed to have difficulty in swallowing.

'Not that there is anything untoward about your involvement, Mr Etchells. You, of all people, will understand the value of money.'

Etchells gulped and swaying slightly, moved to his desk and sat down heavily in the chair. Drawing a piece of Bank writing-paper towards him, he dipped his pen in the inkpot and scrawled a sentence across the middle of the sheet. He then signed it and pushed it towards Isabel.

'Thank you so much, Mr Etchells. That is most gracious of you.'

Isabel swept out without a backward glance.

Kitty was impressed when Isabel returned with the paper. 'What does it say? I can hardly read it.'

'Oh, no matter what it says. It's his writing, on his paper, with his signature – that's all that matters.'

This proved to be the case at the Assembly Rooms. With two tickets bought, Isabel made her way to Northumberland Place where she had been assured she would find a hirer of fancy dress costumes. She allowed Kitty to accompany her as advisor.

The first thing to strike them was the smell of camphor and stale perfume in the small back room. Costumes of all colours, periods and fabrics hung round the wall; shoes stood in boxes in a higgledy-piggledy pile while fans, feather boas and long, trailing scarves spilled out of an overflowing chest. Miss Bouvier, the owner, with dyed hair and heavy rouge on her withered cheeks, bore down on them with obvious delight when she realised that the customer wanted a costume for the ball.

'My dear madam! Have you any idea of the costume you desire?'

'Not exactly. Could you show me a selection?'

The woman ran a practised eye over Isabel's figure and began pulling out dresses from the racks. Each time she gave the gown a melodramatic flourish and let it drape over one arm in what she took to be a flattering pose.

'This is a very popular choice, Madam. A Highland lady of quality. As in the Waverley novels? Sir Walter Scott? Diana Vernon? A heroine?'

None of these references drew any response from Isabel. It was a handsome costume, a white silk gown draped in a blue and green plaid stole which was secured by a large brooch.

'And for the gentleman, a matching costume!' Miss Bouvier whipped out another costume from behind her back, distinguished by a kilt and a large fluffy white sporran. 'It comes with knee-length socks – and a dirk!'

Isabel looked doubtful. 'No. I do not think the gentleman will be wearing fancy dress. What do you think, Kitty?'

Kitty shook her head. Miss Bouvier was undeterred.

'Of course, the ideal choice for the gentleman is regimental dress uniform. Failing that, evening dress. Did you like the Highland costume, Madam?'

Isabel was not sure. In quick succession, the woman displayed ladies' dresses of the sixteenth, seventeenth and eighteenth centuries followed by French, Italian, Spanish, Swiss, Turkish and Chinese. 'Or Madam might prefer the allegorical. A Greek goddess perhaps? Or Dawn? Or Spring?'

Isabel finally settled, with Kitty's approval, on a Spanish lady's dress, red silk with frills and flounces, which came with a black lace fan and mantilla. The boots were extra but Isabel had to have them – red leather, high-heeled and tied with black satin ribbon.

It was a happy woman who returned home in the drizzle, with Kitty carrying the parcels. She was even happier when Randolph arrived early in the evening as Kitty and Michael were leaving. When she told him of the ball, omitting the detail of her visit to Mr Etchells, he was quite willing to accompany her, especially as she had already bought him a ticket.

'And you say Amelia Ford is going?'

'I believe so.'

As the day of the ball arrived, Isabel found she had not left it a moment too late. She obtained almost the very last appointment at the hairdressers.

'So, a very busy time for you,' she said to the coiffeuse at Finigan's.

'Yes indeed, madam. I hear they have sold over eight hundred tickets so there will be many, many ladies wishing to have their hair dressed this afternoon.'

Isabel had brought the mantilla with her so that the hairdresser could fashion her dark ringlets accordingly and advise on the fastening of the head-dress later in the day. The hairdresser thought Isabel's fancy dress very pleasing and an excellent choice for someone of Madam's dark, romantic colouring. Isabel talked more than usual and found she was quite tired when she got home. She spent a couple of hours resting on the couch with her feet up and her hair carefully spread over the cushions. She wanted to be well rested for the evening's dancing.

Kitty helped her to dress before she left for the club. She declared herself well pleased with the effect achieved. 'It fits remarkably well, I think, for a hired costume. And the colour is perfect for you,' she said, tilting the pier-glass so that Isabel could see the full effect. It was true. She looked every inch a beautiful Spanish lady and fluttered the black lace fan beguilingly to prove the point.

As the Assembly Rooms were only a few minutes walk away and the night fine and dry, Isabel consented to walk the short distance on Byrne's arm. The wisdom of this became clear as they neared the venue. Every inch of the surrounding streets was clogged with carriages setting down their finely-dressed passengers. Some of the drivers, no doubt on their owners' orders, had stationed the empty carriages along the kerbsides to await their passengers' return some hours later. This had the unfortunate effect of blocking the road so that no-one else could take their carriage close to the Assembly Rooms' entrance. The air was thick with jeers and shouts, protestations from old ladies and arguments between young men in uniform who were trying to bring some sort of order to the mêlée.

As Isabel sailed into the Assembly Rooms and past its elegant pillars, she felt that this was exactly what she had been waiting for. This was an entry into Bath society, however it had been achieved. She held her head high as Byrne steered her gently towards the club room where they were to meet Amelia Ford and her partner. They were by no means the first there; a group of about thirty young people were gathered, the ladies wearing garlands and trimmings of a particular flower which the gentlemen sported in their buttonholes.

'They are to perform a floral quadrille,' explained Amelia, pointing out the pink roses, narcissi, poppies, azaleas and so on which were featured. Isabel had to admit, although she hated doing so, that Amelia Ford looked extremely fine. She was dressed, she told Isabel, as Marie Antoinette in a sumptuous pink and silver gown of the period decorated with lace and pearls. She wore a full white wig, all puffs and curls, which suited her very well. Her slim figure was shown to advantage in the tight bodice which pushed up her small breasts and made them visible. Isabel tried not to notice that Byrne was noticing them too.

Amelia's companion was a Captain William Stoodley of the 16th Queen's Lancers regiment, resplendent in a scarlet jacket. A pleasant enough man though, in her opinion, let down by a weak chin. She looked with satisfaction at her own partner. There was no doubt that, even against the background of so many men in colourful and impressive uniforms with their gold frogging and epaulettes, Randolph Byrne, tall, broad-shouldered, his pale gold hair shining in the light of the chandeliers, cut a handsome figure in his black evening suit. Isabel gloated when she saw the eyes of other women linger as they caught sight of him.

Although she had not at first welcomed the idea of making up a party with Amelia Ford and her partner, she could not deny that the woman's familiarity with Bath society was an advantage. As they passed through the Octagon and thence to the ballroom, Amelia gave a light and sometimes amusing commentary on the other guests. She pointed out the Mayor of Bath, the Member of Parliament, Mr Gore Langton, the titled ladies and the four baronets in their court dress.

Isabel was pleased to see that there seemed to be a superfluity of officers, always a good sign at a ball, who stood two or even three deep along the wall. Here Captain Stoodley came into his own, identifying the uniforms of the 72nd Highlanders, the 8th Hussars, the Royal Wiltshire Militia, the Royal Navy, the West Somerset Yeomanry Cavalry and so on. 'There you will see Lieutenant-General Gordon Higgins, with his Diamond Order and the Sabre of Honour presented to him by the Sultan,' he announced in a tone of authority. Isabel had completely lost track of who was who but nodded as if she was impressed by this information as Stoodley clearly intended her to be.

She was less pleased to observe how easily Amelia Ford conversed with Randolph and how frequently she made him laugh. She heard her speak of a young lady dressed as a snowdrop as 'looking more like a milk pudding' and he laughed again when she indicated 'the oddness of Hamlet talking to a sea nymph'. As the joke was lost on Isabel, she found it all the more annoying.

Still, dancing the Lancers Quadrille with Randolph made up for all these small irritations – its slow and solemn movement, the graceful bowing and curtseying – surrounded by other dancers dressed as corsairs, mandarins, cavaliers and in many sumptuous costumes from past ages, all in the glittering elegance of the grand ballroom. Isabel thought with delight how Ellen Thorpe would respond when she heard about the experiences of the evening.

The room grew hot. Jackets were discreetly unbuttoned and ladies relinquished the more tiresome accessories of their fancy dress, leaving shawls, hats and capes on the backs of chairs. After supper came more dancing and finally a retreat to the card room for tea and coffee.

'A most successful ball, I do believe,' said Amelia, fanning herself with a silver lace fan. Beads of perspiration glistened on her brow; the warmth of the room gave her pale complexion a translucent glow. Isabel glanced at Byrne and was piqued to see that his eyes were fixed on Amelia's glowing face.

It was now past one o'clock and Isabel was beginning to feel it was time to go, particularly as the hired boots were pinching her feet. The most distinguished guests had already left, others were preparing to go and only the young were still dancing. Whoops and cries could be heard from the ballroom where the orchestra was now playing an eightsome reel.

Isabel, Byrne, Amelia and Stoodley emerged into the cool night air. Even at this hour there were still some lights showing in the tall Georgian houses which surrounded the Assembly Rooms. The streets were almost clear of private carriages; a few for hire stood waiting in Alfred Street. Good nights were exchanged and then Amelia and her escort turned away in the direction of the Royal Crescent. Isabel slipped her arm through Randolph's and they began to walk downhill.

At that moment, Isabel felt a surge of happiness. Whether it was brought on by the absence of Amelia Ford, heightened by the lateness of the hour and the quantity of wine she had consumed, she did not know nor care. She drew Randolph towards her and pressed her breast against his arm, making him turn towards her with a smile discernible in the moonlight. It was not difficult to convince herself that this man belonged to her, now, and perhaps, for ever.

The mood did not last long. Suddenly, above the rooftops in front of them, they saw the unmistakeable signs of fire. Swirling smoke and flame rose high into the night sky and as they drew nearer, came the sound of people shouting and a distant crackling.

'Where's it coming from?' shouted Isabel but Byrne had already broken into a run. She followed him as fast as she could, heart thumping as she realised that they were running in the direction of St James's Street, home of the gaming club. Pushing their way through onlookers, they came to the burning building, the club itself.

Two firemen were directing a hose onto the flames from their apparatus with little effect. Byrne ran up to a policeman standing beside them.

'Where is the fire engine?' he cried. Isabel could not hear the policeman's reply over the roaring. She clutched Byrne's arm.

'What did he say?'

Byrne turned to her, furious, frustrated.

'He said someone has gone for the keys which are kept somewhere else!'

As they watched, the flames crept ever higher. The whole building was now alight, the basement full of black smoke with long ribbons of yellow flame running along the tops of the windows. Isabel was rooted to the ground. Her tiredness and the shock of the fire rendered her incapable of speaking or thinking. All she could do was to stand there, transfixed by the roaring, licking red monster before her. The policeman had pushed the onlookers back, allowing only Byrne and herself to remain in the proximity of the burning building. Even so, they were forced to move back as the wind shifted and drove hot air and smuts into their faces.

The fire engine arrived at last and now more hoses were uncoiled, the water hissing as the jets hit the flames. But it was clear that it was too late. Isabel recalled, though she had not witnessed it, the blaze at George Blezard's mill in which he had perished. The insurance had been enough to repair the damage. Byrne, surely, would have had fire insurance? It could be sufficient to rebuild the club, perhaps in better style?

He was at her side, looking weary, his face and shirt-front smudged with soot, and said something which had not occurred to Isabel. 'I hope everyone got out in time.' He did not have long to worry; Kitty and Michael could be seen on the other side of the road and came hurrying over when they saw Byrne.

'What happened? When did it start?' Byrne's voice was curt, his concern for his staff lessened by the sight of them.

Kitty spoke up, her arm linked through her brother's. 'We'd just come away and were walking home. After midnight. Pickwick locked up. We'd almost got home when someone came running past, saying they could see flames in the basement. So we rushed back. It was well alight. Nobody could go in.'

Behind them came the sound of burning rafters and floorboards crashing through the building, sending showers of sparks into the night sky. By now, the fire had attracted a large crowd, obviously enjoying the spectacle, cheering when a large piece of the roof broke off and tumbled into the street. Byrne shook his head in disgust. Isabel laid her hand on his arm but he did not respond.

'Randolph! I'm going home. Do you want to come back with me?'

'No, no. I'll stay here. And then – I don't know, I'll find somewhere.' He turned his back on her.

'I'll come with you.' It was Kitty. Together they walked back to Old King Street, the acrid smell of the fire heavy in the still night air. When they reached the front door, Isabel was overcome with such a feeling of weakness that Kitty had to find her key and let them in. Her legs seemed to have lost all their strength. Leaning heavily on Kitty's arm, she managed somehow to mount the stairs and then remain standing long enough for Kitty to remove the Spanish lady's costume. As she fell into bed, Isabel wondered, before sleep overcame her, what the consequences of the fire would be. Kitty and Michael would need to find other work and Randolph... What would he do now?

When she woke next day and found it was afternoon, Kitty and Michael were out and she had to make her own tea. After the effort, she went back to bed and reviewed the events of the night before.

The fire she did not dwell on; it was unpleasant and not her worry. No doubt she would find out soon enough. No, it was the ball that she revisited in memory. How splendid it had been ! She would never forget the look of the great ballroom with its chandeliers, thronged with dancers in colourful costumes and uniforms and in the other rooms, people chatting, drinking, eating, laughing. It had been a most satisfying evening and worth every penny. If she had her way, it was the first of many excursions into Bath society. How she would enjoy describing it to Ellen Thorpe!

There was the question of Amelia Ford. She was useful, of course, as the evening had proved, and someone who lived in the Royal Crescent, even in a rented apartment, would always be worth knowing. But she could not ignore the fact that Amelia was an attractive woman whom Randolph seemed to admire. Still, she had not caught her actively flirting with him. In Isabel's opinion, such pale colouring did not suggest a passionate nature; there was an impression of bloodlessness about her that was very unappealing.

Kitty and Michael returned later that evening, bearing food.

'We've seen Mr Byrne. He's staying in a lodging house in St James's Square – someone he knows.'

'How does he seem?'

Kitty was blunt. 'Not happy.'

The dingy hallway of the lodging-house in St. James's Square smelt of stale food and soot. From above came the sounds of thumping, an infant wailing and raised voices as Isabel began to mount the stone stairs. Most of the doors on each landing were shut; through the open ones she caught a glimpse of floorboards, meagre rugs and occasionally a dirty child who looked at her before backing out of sight.

When she reached the top floor, a man in working-clothes emerged from the back room. In answer to her enquiry, he nodded his head towards the room he had just left and went down the stairs without a word, his heavy boots clomping on every tread to the ground floor.

Isabel pushed open the door and found Byrne sitting on a bare mattress with his back against a striped ticking pillow which was dark and greasy with use.

His appearance shocked her. His hair was tousled and two days' growth of ginger-blond stubble blurred his jawline. He was wearing a vest and the black trousers from his evening suit; the rest of his clothes lay crumpled on the floor on top of his boots. He looked at her without interest and drew deeply on a cigar.

'Randolph?'

'Isabel. How nice to see you. Come in.' The words were welcoming but the tone was not.

Isabel edged in, looking for somewhere to sit. There was a single, unmade bed, a rough table with a few dishes on it and a wooden chair on which she perched, drawing her skirts up, away from the grimy floorboards.

'You will excuse my not getting up and offering you some refreshment, Isabel. As you see, I am merely a guest here.' His smile was as ironic as his speech. 'Fortunately, Tom, a friend from the old days, has offered me his hospitality.'

Isabel wondered what 'the old days' referred to. She realised she knew nothing of Randolph's past.

'You are very welcome to stay with me, you know. I could easily get a bed for you.'

'Thank you. But I think it best if I stay with Tom for the time being. I am not sure how long I shall be staying in Bath.'

His words alarmed Isabel. The thought of Bath without him filled her with horror. He must stay!

'Where – what do you intend to do? Will there not be some insurance money to come? Not to rebuild the premises perhaps but to help you set up elsewhere?'

He gave an unpleasant laugh. 'You have a touching faith in my business affairs, Isabel. Would it were well-founded!' He drew on his cigar, making it glow down to the tip and then got up suddenly, exhaling smoke and threw the stub out of the window.

Isabel experienced a sinking feeling. 'You were not insured?'

'To put it plainly, no.'

Isabel's mind was in turmoil. What would he do? She knew of his business interests in London. Perhaps he would go there? The prospect dismayed her. She knew, deep down, that he did not care enough about her to want her to go with him. She did not dare suggest it for fear of hearing the rejection in his voice. There was only one way she could hope to keep him close.

'How much money would you need to set up again, in Bath?'

He turned round briefly and then went back to staring out of the window.

'I don't know. Furniture and furnishing may be got cheap. Not so the gaming tables. I should probably have to go to France for the roulette equipment. Three, four hundred perhaps.'

It was more than she could afford. If only the picture had raised more!

'I wish I had the money to lend you, Randolph. As it is...' She opened her hands by way of explanation.

'Never mind, my dear. I did not expect it.'

She had a uncomfortable feeling that he did. 'So, what do you plan to do?'

'To begin with, a visit to the barber's. Then perhaps a stroll into town. There will not be much point in visiting what remains of the club but perhaps I had better do so. I also intend to call on someone who may be able to help me with funds, possibly going into partnership.' For the first time, he managed a smile.

'Oh, I do hope so! I should be sorry to lose you to London!'

'Yes indeed. Bath suits me very well. Let us hope I receive some good news this afternoon.'

'And will you come to supper tonight? And tell me how things stand?'

'Very well. You will forgive me if I am still wearing the same shirt I wore to the ball.'

'Of course! You lost all your belongings in the fire as well!'

He shrugged. 'These things happen. I have met misfortune before.'

Isabel opened her purse and gave him twenty pounds.

'Buy yourself what you need. And let me know if you need more. I look forward to seeing you later. About eight?'

Isabel planned the supper. Oysters to start with. This was a good day to buy them according to Kitty who knew about such things. Then a beefsteak pie, again from one of Kitty's suppliers, washed down with a bottle of French wine. Kitty continued to oblige; she was going to shop, serve and disappear afterwards. Meanwhile, Isabel went to have her hair dressed and bought some scented soap. Returning home in a more cheerful frame of mind, she found a letter from Ellen awaiting her. After the usual descriptions of the family's health, or rather, in Ellen's case, ill-health, came the following news.

We are pleased to tell you that Charlotte is bearing up well after her bereavement. She is now coming out of mourning and we are hoping she will now resume her social engagements.

These last months have not, however, been unproductive for her. You may have heard that she made a generous bequest to an evening school for mill-girls. Very generous, apparently, and in memory of Sam. According to Grace, who heard it from Maud Crowther, in confidence, Charlotte has inherited considerable wealth, much more than any of us dreamt, from her grandfather, Josiah Gledhill. (I expect, being family, you already know of this.)

No doubt we shall be hearing more of Charlotte's good works. Frederick thinks she could do more with her thousands than give them away but my view is that she has a right to do as she likes with her own money, especially if it helps her in her grief.

Now as to the change in skirts...

Thunderstruck, Isabel could hardly breathe. Thousands!

Her face flushed with rage, she threw the letter to the floor, picked up an ornament she had never liked and hurled it against the wall where it smashed into pieces. She, Isabel Blezard, who had married into that family, who had put up with the clumsy embraces of George Blezard and his stupid domestic ways for nearly two years, *she* had come away with only a few hundred pounds as if she was some mistress, or servant, to be paid off! If anyone deserved some of it, she did!

She stormed downstairs, poured herself a large glass of brandy and drank it down. Unfortunately it only made her hotter.

Later, when she had calmed down a little, she recollected that it was not actually Blezard money but Gledhill money from the father of the first Mrs Blezard, Charlotte's mother.

Her mind was racing. How much might she be able to extract from Charlotte? No good pleading charitable work – that would not convince the girl. Perhaps a touching letter, mentioning illness, necessary medical expenses and so on. Yes, she would try that. However it would be unlikely to warrant more than a hundred or two. No, people like Charlotte would rather spend it on a lot of worthless strangers than give it to family!

Isabel remained locked in this torment for almost an hour. Only the imminent arrival of Byrne made her regain control.

When he arrived, he looked much better, washed, shaven and wearing some new clothes. He seemed pleased with himself.

'So, how was your meeting?' asked Isabel, handing him a drink.

'Good, good! I think it will not be too long before I am back in business. I shall go up to London directly to see about roulette tables. Fortunately my business partner tells me she already has some experience in this field.'

Isabel stared at his smiling face. 'She? Who is this?'

'Why, Amelia Ford, of course! I should have realised she was familiar with the gambling world – she was so at home with it. She says she is delighted at the prospect of our working together.'

A hot wave of jealousy washed over Isabel. This she had not foreseen.

'You are surprised, Isabel?'

'Yes indeed, Randolph. I'm surprised you should have been taken in so easily by her.'

'Taken in? What are you talking about?'

'Well, I have heard the rumours. I'm surprised you haven't.'

Byrne glared at her. The sense of danger, of risk, excited her. There was no stopping her invention.

'Whatever do you mean?' Byrne's voice was rough with anger.

'Why, that she makes a habit of this. Lures men on, makes them think she is going to put money into their concern, gets them excited and then pulls out. Usually leaving them to pay the expenses. She's known for it!'

Byrne looked as if he did not know whether to believe her or not.

'How can you say this? You, who have been in Bath less than a year!'

'I heard it from Charles Lester, the man who dropped dead in your club. He recognised her in the street one day and told me all about her!' There was no possibility of Byrne checking that particular lie.

Byrne bit his lip, walked away and swung round to face her.

'Supposing it were true, what then? What other chance do I have of raising the kind of money I need?'

'Well, there may be another way. And this time, my knowledge could benefit you greatly.' Byrne waited. 'I have just learnt that Charlotte, my stupid step-daughter, has come into considerable wealth, thousands upon thousands apparently, from her grandfather. Her intended husband died earlier in the year and she is relieving her disappointment by making large bequests to charity. I shouldn't think it is beyond your power to go up to Yorkshire and persuade her to contribute to the cause of Randolph Byrne!'

Isabel's voice became more and more shrill. She was conscious of losing control and talking nonsense. Anything, anything to get him away from Amelia Ford!

Byrne was silent for a minute. When he spoke again, his mood had changed.

'Have you ever mentioned my name to her, to this Charlotte?'

'No. Why should I?'

'What are her favourite charities? What does she care about?'

Isabel sneered. 'Children, I suppose. The poor. The usual things.'

Byrne was tense with excitement. 'And she has business friends? This Ellen? Her husband is a business man?'

'Yes. Frederick Thorpe. Well-known in the town. Houses, contracts, investments, that kind of thing.'

A smile of triumph appeared on Byrne's face, though it did not make him more attractive. He stepped forward, lifted her hand to his lips and kissed it.

'Thank you, Isabel. You have been very useful. What is it they say? Charity begins at home.'

Isabel did not know how to respond. She stood, motionless, mute. But deep down she felt a sudden sense of dread, a fearful premonition that she had started something which was now beyond her control. And which left her powerless.

CHAPTER TEN

In the months following Sam's death, Charlotte learnt to value both novelty and familiarity in helping her to cope with her loss.

Novelty came to her in the shape of reading reports connected with education, housing and health, matters she had always heard of but never known about in much detail. Her studies helped to pass the time in the day and in the longer hours of the evening, now, thankfully, remaining lighter with the arrival of summer.

The familiarity of life – the sights and routines – carried her through in a more subtle way but one which was equally important. Walking along the Woodsome valley and up to Castle Hill lifted her spirits and brought her a feeling of calm which she could sense but not quite understand. Although the places where she and Sam had conducted their courtship could bring tears to her throat, she did not avoid them but tried to weave them into memory so as to strengthen it without pain.

An established part of life which continued to console her was one in which Sam had played no part. Sunday morning service in the parish church, which she had attended for most of her twenty years, varied hardly at all. The vicar, curate, choir and congregation followed the words of the Bible and the Book of Common Prayer and sang well-loved hymns from the hymnbook. The unchanging nature of the service was reassuring. Charlotte loved the fact that people had been worshipping in this venerable church for hundreds of years, had met the seasons and faced the hardships of life with the same words of Christian consolation.

On this fine morning, when the sun was warming the ground and the woods were full of birdsong, she stood singing *O God Our Help in Ages Past*, surrounded by the parishioners. Many of them she knew by name. All were familiar. But today, unusually, there was a new face – a well-dressed, handsome man standing in the pew across the aisle and singing lustily in what she could hear was a fine baritone voice. Without meaning to, she caught his eye whereupon he nodded pleasantly and then returned his gaze to the hymnbook.

When the service ended, people stood up and began to move out. Charlotte was sitting at the end of the pew and as she stepped into the aisle, the stranger did the same. A smile, a polite 'After you, madam,' and a pause before he followed her to the church door. He was so close behind her that she could not help hearing his words to the vicar as he shook hands and thanked him.

'A most interesting sermon, sir, and such a fine church! I look forward to attending again next week.'

The congregation moved slowly out of the church, groups of people stopping to chat and holding up the progress of those behind them. Thus it was that she found the newcomer at her elbow.

Close to, she noted the hazel eyes in a clear-skinned face, no beard but a full moustache of the same blond colour as his hair. He was very much taller than she was. Another jostle from behind and he came even closer.

'I beg your pardon, madam. We seem to be in the way.'

'Yes. Perhaps we are.' Charlotte smiled as they disengaged themselves from the throng. When they reached the end of the church path, he turned to her again. 'I wonder, madam, if you could direct me to the Woodsome valley? I am visiting Almondbury for the first time.'

'Of course. I am going in that direction myself. If you would care to accompany me?'

'That would be most kind. If you are sure –. '

'Yes indeed.'

The man put his hat on and together they crossed the road and began walking up the hill. When they reached Sharp Lane, Charlotte spoke again. 'I live down here and then the valley is just beyond that.' They turned left and began descending the steep lane. 'Your first visit to Almondbury? Are you perhaps visiting friends?'

'No, I am sorry to say I have, as yet, no friends in the area. To tell the truth, I am exploring the village because I believe my grandmother grew up here. As I had business in the north, I thought I would spend a short time in Huddersfield and seek out her place of birth.'

'A worthwhile task!' exclaimed Charlotte. 'If you know your grandmother's name, you may find someone who knew her. There are some long-lived folk round here.'

'Ah, I'm afraid that is the problem. Try as I might, I cannot remember her maiden name, if I ever knew it. Her married name was Rebecca

Brown but that may not be helpful. She was still unmarried when she left Almondbury.'

'Oh, I see the difficulty! Still, I am sure you will enjoy your walk on this fine morning. Just continue down this lane. You can go left or right along the valley. Good-day Mr – '

'Brown. Ralph Brown.' He bowed slightly and smiled.

'Blezard. Miss Charlotte Blezard. It has been most pleasant making your acquaintance. Good-day.'

He smiled again, this time more widely, showing good teeth, touched the brim of his hat and walked on.

Charlotte spent most of the day reading and answering letters, glad of any activity that kept her busy. Once or twice she thought of Ralph Brown and wondered what he had made of his walk. Strangers were rare in the village, especially handsome ones wearing expensive clothing. She would not be the only member of the congregation to have noticed him.

Ellen Thorpe came to tea. She embraced Charlotte with a rustle of lilac silk and a waft of perfume.

'My dear Charlotte! How are you? We have thought of you so often!'

'I am very well, thank you, Ellen. And how are you? And the children?'

Ellen needed little prompting to talk about her headaches and her children. Charlotte had not taken to Ellen at first when the family were renting Dartmouth Hall in the village. Ellen came from London, a fact she usually mentioned at least once at every meeting and her air of a superior being amongst provincials had not endeared her to Charlotte. But the more time she spent in her company, the more she saw that behind the fluttery manner and the preoccupation with fashion was a kind-hearted, if rather weak, woman.

By contrast, Charlotte liked the husband, Frederick, a little less. He had an excellent manner, spoke well and could take command of any situation with charm and confidence. But Charlotte felt he cared for very little except his own social and financial success. There were occasional hints too of his fondness for ladies other than his wife. She refused to believe any of them without proof but it was true that rumours did tend to colour one's impression, however baseless in fact.

'Now, my dear, Frederick and I wondered if you were able to dine with us on Saturday? We should so much like to have you with us. It seems such a long time since we were together.'

'Thank you. Yes, I should like that very much,' said Charlotte who knew without looking that she had no other engagement.

Since Sam's death, she had observed almost six months of mourning and taken no part in social occasions. But the time had come to move on. She knew her parents would have approved; Sam would have expressed incredulity that she had sustained her mourning for so long.

'Mostly the usual company, I'm afraid. Although there will be someone you have met before but hardly know.' She looked at Charlotte who obliged by looking interested. 'We have invited a gentleman by the name of Ralph Brown whom I believe you met briefly at church last Sunday.'

Charlotte confirmed that this was so. Ellen was happy to relate the circumstances which led to the invitation.

'You know that Frederick spends every Monday evening at the George Hotel. He meets his business friends, ostensibly for dinner but really, I fancy, for an evening of drinking and gossip. It's a tradition they have kept up for years and when I complain, as I do if he wakes me up coming home very late, he points out that many a good business deal arises from those gatherings. I dare say it's true. I think your father and his cloth merchant friends did much the same thing at the White Hart? However, as I was saying, they were drinking in the bar when a gentleman who was staying at the George, also a businessman, struck up a conversation with him and proved so interesting that Frederick invited him to dine with them instead of dining alone as he intended doing. It turned out that he had worshipped at Almondbury church and made your acquaintance.'

'Yes, that is so,' said Charlotte. 'We met only briefly, of course, but he seemed a pleasant gentleman.'

'I expect he told you of his interest in Almondbury. It seems he travels a good deal in his business affairs.'

'I did not learn very much about him, I'm afraid,' said Charlotte.

'When Frederick told me about him, adding that he was a fine-looking gentleman who knew London well, I thought we should, in the general way of hospitality, ask him to dinner. It works well in making up the eight which I always think the ideal number for a dinner party. A small enough number to have a single topic of conversation at the table and large enough to enable smaller conversations to flourish.' Ellen stopped abruptly and bit her lip.

Charlotte understood why, had in fact been aware of Ellen's lack of tact as soon as the matter of numbers arose.

She smiled and spoke quickly to cover Ellen's obvious embarrassment. 'I agree, Ellen, eight is a good number. So – the Broomfields, Grace, James Hallas?'

'Yes indeed.' Relieved, Ellen rushed on. 'One doesn't like to gossip, of course, but I am a little worried about Grace. I think she may have developed a fondness for James, a fondness I can only think unwise.'

Charlotte raised her eyebrows. 'I have not seen them lately so I cannot say. But I suppose it is not an impossible pairing.'

She thought back to the Christmas Eve party at the Broomfields when James had danced with Grace, to her obvious delight. And James had seemed affected by some tender emotion on the day he had called on her and brought her the daffodils.

Ellen shook her head. 'I fear Grace will be disappointed. We all know a second wife would be good for James but I do not think he cares for Grace in that way. I think that, after this dinner party, I shall try not to invite them at the same time. It will be kinder in the long run.'

When Ellen's carriage had pulled away, Charlotte picked up her journal and filled in the dinner engagement. It was not so very long ago that she and Sam had been to dinner with the Thorpes. She remembered the evening vividly because she had approached it with some trepidation, unnecessarily as it turned out. She must try to push the memory to the back of her mind when she returned to the Thorpe home on Saturday. Perhaps the presence of a newcomer would make it easier.

When Charlotte arrived, the rest of the guests were already in the drawing-room. At one side, deep in conversation, stood Ralph Brown and Seth Broomfield. Charlotte thought how different the men looked even though they were of similar height. Seth's dark countenance was set in its usual glare and his body ill at ease in his clothes. Brown, on the other hand, appeared to be completely composed and cut an elegant figure in his evening suit. He looked up and smiled when he saw her.

James Hallas stood with a lady at each elbow – Jemima Broomfield demure in deep crimson silk, her shiny ringlets bobbing on her shoulders, and Grace Littlewood in grey bombazine, her sharp features softened by her smile.

Charlotte saw at once that Ellen was right. It was distressing to see Grace's eager attempts to capture and hold James's attention. Charlotte watched him respond to her politely and then try to include Jemima in the conversation as well.

When the time came to move to the dining-room, Grace stuck closely to James's side and ensured that she sat next to him at the table. Jemima sank gracefully onto the chair on his other side.

Ralph Brown slipped quietly into the seat next to Charlotte, sitting directly opposite Jemima.

'So,' he said, unfolding his napkin, 'we meet again.'

Charlotte smiled. 'Did you enjoy your walk along the Woodsome valley?'

'I did although I believe I have hardly done justice to it so far. I walked down to – Birks, is it? And then along the Woodsome Road and back to where I left you. I believe I must walk to the top of Castle Hill before I can say I have seen the best view in Huddersfield.'

This provoked a positive reaction around the table and as the soup was being served and glasses filled, the rival claims of local beauty spots and vantage points were put forward. Brown listened and promised to visit as many of them as he could.

Charlotte was amazed at his poise. He seemed perfectly relaxed, despite being a stranger, and responded graciously and appropriately to every suggestion.

'Do you know how long you will be in the area, Mr Brown?' asked Ellen.

'Not exactly but I am at liberty for about a month. Then I intend to travel to Newcastle to look at the ship-building there.'

'Is that your line of business?' asked James.

'Yes, in part, but I also have interests in railways and construction companies. Not here but abroad – South America, Egypt.'

The foreign place-names created a stir of interest. Brown maintained an air of modesty while Frederick satisfied the group's curiosity.

'Mr Brown tells me he has just come back from Egypt where, as we know, construction of an important canal is in progress. Mr Brown, please tell us more. We may live in Yorkshire but we like to keep our eyes on world affairs, you know.'

There was a murmur of agreement, partly lost in the sound of clean plates being set down by the servants. When all was settled, Frederick urged Brown to tell them more, which he did with a pleasing reticence.

'I expect you have heard that this canal, over a hundred miles long, between Port Said and Suez will make communication between Europe and Asia very much easier. Ships will be able to ply the canal without having to sail round Africa or else unloading and carrying goods from the Mediterranean port overland to Suez as they have done in the past.'

Charlotte, who had studied the globe with her father when she was a child, spoke with genuine interest.

'It will be a remarkable achievement when it is finished. It should have an immediate impact on trade, I should think.'

'I hope tha's got shares in it then,' said Seth.

'Unfortunately not,' Brown replied. 'The main shareholders are French, with only a minority share held by the Egyptians.' He appeared to sense that the topic was exhausted because he turned to his hostess and said 'My dear Mrs Thorpe. The last time I tasted such good beef I was in one of the finest restaurants in London!'

Charlotte saw that he could not have said anything more calculated to please Ellen Thorpe.

'How good of you to say so! You know London well perhaps? I myself am from Chelsea.'

'Ah, a most delightful part of the capital! I am more conversant with the City, the business centre.'

'And are you fond of the theatre and the concert halls too, Mr Brown? I sometimes pine for more choice than we have here in Huddersfield.'

'I am very fond of music, Mrs Thorpe, and hope to attend a concert while I am here. Huddersfield is known for its Choral Society as well as for its fine worsted.'

Charlotte was about to say how she had enjoyed the Society's performance of *Judas Maccabeus* but then remembered that she had been with Sam and decided to remain silent.

Some high-pitched laughter from Grace cut across the murmur of conversation.

'Frederick has been telling me about a tramp arrested for begging door to door in Almondbury. He appeared lame until P.C. Ramsden came on the scene whereupon he ran off! It seems he had enormous pockets stitched inside his coat, full of stuff he had stolen! He was sent to prison for a month which I think serves him right!'

'Are most miscreants sent to prison?' asked James.

'Not necessarily,' said Frederick, who seemed pleased to be the centre of attention at last. 'A case I dealt with last week for example. Three men caught playing pitch and toss for pennies on Castle Hill on a Sunday. They were fined 3s.4d each plus costs. No need for prison there.'

'I wonder that men gamble,' said Jemima. She had not spoken before to the whole company. Charlotte thought she looked distracted in some way.

'The unwise do,' said Frederick, 'of all classes.'

'The more fool them,' grunted Seth. No-one else appeared to have any opinion on the subject which was then dropped.

After dinner, the ladies rose and retired to the drawing-room leaving the men to their port and tobacco. As they left, they could hear Seth arguing that if they got the power, the working class would overthrow the constitution, with Frederick and James disputing the point.

'Thank goodness we can leave them alone with their noisy politics,' said Ellen.

When the gentlemen came to rejoin the ladies, Brown came and sat down next to Charlotte immediately.

'Our host has been telling me about your generous donation to the Female Educational Institution. May I say how much I applaud your action? It is just what one likes to hear.'

No further private conversation was possible as they were drawn into the group by their host and hostess. Jemima agreed to play and sing which she did very prettily. All eyes were on her, apart from those of Grace who gazed at James instead.

At last it was time to leave. Seth and Jemima disappeared into the night, followed by James who seemed keen to move away from Grace as quickly as he could.

Charlotte, who was taking Grace home, offered Ralph Brown a ride into town as far as his hotel but he declined, saying a walk would do him good. Charlotte bade him good night, privately approving his decision.

Grace was untypically quiet as the carriage rolled on across town. Charlotte was sorry for her. Although Grace was not a very likeable woman, if she had unfortunately fallen in love with James Hallas, as seemed likely, then she would be suffering emotional pain. And that was something she, Charlotte, would not wish on anyone.

The following day, Sunday, dawned fine and sunny. Charlotte, walking up Sharp Lane on her way to church, thought it quite possible that she would see Ralph Brown again. Sure enough, he entered the church very soon after her and asked very politely if he might sit alongside her in the pew.

During the service they did not speak to one another. At one point, he could not find the psalm until Charlotte gave him her book open at the correct page and received his in return.

The service over, they left the reverent gloom of the church interior and emerged into the bright light and fresh air. The effect was cheering. A group of worshippers was proposing to walk up to Castle Hill. Those who knew Charlotte encouraged her to join them. Finding Ralph Brown at her shoulder, it seemed natural to include him in the invitation. They set off up through the village and then struck out across the fields which led up to the summit.

'I have read somewhere,' said Brown, 'that when one goes to an unfamiliar place, one should go to the highest point so that one can see it as a living map.'

'I have read that too,' said Charlotte. 'I think it was Harriet Martineau who said it. And we are on our way to the ideal spot!'

In a while, all but a few hardy folk were forced to stop talking to catch their breath for the steep ascent. Stopping near the top for a rest, Brown leant towards her. 'May I repeat what I said last night? Your generosity towards those girls' education. I do believe that if one can improve the lot of one's fellow man, then one should do it. Both you and he, or she, are the better for it.'

'Exactly. Then we are of one mind. Are you intending to do something similar?'

'I am indeed, although I have not quite decided on the direction. When I was in London, I visited the improved housing for workers in Whitechapel which George Peabody, the American millionaire, has financed. I was very impressed.'

'Oh, I should like to see them too! It is a fine thing to have done. The condition of the courts in the centre of town, where so many of the poor are crowded together, is shameful. I would not wish you to see them.'

'My dear Charlotte, they will be no worse than in other cities. But I too share your concern. There I am, at the George, surrounded by gleaming mahogany and polished brass whereas I know that the working people live in very different circumstances.'

'So is improved housing your primary concern?'

'I am not sure,' said Brown, looking serious. 'The truth is my heart is more drawn to other areas of need.' He paused, which kept Charlotte waiting with increased interest to hear what he had to say. 'I have made a deal of money, Miss Blezard, a very great deal of money some would say. At the beginning of my business life, I knew exactly what I wanted to spend my money on.' His voice dropped lower. 'I was newly married, very happy, only wanting a family to make my happiness complete. And then my wife, my dear wife, died in childbirth. Suddenly I realised that money mattered very little if it did not bring happiness.'

Charlotte was moved, so moved by his words that she put her gloved hand on his arm.

'I had no idea, Mr Brown. I am very sorry.'

'Thank you, Miss Blezard. Why should you? It is a terribly common occurrence. But you too, I believe, have suffered bereavement. Mrs Thorpe told me, in confidence.'

'Yes. My betrothed, Mr Samuel Armitage, died very suddenly.' She thought too of the loss of her parents. 'I did in fact name the bequest I made after him. In his memory.'

'That is an excellent idea! I think, perhaps, I should like to do something for children. So many of them, poor, sick, know nothing of what life can offer.'

'Oh, I do agree!' cried Charlotte, clapping her hands together. 'It is just what I was thinking of myself!'

'So, perhaps, a Blezard Trust? Like the Peabody Trust?'

'Yes, very possibly. Although I had not thought as far as that.'

'Come,' said Brown, standing up. 'Let us get to the summit of this great hill so that you can educate me as I deserve.'

Laughing, Charlotte allowed herself to be helped up. As they continued their climb, Brown offered her his arm and it seemed both natural and polite to take it.

At the summit, they stood with the town at their feet with its mills, factory chimneys and church steeples while away to the west, the line of the Pennine hills and behind them, the leafy Woodsome valley. Brown declared himself 'impressed' 'stunned' and 'staggered' while Charlotte laughed at his language as she was meant to do.

The walkers now began to disperse and make their way down the hill, choosing the path most convenient to them. Charlotte and Ralph Brown were among those picking their way towards Lumb Lane.

As the descent became steeper, Brown held out his hand to steady her down the slope. As he did so, he looked meaningfully into her eyes for the first time and held her gaze. She found it very disturbing. He spoke softly.

'Do you know what else this view is called, when one looks down from a height, so that one sees the full picture? No? It is called "the angel's view."'

The next moment he had turned away and appeared to be concentrating on the descent to the exclusion of everything else.

Ellen Thorpe, fired by the recent success of her dinner party, was quick to plan another social event. Later that week Charlotte received a note from her. Could she persuade Charlotte to accompany her and Jemima on a picnic at Blake Lea, Marsden? She and Jemima thought that their guest, Ralph Brown, should have the opportunity to see another of the local beauty spots. They would be a small party of six, Frederick being unable to join them because of a board meeting. Ellen would provide all that was needed. Charlotte accepted with pleasure and noted the absence of the unfortunate Grace Littlewood.

The day of the picnic proved fine and warm and it was a cheerful party who gathered at the appointed place and chose a suitable flat piece of ground by the stream with a picturesque old bridge in the background.

Charlotte soon saw that the group was not completely happy. Seth Broomfield seemed unable to relax and consulted his fob watch every few minutes. However, once Ellen's two servants had spread out the travel rugs and unpacked the picnic hampers, even Seth began to enjoy himself.

Half an hour later, the atmosphere had changed, under the influence of ham sandwiches, chicken legs and cordial. Perhaps it was the absence of dining chairs and a table, thought Charlotte. It was difficult to be anything but informal when sitting on a rug with one's skirts piled into a heap at one's side and eating with one's fingers.

Ralph Brown sat beside her, constantly attentive. He took a polite and apparently genuine interest in everyone's conversation, whether it was the quality of French wines, the building of the local Standedge Tunnel under the Pennines or anything relating to London, a topic which always seemed to arise in Ellen's company.

James Hallas lolled on the other side of her, quiet for the most part, chewing on a blade of grass. Across from him sat Jemima who looked flushed and happy. She too said very little.

As usual, Seth looked clumsy and ill-at-ease, perhaps explained by the tweed jacket he was wearing which looked much too warm for the day. Ellen tried to cheer him up by fanning him which he tried to take with a good grace. From time to time he mopped his brow with a handkerchief, consulting his watch yet again. Ellen was trying to persuade him to do something.

'When you go to this dinner at the George – when is it? Friday? Why don't you do as Frederick does – book a room there for the night? Then you can stay up late and drink as much as you like. And avoid waking Jemima up when you get home in the early hours, dropping your boots on the floor!'

Everyone, except Seth, laughed.

'It sounds an excellent idea!' said Ralph. 'I recommend it!'

Seth looked doubtful but then gave in. 'Well, mebbe I'll tek your advice this time. To my mind, there's nowt like your own bed.' He got to his feet. 'I'm sorry but I mun be off, Ellen. Business.'

There was a moment's silence. Charlotte noticed that Jemima said nothing but kept her eyes fixed on the rug in front of her as if trying to commit the pattern to memory. She barely raised her eyes when Seth spoke to her.

'I'm tekking t'carriage, Jemima. Do you come home with Ellen.'

Ellen spoke up gaily. 'Don't worry, Seth. I'll see Jemima gets home safely.'

Seth had to be satisfied with that and stumped off towards the road where his carriage stood waiting.

The five people left continued chatting companionably. Charlotte was delighted to find that Ralph Brown loved music as much as she did and that he proposed attending a concert at the Assembly Rooms which Mr Wood was presenting that week. Would she care to accompany him? She would be delighted to do so.

When they got to their feet and prepared to leave, there was some hesitancy as to who would travel in which carriage. Charlotte had been brought by the Broomfields while Ralph had come with Ellen and the two servants.

'If James will drop me in town, I should be most obliged,' said Ralph. 'Miss Charlotte is most welcome to take my place in Mrs Thorpe's carriage.'

'What do you say, Jemima?' asked Ellen. 'Are you happy to squeeze in beside Charlotte? I'm sure we shall all manage.'

Jemima looked uncertain. James spoke casually.

'I'd be happy to take Mrs Broomfield. I can go on to Dalton after going through town for Ralph.'

'Is that all right, Jemima?' asked Ellen. 'There would certainly be more room that way.'

Jemima agreed. They picked up their belongings and moved off. Charlotte had enjoyed the picnic but there was a feeling of tension somewhere. She could not put her finger on it.

After the concert, Charlotte was gratified to find that she and Brown held similar views about the stronger and weaker points of the performance. And she could not help noticing the admiring glances cast on her companion by other women. They allowed their eyes to rest on him for much longer than was usual. She felt rather proud to be by his side and simultaneously ashamed of herself for such a thought.

'It would perhaps be wise to take my arm, Miss Blezard,' Brown said as they came out onto the pavement. Charlotte needed no persuasion. It was after ten o'clock and in walking to the carriage, they passed several dark alleyways. There was no sign of a constable.

As they walked beneath a street lamp, they heard a groan which came from a man lying huddled against a wall. They approached the heap of clothes cautiously. He proved to be no tramp but a well-dressed individual with good boots showing. Brown stepped towards the figure and gave a startled exclamation.

'Good God! It's Broomfield, I think, Seth Broomfield!'

Charlotte moved closer.

'Yes, it is. What can he be doing here? Aagh!'

A strong smell of alcohol reached her.

'Is he in the habit of doing this?'

'I shouldn't think so – though I have seen him before the worse for drink.'

'Perhaps,' said Brown, kneeling beside him, 'he has been the victim of an attack, a robbery. But I cannot tell without going through his pockets which I think I had better not attempt. We must get him home!'

The Blezard carriage was quickly drawn up alongside and with the help of the coachman, Broomfield was bundled inside where he lay slumped along the seat, breathing heavily.

'Isn't this the night he was supposed to be staying at the George?' asked Charlotte. 'I wonder why he changed his mind?'

'Why indeed?' said Brown.

Charlotte did not understand his ironic tone but did not want to admit it.

The presence of their comatose passenger had a dulling effect on the mood inside the carriage. Charlotte was annoyed. She would have liked to be discussing the music they had just listened to instead of trying not to hear and look at the drunken Broomfield. She hoped he would not be sick.

After what seemed like hours, the carriage turned into the gateway of the Broomfield mansion and along the sweeping drive. There were no lights showing except for the entrance hall.

When they came to a halt, Brown turned to her and spoke quietly with some urgency.

'Miss Charlotte, trust me. Do what I suggest. I will stay with Broomfield for the moment. I would like you to ring the bell and when you are let in, go up to Mrs Broomfield's bedroom. Do you know where it is?'

'Yes, yes, I do,' said Charlotte, bewildered. 'What then?'

'Knock loudly, open the door if you must and tell her her husband is returned. Will you do that?'

Charlotte agreed although she did not fully understand the situation.

The manservant who opened the door a crack looked shocked but when he recognised her, his face relaxed and he let her in.

Holding up her skirts, she ran across the tiled floor and up the ornate staircase. Her feet made no sound as she hurried along the carpeted corridor. Reaching Jemima's bedroom, she knocked on the door.

There was no response and no sound from within.

She knocked again.

A minute, perhaps, elapsed. Remembering Brown's words, she grasped the door-knob and pushed the door open, sending a beam of light into the room.

Immediately there was startled movement on the bed and Jemima Broomfield sat up, her hair cascading over naked shoulders, clutching the covers to her chest. A moment later the man with her reared up, his white body stark in the dim light. It was James Hallas.

Charlotte had no time to be surprised.

'Jemima! Seth is returned!' she declared and pulled the door to.

She was down the stairs and back in the carriage as fast as she could make it.

'Did you warn her?' asked Brown.

'Yes.'

'Then we had best get him inside.'

The task was completed with the help of the manservant who was sent to the kitchen for coffee. By now Broomfield was opening bleary eyes and sitting propped up against a sofa in the hallway.

Brown spoke sharply to him.

'Broomfield! Broomfield! They're fetching you some coffee. Then get yourself to bed. Do you hear me? Good night. Come, Charlotte.'

He took her arm and led her back to the carriage.

Charlotte was in a state of shock. She didn't know which discovery was the most surprising – that she had found Jemima in bed with a man, that the man was James Hallas or that Brown had foreseen the entire situation. She felt very stupid.

'How did you know, how did you suspect that this was happening?'

They were now facing one another in the carriage as it swayed and jolted over some uneven ground. Brown's expression was humble.

'I didn't exactly but it suddenly fell into place. I noticed that Mrs Broomfield and Hallas looked very interested when Broomfield said he planned to stay the night at the hotel. And did you not see how close they sat at the dinner party with their arms often touching?'

'No, I did not. To tell the truth, I was watching Grace Littlewood instead. I'm sorry. I want to laugh but I shouldn't, it isn't comical.'

Now Brown laughed, a deep-throated chuckle. 'Laugh if you want to, my dear Charlotte. At the folly of human nature – which never changes.'

But Charlotte could not. She had just realised how dreadful the outcome might have been if Broomfield had surprised the lovers. Brown's shrewdness had prevented what could have been very ugly and possibly fatal. She looked at Brown who was leaning back against the upholstery with half-closed eyes. 'What do you think Jemima will do now?'

He sat forward. 'I don't know. Finish the whole thing or carry on more discreetly. It depends how serious their feelings are for one another. No wife should leave a rich husband without considering the consequences, social and financial.'

Now it was Charlotte's turn to lean back and close her eyes. She felt horribly young and innocent compared to Brown's worldly-wisdom. How fortunate it was that he was with her! She opened her eyes a little and saw that he had his eyes closed. He really was extraordinarily handsome. His hands, lying relaxed on his thighs, were very fine.

Then she shook herself. This would not do! She had no intention of falling in love with Ralph Brown. She would not be capable of that emotion for a long time. But she was forced to admit that his attractiveness was palpable. Thinking of Sam, she realised that she had felt protective towards him, almost maternal. Brown, however, made *her* feel protected, massively so. The sense of security it gave her was tempting. She could easily understand other women seeking it for themselves.

Next morning Charlotte became aware that the Broomfield incident had affected the relationship between herself and Brown. She felt a greater closeness, a sense that they were conspirators.

On Sunday it felt quite natural that they should sit together in church and speak to Canon Hulbert together at the end of the service. They walked slowly side by side along the church path.

'What is happening tomorrow, Charlotte? Do I detect excited anticipation in the air?'

'You do, indeed!' laughed Charlotte. 'Tomorrow is Whit Monday, our church feast day for the children. All the teachers and scholars of our day and Sunday schools will meet for communion and then there's a jolly procession in the vicarage garden with Lady Dartmouth's brass band playing. After that, they all process to other big houses in the village where they're given sweetcake and a special gift of an orange each. Back to the Hulberts' garden for tea and more buns and then down St Helen's to the Grammar School where the headmaster is lending them a field for games.'

'It sounds splendid,' said Brown. 'I am quite envious, especially of the orange. What part do you play in this?'

'Well, I make a contribution. Nothing else is expected of me but I shall walk along to the field later to see them all enjoying themselves.'

'Do you think, Charlotte, I might call on you then and accompany you to the games field? It sounds a happy occasion. I should not like to miss it.'

'Of course. It will be a pleasure.'

When Brown had walked Charlotte back to her house, he left her, having been invited to Sunday lunch by the Thorpes who wished him to meet other friends of theirs. They both agreed no mention should be made of what had happened on Friday night. Brown appeared reluctant to leave her. He took her hand and held it in his for longer than was customary.

'Till tomorrow then, Charlotte.'

'Till tomorrow, Ralph.'

Charlotte went indoors, more cheerful than she had felt since Sam's death. Not long after, a messenger brought a note from Jemima Broomfield.

Dear Charlotte,

I wish to thank you for what you and Mr Brown did on Friday. I dread to think of the consequences if you had not intervened.

I should like you to know that James has decided to leave the district. It is hard for me to accept this but I know it is the right thing.

I trust you will not speak of this to anyone. Thank you again.

Jemima Broomfield

Having read the note, Charlotte set light to it and dropped it in the fireplace. As she watched it curl and shrink to a blackened wisp, she hoped Jemima would be able to put the affair behind her. But she knew it would not be easy.

Whit Monday dawned sunny and mild, the sky bright blue and cloudless.

Charlotte spent the morning visiting some old people in the parish, taking gifts of food and clothing and listening to their recollections of Whit celebrations past. Their memories were sharp and vivid even now. It was confirmation, if any were needed, she thought, of the joy of communal festivity, especially for children from poor families. These people had grown up at a time when children still laboured in the mills and factories and in the local coal-pits. A church feast day stood out like a beacon in their lives.

When Ralph Brown arrived, he was in a jovial mood.

'What is this, Ralph? The holiday spirit?'

'I suppose it is! I have just narrowly escaped being crushed to the ground by hundreds of happy children intent on swarming down a footpath off the village main street. I was hard put to it to keep my footing!'

'Ah! That would be the children from the Wesleyan Sunday School. They would have been visiting local benefactors and then back to chapel for tea and buns. When you saw them, they were on their way to a field next to Eldon House to play games.'

'I had no idea Almondbury could muster so many children and so many buns! A rival entertainment, eh? I have to tell you I saw evidence of rival oranges!'

Chuckling, Charlotte led Brown along Arkenley towards the school playing-fields. Dropping down to their right was the Woodsome valley in all its June beauty, with its lush green fields and flower-filled hedgerows and rising beyond, the Farnley woods, thick with foliage.

They heard the sound of the children before they saw them, an unmistakeable cacophony of high-pitched voices. In the field the adults stood watching and chatting while the children ran in all directions. The boys in their long trousers were kicking balls or playing games which involved jumping on one another's backs, their jackets unfastened, their caps lost earlier in the games. Some of the girls, in long cotton frocks and with flowing hair tied back, were standing about demurely while others careered about like the boys, shrieking and scattering hair-ribbons as they ran.

Two black-suited clergymen stood talking, both distinguished-looking in their own way. Charlotte pointed them out.

'The one on the left is Canon Hulbert whom you have already met. He took over the living last year and promises well for the parish and the village. The other gentleman is the Reverend Alfred Easther, headmaster of the Grammar School for the past twenty years. A good man, much loved by his pupils. We are very fortunate in them both.'

As they strolled about, Charlotte was greeted by many of the adults and thanked for her contribution to the festivities. Brown, listening, said, 'Do I hear you did not just make a contribution but paid for everybody's tea?'

'Well, Whit Monday is a special day. One must mark it as best one can.'

'I think the church very lucky to have such a generous patron.'

By now they were sitting in Charlotte's garden, the sun beginning to descend in the sky, sending a golden light across the valley. Charlotte had not answered; she did not know what to say.

Brown continued. 'Shall I tell you of my idea? For local children?'

'Oh yes, do.'

'I see, in my mind, a children's hospital – one where mothers can take their sick children and obtain treatment for them, free of charge. I know the Infirmary has its dispensary which does good work but there is no special place for these poor children to receive the proper care and be nursed back to health.'

Charlotte stared at him. He spoke with feeling, as if he found the vision of sick children unbearably moving. He went on. 'Today we have seen happy children, healthy children, running and playing as children should. All children should have that right.'

Charlotte could hardly speak. Her eyes were full of tears.

'On a practical level, Charlotte, I was struck by another thought yesterday when I was visiting the Thorpes. They are planning a short trip to Scarborough next month, just a few days, the sea air always being beneficial for Ellen's headaches apparently. They asked me if I should like to accompany them there on my way north to Newcastle and I agreed. I remembered then that the town was a favourite of yours and wondered, if you do not think it too forward of me, whether you would care to come too. I know the Thorpes would be delighted.'

'I should like it very much, Ralph. Very much indeed. Especially at this time of year.'

'Perhaps we could think of giving children the benefit of that bracing sea air, restoring them to full health. What do you think?'

'Certainly! In addition to a hospital here, one could have a convalescent home in Scarborough for children, and their mothers too, where they could recuperate. What a splendid thought, Ralph! A big country house, in extensive grounds, not far from the sea! It would be ideal!'

Brown looked tenderly into Charlotte's eyes. 'That is a wonderful idea, Charlotte! I salute you!'

Within minutes, they were sitting at Charlotte's desk while Brown drew up some figures. He explained that the Trust, the Blezard Brown Trust, would have to cover not just the capital outlay of the hospital and convalescent home but the running costs which would include the salaries of doctors and nurses. He looked grave. 'We are talking about thousands here, Charlotte, not hundreds.'

'Of course,' said Charlotte who had already estimated a likely sum in her head while he was writing the figures down and adding them up. 'I should expect nothing less. But I can afford it. I shall afford it.'

Brown took her hand and held it between both of his. The sensation was pleasant and she had to admit, thrilling. 'Charlotte, you will be blessed for this.'

Charlotte felt her cheeks go hot. 'You too, Ralph, you too.'

CHAPTER ELEVEN

Time and again over the next few weeks Isabel wondered what Byrne was doing and saying. She was confident of his ability to charm and persuade. There was no denying the strength of his motive.

It would serve Charlotte Blezard right if she fell for his patter. The stupid girl did not deserve the wealth that had simply dropped into her lap. If she, Isabel, had inherited that money, she would have known exactly how to spend it. If she were rich, she would have no difficulty keeping Randolph close to her. Like her, he relished quality – fine leather shoes, well-cut clothes, good wine and fine dining. The only time she had ever seen him untidy had been in the rented room on St James's Square and that had not been typical.

How many thousands would he manage to extract from the gullible Charlotte? Enough, she hoped, to set up a new club and provide them both with a comfortable income. Her intention was to move to a more impressive apartment with a good address. She felt sure she could tempt him to live with her in the Royal Crescent or the Circus. He would surely want more than the two rooms he had occupied above the club which, strangely, she had never seen. His secretive nature both angered and fascinated her.

But now there was nothing to do but wait, something for which Isabel was temperamentally unsuited. She had, however, taken to reading *The Bath Weekly Chronicle* with more attention since the Fancy Dress Ball. The edition which came out a week after the occasion carried an account of the ball with a list of guests. It remained in the house, a well-thumbed copy. There, in black and white, was her name, "Mrs I. Blezard" with the words "Spanish Lady" after it. She amused herself by re-reading the list and ticking off those she had observed. Those she had spoken to numbered only three.

When she was bored, which happened all too frequently, she ran her eyes over the other articles – on the successful introduction of the tread wheel into the local prison and the formation of an Anti-Immorality Association. Bath had its share of kill-joys. One day Isabel had been handed a leaflet in the street by a stern-faced woman in unfashionable clothes. It was produced by a Temperance movement and attacked all those who supported the three hundred places in Bath which sold intoxicating drink. Isabel put it straight on the fire.

The newspaper feature which always interested her most was the news from Paris and London about fashion. This month, she read, the rage for jet beading was beginning to pass away, replaced by the use of flowers and lace as decoration. She was glad to hear it. Fringing around the fichu neckline was said to be very much in favour with young ladies. Isabel looked at herself in the glass and pulled her stomach in. She was sure that, at a mere thirty years of age, she still came within that category. Kitty assured her that she did. She was inclined to believe Kitty – at least, when she said what Isabel wanted to hear.

Nothing more had been heard about the burning down of the gambling club although Isabel suspected that Kitty and Michael knew more than they were saying. Paddy had not been seen since Byrne sacked him. The twins had apparently found jobs as barman and barmaid in the same public house in Walcot. Isabel knew that these establishments ranged from the semi-respectable to the disorderly. The latter sort were a meeting-place for thieves and such-like and often brothels in all but name. Frankly Isabel did not care what Kitty and Michael were up to as long as they continued to pay the rent.

One night she heard them come in by the front door. Instead of the sound of their climbing the stairs, there was silence. Curious, she went out onto the landing to see what was happening.

They were still on the door-mat. Michael was slumped against his sister with his arm round her neck. She was trying unsuccessfully to carry him up the stairs. With Isabel's help, they got him to the second floor. By then, she saw that he was not drunk, as she suspected, but injured. His face was badly swollen, one eye scarcely visible under the puffy flesh.

'What has happened? Who did this?' asked Isabel.

Kitty shrugged her shoulders and made no reply. Isabel knew better than to question further.

Next morning, Michael's eyes were buried beneath a mass of purple bruises. Kitty ran out to the butcher's and returned with a strip of rump steak which she laid tenderly against the swelling. Isabel was amazed, both by the young woman's tenderness and her acceptance of the assault.

For the next few days, the house was unusually quiet. Michael lay in bed resting while Kitty moved about in silence, opening and closing doors without making a sound and tiptoeing between floors. Isabel understood the reason but she missed the sound of Kitty's singing and laughing and the way she would always call out to Isabel whenever she returned to the house. The days seemed longer than ever.

At last! What she had been waiting for! A letter from Ellen. Skipping through the tedious ramblings about the family's health, she found what she wanted to know.

We have acquired an interesting new addition to our social circle, a Mr Ralph Brown, who is in the district on his way to Newcastle. He seems a very successful business man. Frederick is much impressed by him. He has been visiting Almondbury where he believes his grandmother grew up.

We have invited him to lunch and dinner and it was very pleasing to see how well he has been getting on with Charlotte. She still mourns, of course, as is natural, but she looks much more cheerful than of late. I believe they have taken walks and visited a concert together. He is staying in town but goes to Almondbury church to worship with Charlotte.

I must admit I would be delighted to see a serious attachment develop between them, particularly as we have been instrumental in bringing them together. Frederick mocks me but we women understand these things, do we not? Mr Brown must be nearly twice Charlotte's age but that never matters in my opinion.

The four of us plan to visit Scarborough for a few days at the beginning of July and intend to stay at the Grand, the new hotel which we hear is very fine. Am I right in thinking that Scarborough is where you grew up? I seem to remember that George met you while on holiday there.

Isabel threw down the letter. She had been waiting for this, longing to know what it said but now that she had read it, she could feel only jealousy and frustration. She tried to reason with herself. Of course Randolph would make an effort to worm himself into Charlotte's affections. That was the intention. Had he not achieved it, the plan would fail. But reading about it felt like salt in a wound. She longed for him to be here, not in the company of the step-daughter she had never wanted and never liked. *She* should be the one enjoying his company and more precisely, his body.

Could he have made any physical approach to Charlotte? Impossible! The girl was plain and dowdy. It was not to be thought of. But that was easier said than done. Memories of their love-making filled her mind and then to her horror, the memories became imaginings in which Charlotte replaced her in Randolph's arms. Unbearable!

Frantic to escape her thoughts, Isabel threw a shawl around her shoulders and hurried along the street towards Queen's Square. But it was full of families and couples enjoying the summer sunshine, happy in each other's company. After walking determinedly round all four sides and finding nothing to distract her, she went back indoors, none the easier.

Stuffing Ellen's letter behind the clock, she pulled out another that had lain there for over a month. It was from her mother in Scarborough and had been re-addressed to Bath by the family solicitors in Huddersfield. She had written to tell Isabel that her father was very ill. Although they had not seen her since her marriage to Mr Blezard, she hoped Isabel might see her way to visiting Scarborough, if only briefly. Her father wished it and so did she. However, if Mr Blezard could not spare her, they would understand.

Reading her mother's letter again, which she had not done since it arrived, Isabel was thrown into a mixture of feelings. She knew she should have written to her parents when she was widowed and again when she moved to Bath but the fact was that she hadn't. The longer she left it the more awkward it became. She wondered if her father was dead yet. Probably not. It would surely have occasioned another letter.

The idea came to her that she might go to Scarborough and spy on Randolph and Charlotte. And if she thought he was becoming too familiar with the girl, she would let him know that she was watching him. However, she realised he would be furious if she did this. Perhaps best to leave well alone and trust him to achieve what he had set out to do, to cheat the girl out of money she could well afford to lose. How splendid would be his return, exulting and newly rich!

Another wet night.

Kitty and Michael were out and Isabel left to her own devices. Wearily, she picked up the old newspaper again. This time she would count how many men at the ball had been wearing uniform and how many not. But the article failed to hold her; she had read it too often. Idly she turned the page over and saw the word 'Sotheby's' at the beginning of a piece she had not noticed before. With a flicker of interest, she began reading.

The highlight of the auction sale was the remarkable appearance of a Madonna and Child, a newly discovered early work by the Italian painter, Raphael. The expectation was that it would be bought by the directors of the National Gallery who last year acquired a Botticelli and a Rembrandt for the nation. However, as the bidding began, it became clear that there was another interested buyer represented by Mr Grant Lewis, the well-known art dealer. As the bidding rose above eight hundred pounds, the National Gallery representative retired, with obvious regret, from the fray. The painting was secured by Mr Lewis for one thousand pounds. He was unwilling to divulge the name of his client but we note that Her Majesty the Queen has recently completed a collection of engravings of Raphael's work which was begun by the Prince Consort. We venture to say that, if the painting has attracted distinguished patronage, it would not be for the first time.

Isabel felt faint. She did not attempt to stand up because she felt her legs might give way beneath her. Instead, she drew several deep breaths, eventually gathering up enough strength to stagger to the front door, open it and gulp in great lungfuls of air. She tottered back to her chair, took up the paper and read the piece again.

Now an icy calm descended on her, her vision sharp and clear. Randolph Byrne was a cheat and a liar! He had stood in this very room and told her that the painting, for it must be the very same one, had raised only one hundred pounds! And to think that she had given him ten for his trouble!

What further swindle might he be planning? After a large brandy, it came to her. How might he get his hands on everything Charlotte owned, not just a few thousand pounds? Why, by marrying her! The more she thought about it, the more likely it seemed. She re-read Ellen's letter more closely and became surer than ever that this was his plan. She had no doubt he could accomplish it if he wanted to. What did that girl know about men, especially an exceptional one like Randolph? And knowing his talent for disappearing, she was sure he would have no difficulty in leaving the wife and taking the money when he felt the time was right. Having convinced herself that this was the situation, she was forced to face the ultimate question. Would he then come to Isabel and suggest they flee together, perhaps to the Continent, to enjoy his new-found fortune? In a shaft of clarity, she knew he would not.

At that moment, she heard the Nolans at the door and rushed to meet them.

'Kitty! Michael! Come in here!'

The couple entered her sitting-room. As usual, they looked weary.

'Read that, Kitty! And tell me what you think!'

Kitty sat down near to a lamp and began to read the newspaper article. Michael lounged in the shadows. Isabel could hardly control her impatience.

'Well, what do you think, Kitty? Has he swindled me? He told me the picture only raised a hundred pounds! Would he lie to me, would he?'

Kitty looked as if she did not know what to say. Isabel pressed on.

'I know you can't be sure, Kitty, but you've known him longer than I have. Is it the kind of thing he would do? To me, to any woman?'

Kitty looked up, her large pale eyes wide.

'I don't know the circumstances here, Isabel, as you know, but I have to say 'yes'– it is the kind of thing he would do.'

Isabel grasped the newspaper from Kitty's hand.

'That's all I wanted to know.'

When Isabel was in the grip of one of her blindingly hot rages, she scarcely knew what she was doing. Now she felt perfectly in control, so perfectly that she sat down and wrote an appropriate letter to her mother. There was no point in paying to stay anywhere else.

Old King Street
Bath
June 1868
Dear Mother
I have only just received your letter dated April 30th and am distressed

at what you must think of me. The letter was forwarded to me by the family solicitors and must have been held up there. I regret to tell you that I am recently widowed and have come to Bath to recuperate.

I shall come up to Scarborough next week to see you. I hope that Father has made some improvement. With all good wishes from your loving daughter,

Isabel

She was quite proud of the letter. The word 'recently' was an excellent choice.

Privately she hoped her father had died in the meantime and the ownership of the hotel passed to her mother. Something might be made of that.

Having checked that she had enough cash hidden in her secret store, she sallied forth to the railway station, parasol twirling on her shoulder, to enquire about trains to Scarborough.

Looking at the two trunks and four portmanteaux being carried on to the platform at Huddersfield station, Charlotte wondered how long the Thorpes intended staying in Scarborough. Ellen had also brought a maid to help with the tasks of unpacking, dressing her and packing up when they left. Despite this and the presence of her husband, Ellen looked very nervous. She was patting her neck, which was blotched red, with a lawn handkerchief.

'Forgive me, my dear. The expected arrival of a train always affects me in this way. The noise! The steam! Yet I enjoy a holiday as much as the next person.'

Charlotte admitted there was some basis for Ellen's condition. The train roared into the station like an iron monster, screaming and snorting steam. All was confusion – doors opening and slamming shut, passengers getting off and on, children crying, porters pushing trolleys, the guard blowing his whistle, waving a green flag and they were off!

'Oh my goodness!' gasped Ellen. 'What a relief to be on board!'

Charlotte was intent on enjoying every moment and so far was succeeding. Sitting by the window watching the countryside slide swiftly by was one of her favourite experiences.

At her side sat Ralph Brown, good-humoured, attentive, in charge of anything that needed moving or fetching and seemingly willing to take an interest in anything she said.

The journey passed all too quickly for Charlotte though Ellen declared herself weary and ready for her afternoon rest.

The Grand Hotel was not far from the railway station in Scarborough. After loading up one carriage with the luggage and the maid, the Thorpes, Charlotte and Brown boarded another and were soon at their destination. Here a smartly uniformed doorman received them while two porters threw themselves at the bags and began carrying them inside.

Frederick and Ellen knew Scarborough well and usually stayed at the Crown. But this time it had to be the newly-opened Grand, occupying a prime position overlooking the bay. They had read about it in *The Yorkshire Post* who had called it a landmark in seaside architecture.

'The original concept was based on a theme of time,' said Frederick, as they entered the building between rose-coloured pillars. 'Four large domes, fifty-two chimneys, twelve floors and three hundred and sixty-five rooms. But I'm not sure they accomplished all that exactly.'

It did not matter. They stood in a beautiful hall with a domed roof, surrounded by potted palms and a huge jardinière spilling over with flowers. All around were tall, handsome arches and elegant plasterwork but the main focus was the very wide, majestic staircase, with its carved ornamental balustrades, which swept up to the first floor and beyond.

Charlotte was delighted with her bedroom with its spacious private bathroom and sea view. While Ellen rested and Frederick retired to the smoking-room, she accepted Brown's offer of a stroll around the town. He had never been to Scarborough before so Charlotte led him to the Spa.

'I have never seen anything like it,' he said as they admired the building with its vast assembly hall, colonnade with shops and open air bandstand. 'We must come one evening to the music hall.' He also declared himself impressed with the situation of the town itself, its two wide sweeping bays separated by a rocky headland, the site of a medieval castle. 'That too is a remarkable building,' he exclaimed. They were standing across the road from a circular building topped by a dome.

'That is the Rotunda, the geological and archaeological museum,' explained Charlotte. 'It is one of my favourite places. I should like to show it to you tomorrow when we have more time. I think perhaps we should be returning to the hotel now to be in time for dinner.'

Brown agreed to both propositions, causing Charlotte to decide he was the most agreeable man she had ever met. He must have some faults, she thought, as she watched him buying a newspaper from a street vendor, but I have yet to discover what they are.

'Charlotte. Before we join the Thorpes –.' Brown sounded serious. 'I will visit the estate agents tomorrow and see if I can arrange some viewings for the day after. In the meantime, it might be as well not to mention our plans to the Thorpes, until we can reveal something more settled. Do you agree?'

'Yes, of course. I can see the sense in it.'

She tucked her arm into Brown's as they walked back to the hotel. It had somehow become natural to do so.

Isabel had not been back to Scarborough since her marriage to George Blezard almost three years before. She felt no thrill of anticipation or pleasure at seeing her parents again as she walked along the street which lay a quarter of a mile back from the South Cliff. The sign 'Rowe's Hotel' had needed replacing when she still lived there. Now the rust was biting into its surface, hastened by the salt wind off the sea.

It was her father who had had the sign made and affixed to what was really nothing more than a boarding-house. His involvement with the sign was his only contribution to the business which had fallen heavily on the shoulders of his wife, Norah. Isabel had been forced to help with domestic duties which she hated. At the age of fourteen, she donned a black dress and announced that from now on, she would be the receptionist and not the skivvy. A cleaner had been engaged but then dispensed with as Maxwell Rowe began to drink and gamble away the hotel's meagre profits. Isabel and her mother had not starved and had it not been for Rowe's other hobby, women, they might have been happy enough. But Isabel itched to get away and when one day, George Blezard, a widowed mill-owner from Huddersfield, had come to stay, she had decided he was the way out of her humdrum life.

It was not her fault that her plan had misfired. George Blezard was simply not the very rich man she thought he was. The fact that he chose to stay in a cheap hotel rather than one of the grander ones along the Esplanade had not alarmed her. She imagined he might be careful about how he spent his money, thrift being a quality as often found amongst the rich as amongst the poor. But the deed had been done and she had left Scarborough for the hills and valleys of the West Riding. Since then she had barely given a thought to the parents she had left behind.

She pushed open the creaking gate and went up the crumbling path. Her mother opened the door, the same pale, tired-looking woman as ever.

'Isabel! It's good to see you.'

Isabel nodded and walked past her into the hall.

'We've no visitors yet,' her mother said. 'It's still quite early in the season. It's just as well, with your father being ill.'

Isabel followed her mother up the narrow stairs and into a first floor bedroom. Her father lay in bed, his eyes closed, his face white and gaunt, his bony fingers clutching the sheet to his chest.

'Maxwell! Isabel's here.'

He opened rheumy, red-rimmed eyes. There was no word of recognition, only a faint murmur. Her mother picked up a beaker of water and held it to his lips, propping him up with her other arm. The whole room smelt of sickness. Isabel could not wait to get out.

Downstairs she drank some tea. Her mother spoke to her in the same timid, unassuming tones she had always used and which Isabel had always found unreasonably annoying.

'What would you like to eat? Shall I get some chops?'

'No, thank you,' Isabel replied. 'I shall be dining out.'

At the Grand Hotel, the four guests were in high good humour as they sat down to dinner. Attentive staff stood ready to serve them in the elegant dining-room; cutlery and glassware sparkled on smooth white table linen. Ellen in particular felt completely refreshed after her nap, her husband obviously happy at this rare state of affairs.

'I had such a lovely sleep! It must be the sea air having a beneficial effect already!'

'Have you any plans for tomorrow?' asked Frederick.

'I should like to show Ralph the Rotunda at some time,' said Charlotte.

'Is that the red and white building, foreign-looking, with arches and a dome?' asked Ellen.

Frederick laughed. 'You can tell my wife has never visited it. No, my dear, that is the Turkish Baths.'

As the laughter subsided, Brown made a suggestion. 'Which would you prefer, Frederick? A swim at the Turkish Baths or the real thing in the sea?'

Frederick looked doubtful. 'The sea will be very cold indeed, Ralph. It will be nothing like the Nile, believe me!'

'All the same, it seems a pity not to take advantage of the sea while we are here.'

'One swims in sea-water, of course, at the Baths,' said Frederick. 'Warmed to a comfortable temperature.'

Charlotte could see he was not at all keen to enter the North Sea at this time of year. She did not blame him.

'Oh, do swim in the sea!' his wife begged. 'Then Charlotte and I can watch!' That seemed to decide it although the look Frederick shot his wife was distinctly unfriendly.

'A brief dip then?' Brown suggested. 'I think honour will be satisfied with a very brief dip. When we feel the temperature, I suspect we shall be very glad to return to dry land.'

'Very well!' agreed Frederick, obviously knowing when he was beaten. 'I think this feat of heroism calls for a celebration!' He raised an arm which brought a waiter to his side immediately. A few words were exchanged while the others studied their menus. Moments later, the waiter pressed his thumbs and the champagne cork flew up with a satisfying pop. Frederick raised his glass 'To Scarborough!'

'To Scarborough!' echoed the others, raising theirs likewise.

As Charlotte turned towards Brown to touch his glass with hers, she was amazed to see his face suddenly lose its colour and his eyes widen with shock. The glass dropped from his hand, sending a watery golden stream across the tablecloth.

At the same moment, Ellen exclaimed 'Isabel! What a lovely surprise!'

Charlotte turned and was astonished to see Isabel standing behind her. The surprise was not pleasant. She had not expected to see her stepmother ever again and certainly did not wish to.

Isabel had not altered at all. She was, as usual, beautifully dressed, this time in deep rose pink, the bodice tight over her bosom, her glossy dark hair decorated with an artificial rose in the same colour. Her smile was mocking; her gaze, strangely, directed at Brown.

'Yes, indeed, Ellen. I hope it is.'

She nodded briefly in Charlotte's direction.

Frederick sprang into action.

'Isabel! How good to see you! You will join us, of course!' One waiter hurried to bring another chair while another two whisked off the wet tablecloth and began re-laying the table with five place settings. Isabel sank into her chair.

Charlotte felt extremely irritated that she was still looking at Brown. She spoke to gain her attention. 'Isabel. What brings you here?'

Isabel assumed a melancholy expression.

'Not the best reason, I'm afraid. I came to see my father who, I'm sorry to say, has not long to live.'

There were murmurs of sympathy.

Isabel sipped her champagne. 'But this must not be allowed to cloud your evening. My father has had a good life. He would be the first to say 'Enjoy life while you can.' I fear I interrupted your toasting.'

'It was, simply, to Scarborough,' said Frederick, 'which is of course familiar to you. My dear Isabel, may I introduce Ralph Brown?'

Isabel extended her hand. Brown touched it briefly and then returned to studying the menu.

It was an excellent dinner, calling forth much praise from the diners. Charlotte realised that Ellen must have written to Isabel, telling her they were coming to Scarborough. Whether Isabel had timed her visit to coincide with theirs was not made clear.

She noticed that although Isabel looked at Ralph Brown frequently during the meal, he did not look at her. Usually men did look at Isabel. Her appearance and her behaviour encouraged it. On this occasion, Charlotte was grateful for the omission. Instead, he was especially attentive to herself and Ellen, which was pleasing.

By ten o'clock, Ellen declared herself ready for retiring after a day of so much excitement. Charlotte, though not tired, was happy to leave the table. She had found the unexpected presence of her step-mother a strain. She thought Isabel might have offered her condolences for the death of Sam. Ellen would surely have mentioned it in her correspondence. However, she did not. Charlotte was annoyed but relieved when she realised how false any expression of sympathy from Isabel would sound.

As they moved out of the dining room, Charlotte was surprised to see Isabel accompanying Ellen upstairs to the bedrooms. Scraps of conversation made it clear that Isabel very much wished to see the interior of the Thorpes' bedroom and that Ellen was just as keen to show it off. As they came to Charlotte's room, she bade them all good night, unlocked it and entered its welcome solitude.

Isabel stood silently as Frederick unlocked their bedroom door. She watched Byrne walk further along the corridor and let himself into the room at the end.

'Here, you see, Isabel, how charming everything is! We really are most comfortable!'

Isabel followed Ellen inside and made suitable noises of appreciation as she indicated the furnishings, the bathroom and the view from the window. The sea, a dark grey, rippled silver in the moonlight.

'Thank you so much, Ellen, for showing it to me. Yes, it is delightful. I will say goodnight now. I look forward to our shopping expedition tomorrow.'

Isabel closed the door and heard Frederick lock it behind her. There was no-one in sight.

Stealthily she glided along to the room at the far end and knocked at the door. There was no response at first and then it opened. Byrne kept one hand on the side of the door, blocking the entrance. His expression was not welcoming.

Isabel bristled. 'If you want people to see me standing here...'

He stepped back and let her in. 'I hope you're not expecting me to say your arrival was an unexpected pleasure because it wasn't.' They stood facing one another, neither at ease.

'Obviously,' said Isabel. 'But I must congratulate you. You have put on a good show.'

He shrugged. 'What do you want, Isabel? Can you not see how stupid your intrusion is? A few days more and I should secure what we both want.'

'And what is that, I wonder? Possession of Charlotte Blezard's money? Or her person?'

'What are you talking about?' Byrne said crossly. 'That was never part of the plan.'

'But perhaps it developed that way. According to Ellen – '

'What does she know about it? She only sees what I choose to let her see in public.'

'Of course. And she does not see you in private, does she? Who knows what you get up to when you are alone – with the heiress.'

The expression on Byrne's face altered. When he spoke, his tone was soft. 'I assure you, my dear Isabel, that there is nothing of that sort to worry you. You would expect a little of that, surely, to gain the girl's confidence but beyond that...' He took a step towards her and put his hands lightly on her waist. 'Do you think anyone who has known Isabel Blezard would exchange her for her step-daughter?' He bent forward with the obvious intention of kissing her but she pulled away and put herself behind a high wing chair, resting her hands on its back.

'How do you expect me to believe you, you, a liar and a cheat?' At these words, he moved towards her but she edged her way round the chair, keeping it between them. 'I shall never trust you again!'

'What is all this?' he said wearily.

'I read about it – in the newspaper.'

'What newspaper? What did you read?'

'About the sale at Sotheby's. The painting! My painting! The one you said raised only a hundred pounds!' Isabel's eyes were blazing. 'It went for a thousand, I saw it!'

Byrne's expression did not alter. 'Ah, now I understand,' he said. 'I see where the mistake occurred.'

'What mistake? You can't lie your way out of this one!'

'My dear Isabel, I have no intention of lying. I simply need to tell you what happened at the sale. How many paintings do you think were there that day? How many of the Madonna and Child? This favourite subject, painted by scores of painters over hundreds of years?'

Isabel was forced to say, 'I don't know.'

'Exactly. You don't know because you weren't there. There were half-a-dozen including yours. I looked at them all and though I am no art expert, I could see that one of them was outstanding, far superior to any of the others. *That* was the Raphael, the one that went for a thousand pounds. Your painting, and the others, went for anything from twenty-five to a hundred pounds. Yours was one of the better ones.'

Isabel did not know what to say. Part of her wanted to believe him; another part held fast to the idea that this was just one more of his lies. If he could lie to everyone else, why not to her?

'There is a lot here at stake, Isabel. The day after tomorrow Charlotte Blezard and I will visit possible houses, the first step in the charitable scheme I have outlined to her and one which she seems ready to accept. Trust me, Isabel, trust me!'

She stood still while he came round the side of the chair and leant against her back. She felt his body warmth at the same time as she felt his hands cupping her breasts and his lips on her neck. Unable to resist, she responded, leaning back, parting her legs as she felt him pushing behind her. They remained like this as long as they could till frustration overcame them and they were in danger of falling. Isabel felt herself turned round and his moist mouth on hers in a long searching kiss that left her dizzy with desire. A few stumbling steps brought them to the bed. Isabel found all her bodice buttons were undone and Byrne's head on her breast, seeking her nipple. She stroked his hair and the back of his head and found her body arching towards his. A few minutes more and he was inside her and they were rising and falling together, her ecstatic cries seeming to come from somewhere outside herself.

Later, she had no idea how later, she opened her eyes. Byrne leant over her and stroked her cheek with his finger. 'So you see, my dear Isabel, there is no need to worry, no need at all.' He leaned forward and kissed her throat, making her shiver with pleasure. 'But I'm afraid, my dear, that you will have to leave. Chambermaids I do not care about but we would not wish our neighbours, the Thorpes, or the virtuous Miss Blezard, to know that you spent the night in my room, would we?'

All the time he was talking, he was lifting her off the bed and handing her under-garments. She had no option but to dress, although she was not fully awake. She fumbled with her stays until Byrne's strong warm hands came to her rescue. At last she was dressed. Byrne lifted her shawl and draped it over her head and shoulders.

'There!' At the same time, he was propelling her towards the bedroom door. A quick glance up and down the corridor and then he took her by the hand and led her to the top of the staircase. The vast hall beneath them was dimly lit by shaded lamps. A solitary clerk dozed behind his desk. Moments later, she was outside the main entrance.

'Shall I come with you?' he asked, still holding the front door open.

'No. no! Best go in. I know the way.'

The streets were deserted, the only sound the soughing of the sea on the shore below. As she approached Rowe's Hotel, with its light burning in the hallway, she realised that her mother must still be waiting up for her. Sure enough, the older woman was resting on the sofa in the parlour, half-asleep. With an effort, she roused herself.

'A good evening, Isabel?'

'Yes, indeed.' Isabel put her hand on the banister. 'Father – is there any change?'

Her mother shook her head. 'No. No change. I bid you good-night.'

'Good-night, Mother.'

Isabel reached her bedroom and began to remove the clothes she had so recently donned. Sinking into her pillow, she experienced a strong feeling of contentment, of serenity almost, which had eluded her for so long. Randolph Byrne did love her – or as much as a man like him could love. They were a well-matched pair. He must know that as much as she did. Passionate, greedy, ambitious and ready to do what had to be done to achieve those ambitions. They wanted the same things in life and together they would enjoy them. How could she ever have doubted him? Charlotte Blezard's only attraction was her money. She was sure of that.

CHAPTER TWELVE

The next day was as sunny as the one before and whatever Frederick Thorpe might have wished, a dip in Scarborough Bay seemed inescapable. The four of them arrived on the beach, the men carrying capacious bags. While Ellen and Charlotte waited, they disappeared into two bathing-machines which had been wheeled close to the sea on the part of the beach where the men swam. No-one else was swimming. Further down the beach, there were some determined paddlers, whole families amongst them. There was, as always, a stiff sea breeze; Ellen wished she had brought a warmer shawl.

Frederick and Brown appeared, the former jumping up and down and slapping his fore-arms across his chest to keep warm.

'My God, Brown! I should have insisted on the Turkish Baths!'

Frederick Thorpe seemed to have lost some of his poise along with his clothes. He did not cut a very prepossessing figure, his thin white legs looking odd emerging from his short-legged costume. By contrast, Ralph Brown was as attractive without his clothes as he was with them, more so if Charlotte dared to admit it.

She had never seen a nearly naked grown man before, even at this respectful distance. She hoped her embarrassed pleasure was not obvious. His tall, muscular body was a creamy golden colour, his shoulders gleaming like satin in the sunlight. His close-fitting costume showed off his flat belly and strong-looking thighs.

He seemed perfectly at ease and set off towards the sea at a run. When the water was waist-high, he launched himself forward, his powerful strokes driving him through the water. Then he turned and swam on his back until Frederick reached him.

It was quickly over. The two men returned to the beach, Frederick shivering with cold, Brown appearing to enjoy the sensation of the sea water running down his body and into the sand. They disappeared into their bathing-machines, emerging a few minutes later, dressed and with a dry hotel towel round their necks.

'I think honour has been satisfied!' Frederick said as he rejoined his wife. He looked considerably happier than he had done half an hour before.

Ellen tucked her arm in his and told him he was her hero which made him look even more pleased.

'You seem accustomed to the sea,' Charlotte said to Brown as they walked back.

'I grew up by it,' he said.

Charlotte would have liked to ask where but was too shy to ask. At the hotel, hot soup was called for and consumed after which the Thorpes retired to their rooms to rest.

Isabel had slept badly, fuddled by strange dreams, woken by the early morning sounds of the town, then falling into a deep sleep and waking in the middle of the morning.

Last night's euphoria had disappeared entirely. How could she have been so stupid as to believe everything Byrne had told her? His skill as a liar was proved by the ease by which he had infiltrated the Huddersfield group. They had all taken him at his word. How could she, who knew him better than they did, have swallowed his tale about the picture at the London auction? His story, that there had been several paintings of the Madonna and Child, and hers one of the poorer ones, must be untrue. She ought to have checked up on him, found out a list of all the items that were in the sale that day. She was sure that had been the case when Charles Lester helped her sell those items of hers in Bath. The words came back into her head – 'Lot 37 : Gold and silver writing-set.'

Isabel sat up. She would ask Byrne for the sale list to prove his claim. If he refused, she would be right to be suspicious. She would contact Sotheby's and find out for herself.

With her mother hovering in the background, Isabel sat in the poky dining-room, breaking her toast into little pieces. If he was lying about the picture – and the more she thought about it, the surer she was that she had been cheated – then he could just as easily be lying about his feelings for her and his intentions towards Charlotte Blezard. She was forced to acknowledge that love-making was not evidence of love, certainly not where men were concerned.

She felt a slight pang of something that might have been guilt when she thought of her husband, George Blezard, widowed and lonely, who sat in this very dining-room not so long ago and succumbed to her charms. She was fairly sure that he had loved her whereas she ... Perhaps Randolph Byrne was punishment for that.

Her musings made her uncomfortable and she stood up abruptly. Her mother came forward.

'Have you had enough, Isabel? I can make you some more toast if you wish.'

'No. No, thank you, Mother.'

Once outside in the fresh air, Isabel felt her head clear. As she walked, the matter of the picture, which had gnawed at her earlier, gradually came to seem less important. It had been almost certainly a trick, a financial sleight-of-hand she might have practised herself. If Randolph Byrne were to be hers, she would overlook it. Perhaps, in time, they would laugh about it in recollection. It was a trifle compared with the greater issue at stake – that of his intentions towards her. If he were telling the truth, that his dealings with Charlotte were entirely financial, then she would forgive him. She had enough confidence in her female powers to believe she could hold him, at least for a while. From what she had seen the previous evening, when they were all dining at the Grand together, his treatment of Charlotte had been merely courteous, nothing more.

As she walked downhill towards the hotel once more, her spirits rose further. If she could observe the couple together, it would surely confirm her impression of their relationship.

Charlotte and Brown met downstairs in the foyer by arrangement, Brown positively glowing with health as they emerged into the sunlight and turned in the direction of the sea.

'Its circular plan is designed to interpret William Smith's great discovery of the stratification of rocks,' said Charlotte as they entered the Rotunda.

'I can see I shall have no need of this,' said Brown, indicating the explanatory leaflet he was holding.

'Oh no, do keep it!' said Charlotte. 'I only know this from my father. He was very interested in all aspects of science.' As was Sam, she thought. An image of his face came into her mind. This would have been his favourite place in Scarborough, she realised, had they visited it as they intended after their marriage.

The thought quietened her. She walked alongside Brown as he stopped, observed the exhibits and read out extracts from the leaflet about the coffered dome, the stone lantern and the upper floors with their craftsman-made mahogany showcases. Downstairs they looked at the collection of antiquities in the one-storey wings, each in a bay affording privacy to the visitors.

Brown continued to make intelligent observations about the exhibits. It suddenly struck Charlotte that these were almost exactly the comments Sam would have made. The idea disturbed her and would not go away. Desperate to change the subject, she stopped in front of a marble bust of a scholar from the ancient classical world.

'I always think that however skilled the sculptors, they never quite manage to make the man's beard realistic,' she said.

'Charlotte, I am bound to agree with you,' he replied.

Charlotte suddenly found herself saying something she had wondered about ever since she had met Ralph Brown. 'I wonder why you do not wear a beard, Ralph. Most men do these days.'

Brown appeared slightly embarrassed, as if Charlotte had breached defences he normally kept in place.

'You are right. I do not. To tell the truth, Charlotte, I look distinctly odd if I do. My beard, strangely, is ginger, not fair like the hair on my head or moustache. So – yes, it is sheer vanity that makes me shave my chin. Or have it shaved for me.'

The smile he gave her was intimate, dazzling.

Charlotte was completely unnerved. The reference to a ginger-coloured beard brought the image of Sam back into her mind so powerfully that she could remember not just the appearance but the exact texture of his beard against her face. Brown's smile penetrated her weakened reserve and she found her lips trembling. A moment later, she burst into tears.

At once Brown came close, putting one hand gently on her shoulder and the other under her chin, tilting her face towards him.

'My dear Charlotte, what have I said to distress you so?'

Charlotte began to explain. 'My betrothed, Sam Armitage – he had ginger hair – it was...' Then she gave way to sorrow entirely, sobbing so violently that her body shook. She allowed herself to be drawn into Brown's arms and pressed against his chest with his arms firmly around her. He held her there until her sobs died away.

'I am so sorry, Ralph. Please forgive me.'

'Forgive you? It is for you to forgive me.'

She looked up into his eyes and saw only tenderness. The next moment he had bent his head. His lips were on hers and she was kissing him in return. A deep sense of well-being ran through her. At last he released her and stood looking down at her with an expression she found quite unfathomable.

Aware now that they were in a public place, Charlotte scanned the room. There was no-one about. Brown understood her at once.

'Never fear, Charlotte. I think we are quite safe. I do not think the fossils will talk.'

She managed a weak smile and put her arm through his as they walked to the exit.

Isabel, the unseen watcher, could not move. A hot wave of jealous anger rose in her chest and threatened to choke her. How could she have believed anything he had said? The man was a selfish monster who cared for no-one but himself. His intentions were clear. He would marry the insipid heiress, strip her of her wealth and then abscond with it! Or – and the second possibility was more painful than the first – he would marry her because he had, by some quirk of fate, fallen in love with the woman.

The thought was unbearable. It could not be true! But there had been something about the way he had taken Charlotte in his arms, kissed her and looked at her! The stupid woman was obviously in love with him. How could she be otherwise?

Isabel did not know how long she stood there. Seconds? Minutes? But she knew what she was going to do. Randolph Byrne was not going to get away with this. The winning cards were in her hand and hers alone. She would unmask him and destroy his plans, whatever they were. Of one thing she was sure. That mouse Charlotte Blezard was not going to have him. Impelled by a surge of vengeful energy, Isabel swept out of the Rotunda and made for the beach. In the distance she could see two familiar figures walking slowly, close together.

'Would you like to go back to the hotel, to rest?' Brown asked.

'No, no, thank you. I think some fresh air would be better,' said Charlotte, taking deep breaths. They picked their way amongst the throng of people now leaving the beach. A chilly breeze had sprung up as the sun vanished behind the clouds. Dogs stood, legs splayed, barking at the waves and a few children played on, refusing to heed their parents' calls. Chairs, baskets and rugs were folded, lifted and carried away as the tide began to come in. The heels of Charlotte's boots sank into the damp sand which clung to the hem of her long crinoline skirt.

'Is this far enough?'

'No. Let us go a little farther. I would like to be away from people for a little while.'

Charlotte still felt shaken by the torrent of emotion which had engulfed her. They walked along the beach for about two hundred yards and reached a stretch where they were completely alone. The two of them stood silently, looking out to sea. Brown's left arm was round Charlotte's waist. His right hand rested on her right shoulder. Gradually the sense of weakness left her. She felt warm and safe in his embrace.

As they stood there, the sky became darker, the wind keener. On the horizon a grey, then blue-black, cloud appeared, coming nearer and nearer until it blotted out the light over the bay.

Charlotte shivered. In response, Brown opened his jacket and drew her towards him so that she stood enveloped by the tweed and by his body heat against her back.

Now the wind came ripping and screaming across the sea, lashing the waves into uproar so that they thundered ever louder on the shore. The surf boiled and growled. The incoming tide spread its angry paws further up the beach until it came within a few feet of where they were standing.

Still they did not move. Charlotte could feel Brown's heart beating strongly against her spine. She did not want the moment to end. She felt warm and utterly secure in this man's arms. No matter what dangers life might throw in her way, with this man she could face them all.

The squall had reached the harbour. In the distance they could see the fishing boats rocking about as the swell hit the harbour wall. Then, as quickly as it had come, the summer storm subsided. The wind died down and gradually, the dark clouds moved away from the sun, leaving the sky clear with a strange silvery light.

'Charlotte!'

She turned her face towards his, now so close that she could see the brightness of his eyes and the moistness of his lips.

'Perhaps we should go back to the hotel.'

'Yes, perhaps we should.'

But neither of them moved. As Brown bent his head lower, she prepared herself to meet his mouth with hers.

Suddenly, she felt Brown start and drop his hands. He was staring over his left shoulder, back the way they had come. Turning, she saw a dark figure advancing on them, small at first and then growing larger. Her cloak and skirts were swept by the wind, blown upwards and tossed to and fro, bat-like, by the strong gusts. Slowly she made her way towards them, arms flailing as she tried to hold still the flapping bonnet. It was Isabel.

Charlotte looked up at Brown's face and was surprised to see it flushed with anger. He dropped his arms, releasing her from his embrace. Isabel came on until she was only a few yards away.

She said nothing but simply glared at them, showing her teeth, her eyes sooty holes in her pale face. For a moment there was silence. It was broken by Isabel.

'A touching scene! What a charming couple you make!'

Her words were sharp-edged as if cut from ice.

Charlotte stared. She did not know what to make of this. She looked at Brown but his face was turned away from her.

Isabel went on, her mouth twisted, her face ugly.

'But do you know everything about this man, Charlotte, this – Ralph Brown?' She spat the name out as if it were filth.

Stunned, Charlotte clutched at Brown's arm for support. A feeling of dread gripped her heart.

For the first time, Brown spoke. His voice sounded choked.

'Isabel! This is not necessary!'

'No?' Isabel's eyes sparked, the colour returning to her cheeks. 'I disagree. I think Charlotte should know the truth. Charlotte, my dear, I feel I must save you from this impostor. You should know, as I do, that he is only interested in your money.' Her face was a mask of malevolence. 'And that his real name is Randolph Byrne. Perhaps he did not tell you that.'

Charlotte felt as though the ground was dropping away from her. She let go of his arm and twisted away. Daring to look at him, she saw his face was ashen. He did not speak. His silence seemed dreadful proof of Isabel's claim.

As control began to return to her limbs, she knew she had to get away. She began to stumble forward, away from Brown, away from Isabel, and back along the deserted beach. She had taken only a few steps when Brown's voice rang out behind her.

'Charlotte!'

She could not stop herself from turning back. His handsome face was strained.

'They were not all lies, Charlotte! Believe me!'

A sob rose in her throat. Gathering all the strength she could muster, she seized her skirts with both hands and forced herself across the beach as fast as she could. Her boots sank into the sand at every step but the impulse to escape drove her forward.

When she reached the path to the hotel, her way was easier. But now there were people about her and she feared her face would tell all. Desperate for concealment, she blundered between guests at the entrance. At last she gained the haven of her own room.

Isabel watched Charlotte's attempt to get away and followed her stumbling progress along the beach. Rich, stupid girl! She had only herself to blame. She needed to learn the ways of the world. Satisfied with what she had done, she turned to face Randolph. His face bore a ferocious look of such hatred that it transfixed her where she stood.

'You fool! You bitch!' he hissed at her. He pushed past her, fetching her a stinging slap around the face with his open hand as he did so. The blow sent her reeling so that she staggered and fell onto her knees.

Getting up was not easy. She caught the heel of her boot in the hem of her skirt and was sent sprawling. Dragging herself upright, she found herself covered in gritty sand. She tried to brush it off but found she could not get rid of it. Her mouth was already beginning to swell up.

She stumbled along the beach, straightening her bonnet and endeavouring to walk in a dignified manner as she neared other people. Byrne had disappeared. She felt dishevelled and out of control. Thankfully there were not many about as she made her way along the back streets to the hotel. She did not regret what she had said and done but the feeling of satisfaction was ebbing away fast.

She was in no mood to be pleasant to her mother when she opened the door. The older woman's face was white and drawn. As Isabel came in, her mother remained holding on to the door, as if for support. When Isabel turned impatiently, she shut the door carefully, so that it made no noise.

'Your father. He's gone. About an hour ago.'

Isabel's instinctive reaction was one of annoyance. Hadn't she had enough this morning? And now this! But she struggled to hide the feeling. She knew the situation called for a kinder response, conventional and comforting. With an effort, she composed her face to express sympathy.

'I'm very sorry, Mother.'

Her mother turned and mounted the stairs. Isabel had no choice but to follow her.

Her father's body lay against clean bedlinen. It looked as though her mother had already washed him and laid him out. The bedroom had been cleaned and all traces of the invalid swept away.

Isabel forced herself to look at the figure before her – the sharp, waxen features, the closed eyes and the thin, greying hair. It did not seem as if it had ever lived. There seemed no connection with the warm, dark-eyed, laughing man she had loved as a child – and had despised as a woman.

Her mother took Isabel's silence for grief and patted her shoulder.

'He is at peace now. That is what we must think.'

As they moved out on to the landing, however, Isabel's thoughts were moving in a completely different direction. But they were not ready to be presented, at least, not yet. Her mother put her hand on Isabel's; she managed to stop herself from pulling away.

'You will stay for the funeral?'

'If I must. I'm sorry, Mother. I have had a trying day.'

'So have I. But you will understand. You have been widowed yourself.'

'Indeed I have,' said Isabel. 'I will just rest for a while. And I will have a tea tray in my room as soon as possible.'

'Very well,' replied her mother, moving to the scullery as she spoke.

Isabel began to mount the stairs. Her experience on the beach was already dropping away from her. She felt pleased with herself. She would begin, as soon as she could, to suggest that her mother should sell the hotel and move to Bath. It should not be too difficult to release some of that money, perhaps to move to a better address. If Kitty and Michael were to remain with her, paying rent and offering services, so much the better. Her mother's presence need not impinge too strongly on Isabel's way of life. If she handled it properly, it could well turn out to be advantageous.

Charlotte did not know what to do with herself. It was no time for tears. Her brain was whirling. Recollections of the times she had spent with Brown returned to plague her – moments of joy when she had felt liked by him, admired and perhaps even loved. She was forced to admit it. And it had all been a lie! All the talk of charity, of doing good, it had all been false! What a fool she had been! If his name was false, then everything about him must be the same. She had heard the term 'confidence trickster'; she had never imagined she would be duped by one.

The minutes passed and her rapid heartbeat slowed down. Common sense came to her aid. Who else knew the truth? She was sure the Thorpes had believed all he said, as she had. She was not alone. That must be some consolation. But there was a difference. She knew, as she stared at her face in the mirror, that Ralph Brown/Randolph Byrne had insinuated himself into her feelings. That might take longer to overcome.

She sat in an easy chair looking out at the sea with the window open and a warm shawl around her shoulders. An hour later, she felt very much better. What had she suffered, after all? A few dents in her self-confidence but these could be recovered from, given time and determination. He had not got his hands on any of her money and indeed, would have found it hard to do so. He did not know she had inherited not just Josiah Gledhills's money but his hard-headed financial sense. She would not have laid out a penny for this trust without legal protection. She thought she would change her solicitors when she got home. There was something about Silas Crowther that she did not like. There would be other solicitors in the town who would be glad of her business.

There came a soft knock at her bedroom door. It was Ellen, looking concerned.

'My dear! I am glad to have found you in. Such a pity! Mr Brown has received a letter by the afternoon post to say that he is wanted in London urgently. He called on us a few minutes ago and asked me to tell you and give you his apologies.'

'Thank you, Ellen.'

There was nothing else she could say at the moment. She must speak to Frederick as soon as possible. He could break it to Ellen. Pray God he had not invested any money in one of Brown's projects.

'I think, Ellen, I will not come down to dinner tonight but will take a light supper in my room. I am a little indisposed. Please give my apologies to Frederick.'

'Oh my dear, I do sympathise! Will you let me bring you one of my powders? They are excellent for headaches and dyspepsia.'

'Thank you, Ellen. I think an early night will set me right. I think however I will return home tomorrow, a little earlier than planned. You and Frederick, I know, will be staying a little longer.'

'Oh, yes, my dear, if only because we are visiting friends in Whitby tomorrow. But will you be able to make the journey on your own? Would you like Mary Anne to come with you?'

'No, thank you, Ellen. That is very kind of you but I shall manage.'

When Ellen had gone, Charlotte looked at her fob watch. If she was quick, she could catch the last post.

The Grand Hotel
Scarborough
7th July 1868
Dear Hannah

I feel so foolish. I have learnt that Ralph Brown, whom I told you about, is not the man I thought he was. It seems that he came to Almondbury expressly to take advantage of me, or more exactly, my money. He is a trickster, known to Isabel, rather better known, I imagine, than any of us realised.

Frederick and Ellen are staying here a little longer but I should like to come home tomorrow, Thursday. I plan to catch a train that will have me

arriving in Huddersfield at 7.00.p.m. Please could Ben meet me?
In haste,
Your friend,
Charlotte

Next day there was no sign of Isabel or of Randolph Byrne, as Charlotte knew she must now call him.

While Ellen was preparing to set off, Charlotte had a quiet meeting with Frederick. He was taken aback by what she told him.

'Good God! Well, he had me taken in, I have to admit, Charlotte. So all that, about the canal, ship-building, the grandmother from Almondbury – was that all lies?'

'I imagine so, Frederick. I think the best we can do is to put it behind us. I do hope you had not invested in any of his projects.'

'No, but I was thinking of doing so! My God! What a narrow escape!'

Charlotte had never seen the self-assured Frederick so shaken.

'Perhaps you could break it to Ellen? Perhaps tomorrow after I have gone? She will be shocked to know of Isabel's involvement, which we can only guess at.'

'Yes indeed. Charlotte, I hope –.' He stopped and looked distressed. 'I hope, we both hope...'

'It is quite all right, Frederick,' said Charlotte, amazed at her own calmness. 'There is no damage done there, I can assure you. There might have been but there wasn't.'

Frederick looked genuinely relieved.

'I am glad of that, my dear, very glad.'

Charlotte boarded the train in a mood very different from that of two days ago. This time the journey seemed purely mechanical, simply a matter of getting from one point to another. However, despite her low spirits, she roused herself to appreciate what was outside the window – the open landscape, the view of York Minster and the sun setting as they entered the West Riding. Before long, the buildings of Huddersfield could be seen and then the train was puffing its noisy way into the railway station.

She had never been so happy to see Ben Haigh as she was at that moment. She saw him standing hesitantly on the platform several seconds before he saw her. His smart appearance took her by surprise. He wore a well-fitting coat of good cloth which revealed his broad shoulders and upright stance, newish breeches and leather boots. But it was his hair that most transformed him. Charlotte was used to seeing it tousled and long on a working day. Today the fair curls looked freshly cut and washed. She felt a rush of affection for him when their eyes met.

Blushing, he busied himself with her portmanteau which he picked up as though it weighed nothing and tucked her small bag under his arm, offering her the other. They walked out through the columns of the station entrance and down the stone steps to where the Haigh pony and trap was waiting. The pony set off when Ben made a clicking sound in his mouth and they began their journey towards Almondbury along the town streets, across the canal and then up the steep winding lanes that led to the farm. Ben said little which suited Charlotte's mood.

When they arrived, Charlotte allowed herself to be enveloped in Hannah's plump embrace. It was like being a child again. She was surprised to find how hungry she was and ate with relish, Ben following suit.

'It's grand to have you back,' said Hannah.

Charlotte looked from one pair of blue eyes to the other. 'It's grand to be home,' she said. And she meant it.

Printed in the United Kingdom
by Lightning Source UK Ltd.
133556UK00001B/73-315/P